Jonathan Lyons

In a surreal twenty-first century full of androids, binaries, Morlocks, chip trippers, black
acid rain and StellarNet obsession, we meet
Cage, a private detective down on his luck.
Kicked off the prestigious Old New York
Police Force after having gone up against
Expedite, the most powerful computer corporation in the world, he is struggling to make
ends meet when fate seems to lend him a helping hand. Fragile Janice Gild comes to him
with the story of the death of her brother
James, a death so bizarre, Cage can only
begin to guess at the method of the gruesome
killing, and the motive behind it.

Soon Cage's path is littered with the burnt
remains of a seemingly unconnected group
of people. Only James' ex-girlfriend, the
inhumanly lovely Jonny Cache, can shed any
light on the victims who have been made to
burn....

About the author

Jonathan lives in Austin, Texas, where he works as a computer expert. This is his first novel.

BURN

Jonathan Lyons

Domhan Books

ISBN: 1-58345-442-X harcover
1-58345-443-8 paperback
1-58345-444-6 disk
1-58345-445-4 ebook
1-58345-446-2 palm
1-58345- 447-0 Rocket
1-58345-636-8 Microsoft

Published by Domhan Books
9511 Shore Road, Suite 514
Brooklyn New York 11209

Printer by Lightning Source, TN
Distributed by Ingram Book Company

one

Outside, it rained black again.

Outside, it was still dark, still the dirty gray near-night of the best-lit days of Old New York.

Cage paused in the doorway of *Gotham George's*, and licked the cold, tangy rain from his upper lip as he mopped it from his hair, his brow, his stinging eyes. He'd lost his umbrella somewhere along the line, and hadn't bothered to replace it yet, despite regional Civic Environmental Authority warnings not to venture out without at least level-three precautions.

Right, he'd thought, when he'd seen the flashing warning in the lower-right corner of the video billboard outside his office: *Every-one drops everything and straps on a filter mask when CEA tells 'em to, too.*

His black non-react trench coat, he noticed, had gone ashen over the past few months. So much for non-reactive.

Cage had stepped into a new chuckhole in the walk between the office and *Gotham George's*, and his footfalls were punctuated with a cold *squish* every other step.

He ventured past the tarnished, brass *GG* logo, into *Gotham George's* and found Donatelli Three minding bar.

Old, old jazz, music from before Cage was born filtered through the bar, while a permanent cologne of cigar smoke and hydroponic tobacco 2942, and spilled beers from a hundred-plus countries fill-ing the place.

Cage waved an index finger at the bartender. "One finger!" he yelled to Donatelli Three over some cacophonous sex-partnering gameshow Netcast. He chose a seat shrouded in some of the place's permanent shadows, away from where most of the tavern patrons wandered. Cage pulled off the ash-colored trenchoat, draping it over the opposite side of the booth to dry.

On the 'Net set a timer counted toward zero, while a couple copulating on stage before a live studio audience kept at it while contestants vied to replace them. The audience was enthusiastic, to say the least.

Donatelli Three ran Cage's profile. "Laphroaig? A bit of the old medicinal spirit?" asked the bartender. This elicited a nod. The bartender's memory was as reliable as that of Gotham George himself.

"A double is only one more Ennay, Mr. Cage," Donatelli Three informed him, its conspiratorial-smile algorithm running over-time.

Smiling the smile of friendly surrender, Cage waved two fingers in the air, gesturing for the double. He tugged his brown, texture-woven vest forward, loosening the double-Windsor of his plain, black tie.

As he savored the peaty single-malt in his mouth, he felt a familiar tremor along his left hip. He ignored the summons, taking another long pull on the glass.

Gotham George's was an all-hours joint. Decades of sloshed drinks were chronicled in lacquer-like layers in the ancient, worn tile of the tavern floor, like rings in the tree cutaways Cage had seen in museums as a kid.

"Like to weather the storm, if you don't mind, Donatelli," he said.

"You always like to do so when business is quiet," replied Donatelli Three's smooth voice, in a flat, nonjudgmental tone, from a small lamp near Cage in the dimly lit booth. Donatelli's lips hadn't moved. It hadn't turned from loading glasses and pitchers into a sterilizer ten yards away, and it creeped Cage out a little when his bartender multi-tasked.

When the tremor came again, Donatelli Three turned, looked at Cage as though sizing him up, and said, "Someone's trying to reach your Personal."

"Yeah," said Cage.

"Do you think it's her?" asked Donatelli.

Still reading my profile, Cage thought. *Not like I haven't told it the whole story a hundred times.*

But his bartender prodded its regulars like this. It was in its programming.

Cage said, "Another Laphroaig."

The bartender complied. "It isn't Cin, Cage; she's a Climber. You know that. Someone's trying to establish a StellarNet conference with you. Work-related, I'd wager, from the looks of the referring URL," the lamp speaker said as the bartender decanted Cage's order. Again, Donatelli's lips did not move.

"And you seem to have forgotten your tab recently, Mr. Cage," Donatelli's voice issued from the bartender itself this time. "Gotham George will certainly remember."

Gotham George has enough of a downpayment in my insurance retainer, thought Cage. But he wasn't about to say that to Donatelli Three.

Not certain whether to be relieved by the news that it wasn't his ex, or put off with Donatelli's candor, Cage jerked his Personal from its left-hip holster, activated the little hand-held unit, and set it down on the bar.

"Cage here," he said.

two

On the tiny screen, a pixelated image loaded, gaining resolution and clarity: A gum-popping girl in her late teens or early twenties, deep-oak colored roots tinged lighter at the ends, appeared.

Caught out in the rain, Cage thought. *She's due for another tint job.*

An identifier key — his — in the upper-right corner told Cage it was Effie at the office. Across the lower portion of the screen, an ad began to scroll past: "Need to get there fast? Catch the Bullet! Low-orbit travel beats jet airliners hands down!"

A small, stylized company logo followed the text of the ad across the screen of his Personal, followed by an online address.

"Cage, a woman has contacted us who *most* urgently wants to meet with you."

"Woman?" Cage asked. "What woman?"

"One Janice Gild," Effie said, reading from a profile. "The image's kinda dark on your end — do you want to enhance the transmission?"

"No," Cage said, "Just patch her through, would you?"

With a shrug, she disappeared in a screen flicker, and a new datastream-carrier image loaded: a woman of maybe early middle-age, not in particularly good or particularly bad shape, white-collar clothing template in rose red.

"Mr. Cage, my name is Janice Gild. I wish to employ your services to investigate a death."

"Police investigate deaths, lady. What makes you think I wanna get in their way?"

Gild squirmed in discomfort, "I'd, er, I'd rather not discuss it on an open conference. Perhaps a private meeting? At your office, perhaps?"

"I'll be out of the office for a while," Cage said, but knew he'd make it back. "This evening?"

With a nod, Janice Gild's image flicked out.

Cage folded down the screen hatch of his Personal and holstered it. He sipped his scotch, remembering, the way Laphroaig always made him remember. Like he was trying to find out what went wrong some time along the line; like he could go back and fix everything if he knew exactly when it had been that the tide had turned. Like it was just a puzzle he had to solve.

A long time ago, Cage had been a career man. A career cop, a detective with a wife-to-be and a good partner and a retirement plan with Expedite Corporation, corporate sponsors of Old New York's police force. The same wave of corporate and political intermingling that had let big-money sponsors introduce science-class literature into public schools — literature from oil companies, for example, arguing that coal and oil were forms of solar energy — and had opened government branches to privatization.

Social Security had been handed to a Japanese mega-investment company's stateside affiliate, raising tensions between the Mafia and Yakuza in North America. Environmental regulation had moved from the taxpayer-funded EPA to the Central Environmental Authority Inc., which had marketed the air-filtration masks and non-react-coating polymers and tap-water purifiers it advised people to use when it posted its public-service warnings of particularly bad smog or acid rain or water-system contamination.

And over the decades, while calculated political nit-picking stalled action on global warming, greenhouse gas emissions, disposal of dangerous wastes, and what have you, the planet's environment had shifted. In some places, the heat had risen, sending up more fog and mist to mingle with the smog of the cities and roam the globe. In other places, temperatures had plummeted as the Earth slouched, wounded, toward some new and bizarre equilibrium.

That was when Nightfall had come. When the sun had slowly dimmed over much of the globe, masked by the thick, permanent smogs. Businessmen full of self-interest told politicians, with obese monetary reminders, that the sun still shone on much of the Earth's surface, and that this was no call for environmental radicalism.

In the New York City of old, where newscasts at the turn of the millennium still proclaimed the day clear and sunny when cameras that were pointed across at Manhattan could muster only a smoky silhouette, the change crept in slowly. It had had enough time to

9

become the norm before Gotham's denizens even realized that the sun had stopped coming out.

The well-to-do began to relocate to permanent synthetic islands in the South Pacific and Indian oceans, islands like New Metropolis One, where a lack of government meant less-stringent environmental regulations. No one would fine them for failing to recycle. There would be no fiascoes over sewage treatment: They had an ocean to take care of these problems.

Cage had wanted to save for a future there, where children he might have some day could play in the sun. But in one day, he had lost his job, lost his future wife — hell, he had lost his whole future.

Gazing a little deeper into the amber depths of his tumbler, his crystal ball in reverse, showing his past rather than his future, Cage recalled deciding to look a little deeper into the death of Joseph Fuhlber, an Expedite Corp. computer scientist, than Expedite Corp. had wanted. Cage had gotten as far as uncovering the death of that scientist's partner amid suspect circumstances when he had found out exactly why news journals and Net sites had long since stopped printing unfavorable editorials about their larger customers: Because the ones that did so lost funding from those sponsors and, in an already competitive market, went belly-up.

The police weren't looking into the partner's death, either, despite a bullet wound to the head identical to the one that had felled Fuhlber, a deadly, blood-splashed cranial abyss that said *murder* to Cage before he'd seen any other information: The angle was all wrong for Dr. Marianne Olaf to have fired the fatal shot herself. But the cops had closed both cases, ruling them both suicides.

Hell, even his partner, Murphy, who Cage had thought wasn't afraid of anything, had had the sense to get out of that murder investigation, though his departure from Cage's side had seemed sudden at the time, though innocent enough.

Only on the mostly abandoned Internet of old — the hard-wired, sluggish, aboriginal ancestor to today's orbiting StellarNet — did rogue news sites publish news or editorial articles that were in any way critical of Expedite.

Cage was a detective who couldn't make the pieces of the puzzle fit in the couple's deaths, and didn't appreciate the warnings from superiors, Murphy, other cops — even Cin — to drop it.

So Cage had been dropped instead. *A loose cannon,* his chief had called him, the same chief who'd held him up as a model for other detectives at a policeman's ball only four months earlier.

Ever since then, he'd managed a slim paycheck in private investigation, slim, but generous enough that with a little juggling he could get by while paying rent for an office near the Old Gotham Quarter and paying Effie to watch his Netmails and conference requests. It wasn't much of a life, but so far he had been lucky; at least it was a life.

Cage downed the last of the scotch coating the glass and nodded to Donatelli Three. Holding a newspaper from the bar over his head to fend off the acidic drizzle, Cage struck out into the smudgy, rainy day.

three

"Six hundred thousand?!" barked the suit, a pudgy, ruddy, sweating, male customer of maybe fifty years. His plaintive cry echoed flatly, competing with the dismal patter of a cold day's rain against the panes, leaking in streams through the roof of the abandoned warehouse they'd chosen for their meeting. "Cache, that's *triple* the agreed-upon fee."

A trump-card smile spread across Jonny's face.

At nearly two meters, the sleek brunette in the slick black NoGo leatherlook coat, polluted rivulets streaming down its surface, was able to hold down a lot of personal real estate in a conversation; she was much more imposing than the hired muscle the suit had brought in case of trouble. More imposing because of her lithe, agile strength. More imposing because of her distracting beauty.

More imposing because she had it.

Jonny was a woman of contrasts: close-cropped, raven-black hair complemented likewise ebony eyebrows and lashes and lips of a dark, deep, nearly brown red against the even paleness of her skin and her razor-sharp facial features. She was not voluptuous, but her hips were present (and presented) with an attitude. She was not comic-booklike, basketball breasted. Far from it. But there was no denying the feminine in her profile.

"The economics of the situation have changed," she said. "Two hundred thousand Ennays was a fair trade back before I held the only copy of your transaction records, Watzke. Now I have it, and no one else does. For the moment."

Watzke sat at the old table weighing the threat, his Personal on the counter before him. He mopped sweat from his upper lip with his sleeve, his arm brushing his filter mask as ruddy anger swelled his face.

Men of power weren't used to bowing to the will of women, Jonny had noted. And a suit like Watzke was a man of power.

Regional vice president of multinational conglomerate Ameribank, a man in a position to know about and take advantage

12

of the occasional market windfall, and he had done just that. But then he'd gotten thinking about the openness of StellarNet, and decided he'd wanted a clean record uploaded to replace his polluted original.

He'd needed a Netrunner of rare talent, someone who could get in and get out of the Ameribank Central Data Reservoir without disturbing the security measures which would need bypassing.

He'd needed someone who'd had their hardware augmented — built for speed and stealth — to do the job.

He'd needed Jonny Cache.

"You got the only copy, huh, Cache? So how 'bout I shoot your synthetic ass? Take care 'a my problems? Take home with me that briefcase Oscar-there's keepin' safe?"

Hired muscle shifted, ready to go for his thigh-mounted, holstered weapon, a features-laden, overly automated flak-spreader done up in flat black duraplex that could make a combat shock trooper out of a five-year-old.

Cache, smile widening, stepped forward as though bulletproof.

"'Cause I'm bulletproof, suit," she purred. "'Cause I'm set to Netmail the file to news sites all over StellarNet the second Gigantopithicus, there, goes for that toy on his leg."

She had him. She knew she had him. Watzke knew she had him.

The suit deflated with a long, labored exhale. "Oscar, hand the lady the briefcases. Both of 'em."

Jonny kept her smile in check. Best not to look like a total beginner, she thought. After a hardware-accelerated inventory of Watzke's cash-laden briefcases, Cache took a seat at the table before the suit's Personal. She stared intently for a moment, then stood.

"All yours, suit. Keep Anabolic Kong there in check until I'm gone, and I'll burn your file, as per our arrangement."

"I didn't see you change nothin'," Watzke said.

"'Course not, suit — infrared link. I can see it just fine, but you can't," she said, loading the N.A.T.S. bills into her own satchel for travel.

"You boys play nice," she said, slinging the satchel over her shoulder.

And as she walked toward the warehouse's doors, rusted im-

13

mobile from decades of caustic rain and lack of upkeep, she found herself singing along with her internal playback of the song that always came to mind when she was about to run her memory-burn app: "Ring of Fire," recorded by her near-namesake in a more sun-lit, bygone era.

Donning a set of spectrum-sweep-capable shades, she struck out into the smudgy, rainy near-night.

four

Cage made his way down the block, keeping close to buildings and under awnings. There wasn't much mainland commerce these days, less where Nightfall meant that the night never lifted, even less so in the little side offices of a run-down borough with no chance of flashy front-door access. Cage could pay the rent, even on time, mostly. And the building's owners weren't interested in kicking out a rare paying tenant in this area.

Off the beaten track and up two flights, Cage had found an affordable option and put an unusually human twist on things: As companies began to realize how much profit went into real workspaces, the virtual office had loomed large in the corporate cost-cutter mindset. *Office* not being preceded by *virtual* was the exception around these parts these days.

Thumbing the lock of the ground-floor entrance, Cage stepped into the dark hall, a landing at the base of the stairwell. A single, pale bulb dangling overhead, about fifteen feet up, shed the only light in the grim building. He gave the newspaper a perfunctory glance, finding the newsprint and ink had been no match for the caustic drizzle.

He noted another set of wet tracks — small and narrow-toed; a woman's — leading up the stairs.

He pushed his hands back through his short, wet, brown hair and began the climb to the office.

He reached the building's third story, making his way down a long hall like a tug cruising an old boatyard, a permanent dock for retired ships: Cage's agency was the only occupied office on the floor. He made his way down the long hall, passing doors with names in paint faded, flaking, in some cases blotted over with white primer. The light in his office was on, as was a small lamp lighting a sign hanging out into the hallway, over the office door, reading simply: "Cage Detective Agency."

As he strode through the aging front door bearing his name in hand-painted lettering, Effie greeted him. Effie: His Girl Friday with her number-crunching mysticism that kept the business mostly out of the red and kept its services from being disconnected.

"Ms. Gild beatcha back, Cage," she informed him, checking him over to make sure he was ready to meet with a client. "You're no suit, Cage. Look like you weren't even expecting business today, but you'll probably be OK," she said. His tie had become rumpled in the wet weather; she quickly straightened and tightened it.

The office was divided into a greeting area, where Effie sat behind a desk and answered Netmail, conferences, and so on; and a back office. The wood, though old and visibly in need of refinishing, lent the office a certain musty sense of the prestige of a booming bygone time downtown. Cage's home base was the back office, and he could see Janice Gild was already waiting within.

Cage ran a hand across his two-day stubble, ran a hand back through his hair again, and headed for the inner office, taking a seat in his chair and desk, directly under an ancient, slow-moving ceiling fan and lamp.

Janice Gild sat in the chair with an easy posture; she felt at home. Her rain-repellent gear hung in the corner on an old coat tree, next to an old cardigan that Cage and Effie rarely disturbed. Outside, the rain kept up a steady hiss, like the sound of an AM radio when the station its tuned to signed off for the night.

"Mr. Cage," said Gild, "I understand that you've found yourself here after a fall from grace, as it were."

She knew about Expedite.

"My past has nothing to do with how I handle business these days, Ms. Gild."

"Janice," she said with a little flick of the edges of her mouth — a smile? — he didn't know. "It does to me, Mr. Cage. My brother, James Gild, died under unusual circumstances in his apartment twelve days ago, and the police have dropped the investigation."

Cage swallowed. Even today, Expedite was a looming menace in his world. He had no problem with investigating, but Expedite controlled StellarNet. They were hip-deep in the pockets of politicians all over the globe, with plenty of dirt on everyone who made a bogus transaction, pr made a conference to someone they might not like the rest of the world to find out about. Anyone who bought something illicit at some point or another. StellarNet linked all, making supposedly transparent actions — renting out a room at a D.C. hotel over lunch hour, for example — all traceable to people in the right places, with the right capabilities.

And this David remembered his bruising at this Goliath's hands.

"You know Expedite's got its hands in everything, don't you Ms. Gild? StellarNet access, credit and debit functionality at businesses. Whole governments heel like Fido when Expedite calls. A sideways glance from them can be devastating."

"As you well know, Mr. Cage," she said.

Cage sat back in his chair, sliding out of the sphere of light from the lamp overhead, watching Gild. A rhythmic *click-clack, click-clack* from the ceiling fan kept a cadence as he considered her.

As the gulf of silence yawned between them, beginning a *danse macabre* with office shadows, Gild broke the spell: "It's the strangeness of the case that's put off the police, Mr. Cage, not Expedite," she said, crossing a set of athletic, eye-drawing legs.

"'Strangeness,' Ms. Gild?" he asked, sitting forward now, leaning his elbows on the desk, his eyebrows arching in query. "What 'strangeness'?"

"He was incinerated in his own home."

"Apartment fire?"

"No," she said. "The condominium didn't burn."

"A break-in? Deliberate attack?"

"No," she said steadily, "there were no signs of forced entry. And James was a very to-himself sort of person."

"Any enemies? Anyone he'd been having trouble with? He have a fling with the wrong guy's wife, maybe?"

"No, Mr. Cage," she said firmly. "James had no obvious interest in having a sex life, as far as I could tell. He was a retired programmer."

"Retired?"

"An early retiree. He was forty-two years old."

Cage contained his surprise.

"How did he manage that?"

"Profit-sharing stock from a project he helped to engineer early on. He sold it and retired, but he loved composing code — I never understood that quirk — and so he worked as an independent contractor, when it suited him."

Cage regarded her. She was an attractive blond-haired woman of young-enough appearance; he gauged her at age forty-four.

"How much of a difference in age was there between you?" he asked.

"About seven minutes. He was my twin brother, Mr. Cage. And the police have given me no answers, brought me no closer."

"I'll need to do some homework, and I'll need access to the scene of his death."

"His will left me with plenty to cover your expenses, Mr. Cage; and I now have ownership of his condominium. Mr. Cage, I just want answers," she said, handing him an envelope. "Crime scene photos."

"I'll see what I can do," he replied, "but I have to be up-front with you: On a corporate whim, Expedite crushed me like a fly once; if they're involved, if they so much as bat an eyelash in our general direction, my investigation stops."

With a nod of acquiescence, Cage found himself gainfully employed again.

As she stood to take her leave, Cage caught sight of her for the first time: a five-foot-four blonde, the rose-red executive number she wore making nearly every move she made make her every curve call out to him.

Well, Cage thought, surprised at the strength of his reaction. *It has been a while.*

When she was gone, Effie walked into Cage's back office.

"Business, Cage?" she asked, loosening his rumpled tie and its day-old knot.

"Business, Effie. Weird business, but business."

"Your Olds is on the roof, Cage. I refueled it earlier."

"You didn't need to do that, Effie," Cage said with a smile.

"I get bored when it's slow, Cage, you know that," she said dismissively. "Go on. You've got a case to solve."

He pulled a tiny chip, his boost sample, from the top drawer of his desk and from its case. Flipping the camouflaged, skinlike flap covering the slim, metallic reader orifice embedded in his skull behind his left ear, he slid the sample chip into place.

Cage remembered when he was younger, and the term had

been Reader™ — copyright held by a small neuro-engineering startup. But Pendergrast Technology and Statesman Register — Expedite subsidiaries — had designed their own versions — and who had the money and clout to challenge Expedite? — and the term had gone the way of rollerblades. The heavy, loamy weight of the scotch on his brain began to wear off almost as soon as the sample booted.

five

Cage was wide awake now, the boost sample working its magic, reducing the effects of the scotch to a smoky aftertaste memory as he initiated the land/park sequence in the Olds and began his descent through the filthy nighttime air and sooty, black rain.

He looked over the old-style photo prints from his new client: Black and white, exposed with so much contrast that he saw only a charred black circle in the center of a mattress. A still-shod foot, the ankle still ringed by a pair of slacks, lay untouched from the toe to a carbon-black char just above the ankle. The black cauterization met the edge of the fore site.

The condo was uptown enough that Cage caught a whiff of money in just hearing the ZIP code. The rooftop was set up for a vertical landing onto a reinforced plate, the cars meant to taxi into reserved, covered stalls. But even the rooftop smelled of extras: Ancient-Roman-influenced columns supported the protective overhang. The entire landing area wasdecorated in similar periodic reference. A pair of towering gods in simulated marble (not marble, Cage knew, because of how well the material resisted the rain) stood bearing the weight of the roof of the covered parking stalls.

Cage's office, by contrast, had only the Aerial Traffic Authority-mandated landing plate and lighting sequence.

James Gild must have been part of a pretty damned successful programming project to afford these digs.

With Ms. Gild's access card, Cage let himself into the building after parking, and made his way toward the late Gild's domicile: No. 101.

The yellow police "No Entry — Crime Scene" tape criss-crossing the entry to Gild's condo had been neatly razored in two and rejoined so skillfully that only on close inspection could he see the seam.

Someone's dropped by to see the late Mr. Gild's place, Cage thought.

He dusted the card-access panel for prints, finding what he'd anticipated: a chorus of smears and partial prints — *clumsy flatfoot bastards*, he thought — and nothing to indicate that any of them was more important than the others.

With a swipe of the card and a command — "Lights" — Cage found himself standing face-to-face with a brightly-lit facet of bachelor life that in some ways mirrored his own. He dismissed an unforgivable stomach rumble when the aging, smoky restaurant-like smell of the air in the condo first hit him. The apartment's air cycling and replenishing system must have been shut down for some time: The smell of kitchen mingled with the thick, dusty, scent of disuse.

Then Cage spotted another indicator of James Gild's evident financial success: a small, immaculately-kept bar constructed of real wood, stained dark and sealed mightily against damage. Cage hadn't seen enough wood in presentable condition in his time to be able to discern the type of tree from which the bar had been fashioned. But it was pretty impressive all the same.

The decoration of the place wasn't the uniform, themed, structured sort of project Cage had come to expect. Gild had artifacts from every phase of his adult life: A comfy old chair that spoke of twenty-something bachelorhood; an AV unit, the size of which suggested to Cage that Gild had rarely bothered watching anything on it; an old, sprocket-shaped living room table that needed refinishing. A bachelor's odds and ends.

On a dark, ancient, cherry-woodlike duraplex stand in the main room stood a small collection of photos, arrayed on an old, translucent, gold-colored scarf that had been draped decoratively over the stand — by Janice Gild or an acquaintance, if the rest of the decor were any indication.

Cage leaned over to peer into the old, tarnishing frames: Janice and James Gild together, much younger. Gild's graduation walk. A pair of old photos depicting a fifty-something couple — the Gilds' parents? He passed his hand before the two photos of the couple, but nothing happened.

He turned to a photo of James Gild with a strikingly attractive young woman, perhaps twenty-five, with long, dark hair. Both smiled. Next to the frame was an empty indentation in the scarf where another photo had once stood. When Cage passed his hand before the frame, the picture activated, skipping to its start frame, and Gild

21

said: "This is her first day at her new home, so welcome to my new housekeeper and companion, Jennifer Four."

In response, the woman smiled and looked out from the frame. She gave the vacant smile, Cage noted, of an android that hadn't patterned to its owner yet.

Then it stopped, set at the frame he'd first seen.

Cage rubbed a hand over his bristled chin and turned to delve deeper into the dwelling. No one had told him about any domestic unit. Maybe the sister, Janice Gild, didn't know her brother's dirty little secret. James Gild probably hadn't mentioned it to her. Domestics were playthings of the well-to-do, but not the sort of possession a guy usually bragged about.

In Gild's bedroom, Cage found the inexplicable: The center of the bed was a fearsome black crater, the scorch mark, presumably, of Gild's explosive final moments.

There were no indications of smoke or heat damage to the ceiling above the bed, nor had an apparently intense fire go beyond an almost perfect four-foot circle. The detective found himself wondering whether this would be the most horrific way for a human being to die; fire had always struck him as the most pain-filled manifestation of death. Even minor burns had seemed excruciating, the sort of pain you didn't want to repeat if you could avoid it.

But it looked like this must have been over with very quickly. The fire alarms within the condo hadn't even been set off.

Cage scratched his head, unholstered his Personal, aimed, and collected a few images for his own analysis.

On the nightstand near Gild's scorched bed, Cage found a snifter, which had left several hard rings on the table; Gild had taken a drink to bed with him.

He leaned in and sniffed the air over the glass. *Brandy*, he thought.

Cage picked up a book resting on the nightstand and examined it. One of the first few pages was turned down.

Moving around to the far side of the bed, Cage found himself looking absently through the greasy smear of the rain on the man's bedroom window, out into the drizzle, into the darkness of the night, into — into a window in a building across the street, to a backlit, overcoat-clad figure who'd just realized Cage had spotted him. The figure put something down — A camera? Small telescope? — and disappeared.

Cage cleared the fire-pocked bed, flung the door open and plowed into an appalled pair of residents and another pair, probably their guests, cheery and clean, all clad in white tennis sportswear. Lunging up from the floor, Cage made for the roof.

He exploded through the stairway door and out onto the landing strip. Firing a quick look at the adjacent building, Cage heard the high-pitched whine of a car's engine — a little one — climbing higher and higher; a car beginning its liftoff sequence.

He bolted for the Olds, and — opting to risk Aerial Traffic Authority wrath to save time — fired up and lifted off without clearance from the building's parking attendant.

In the pits of his bowels he felt the superlow-frequency *thummm* of the engine firing up.

Through the steam and drizzle Cage could just make out a small, sporty car rising from the other building, spinning to the east, and veering off.

Man's in a dangerous hurry, Cage thought, punching his accelerator and bringing his car up to speed.

The small ones had an advantage over a cruiser like Cage's Olds, he knew: They were more maneuverable and could squeeze into tinier spaces. But they couldn't match an Olds for power, and Cage slowly gained on the car.

But the fleeing observer wanted no part of Cage's attention, and left the traffic altitude, diving for the street below.

Cage followed suit, plummeting after the little car he could now see was a Huang-Sen, plunging between buildings after it, buzzing bums and hookers and røgue-bøyz and NewSchool Grrls in alleys and back avenues all they way up to 115th Street.

The two cars hurtled around the tight corners, around buildings, following the streets below.

Cage got up close to the little Huang-Sen, but the smaller car slipped aside like the fish simulation models he'd seen, bolting for the river, kicking up trails of water spreading out from the car's path like anorexic tidal waves, shooting fifty feet into the air, then dissipating into mist.

He was going for the old train bridge at Evans.

In disuse for years and abandoned by the once-prosperous rail-road that owned it when the North American Trade Sector was opened to what suit poobahs called "borderless trade," the old bridge sat, decaying, a blighted, crumbling meter stick for the city's own decline, the occasional brick dropping into the foul, lifeless waters below, the occasional street adventurer drunk on anti-freeze falling through while trying to cross the failing structure.

Cage watched as the Huang-Sen dived for the bridge; the pilot was going to try to swoop under the old fossil. Cage pressed him, knowing the Olds had no chance of clearing a tango with the bridge, and gambling the Huang-Sen wouldn't be able to pull it off, either.

Cage pushed up to the Huang-Sen's tail and stuck to it, but the pilot wouldn't pull out, wouldn't pull out, just kept bearing down on the rusted old structure, and Cage stuck to him, stuck to him, trying to get a clear shot of the man's rear bumper, when he knew, he knew the pilot wasn't pulling out and he knew that if he let him out, he'd keep up his flight, and he took the gamble and stuck to him, close to him. When the roof of the little Huang-Sen made a spark on the underside of the bridge and cleared it, Cage knew he'd be lucky to get out alive.

And there was nothing but water and tail-lights and the Olds skipped like a flat rock expertly flung over calm water, and Cage fought, fought to get it under control, fought to make sense of his dashboard readings over the shaking and thunder as he plowed through the water and then it was …

Quiet.

Shaking his head, Cage looked skyward; the little Huang-Sen's taillights shrank almost until they became a single red dot, then banked sharply away, speeding into the smog and the night.

He flipped the ignition switch and the Olds turned over. Looking around, he saw that he'd come to rest on the river's surface, that the car had held together, and its structural integrity hadn't been breached.

He was afloat. He keyed the liftoff sequence and, hearing sirens in the distance, killed his lights and flew the Olds below the altitude of the skyline, back to the office building.

Effie met him in the rooftop hangar with a hot cup of joe.

"Janice Gild called. She says there's been another burn."

six

Jennifer Four was your average, perfectly proportioned, sexy android. It was built for realism, a takeoff on the old Helen O'Loy scheme, but modernized. The Jennifer Four had been designed to be a domestic unit: Dishes, housekeeping, sex. Expedite's slogan for its indispensable domestic possession: "You'll Never Go Back."

With a permanent link to StellarNet, a recall order could be issued, forcing the android to return to Expedite in cases of malfunction, a sort of digital homing beacon.

It had been purchased by a lonely retired programmer named James Gild.

He'd chosen this design, a composite constructed of a dozen or so female models, a final product that he found profoundly sexually appealing.

It had smallish, rounded, firm breasts, a long spill of raven-black hair complementing likewise ebony eyebrows and lashes, and lips of a ruby red, contrasting the even paleness of its skin and razor-sharp facial features.

Expedite's domestic androids inadvertently became the source of a new disease in an age of lessening interpersonal contact: Sumner's Syndrome. The ultimate lonely guy — or lonely gal — disease.

Sumner's Syndrome arose because the programming — the hardware and the software together — produced great sex. Better than the real thing, some owners insisted. The android's interpretive code and hardware reacted to and adjusted to owner's input, physical and vocal reactions, skin temperature, pulse, orgasm. Expedite referred to the process of learning and adjusting the hardware/software sexual compatibility programming to that of the android's owner as *mapping* the owner's sexual profile.

After having had the sexual company of the perfectly sexually matched android mate, over the course of enough time, some people found that they couldn't cope with the cooperative pleasure-seeking dialogue of touch and talk shared by actual people having sex.

They'll Never Go Back.

Gild hadn't dated; interactions with people, in person, had made him feel watched; he dreamt CIVRML; he could hardly believe anyone had ever used BASIC; the spiraling, interleaved machine prose of artificial intelligence — AI — was his favorite writing mode; he daydreamt in Pascal and practically spoke C++.

So the android had seemed the proper solution at the time: Its intercourse-interpretation algorithms made it responsive in bed — very responsive — and he could return to his work when he wished without hurting its feelings. All very efficient.

As weeks with the android became months, he had begun to realize that he hated its impersonal sterility, its distant stare, its lack of humanity, and he had begun studying its design.

In his workshop at home, he had integrated new processors into Jennifer Four, interleaving their data-handling abilities in a commingling strategy he'd only theorized before, and, after months of scrying, had written new capabilities into its interpretive programming.

On rebooting, Jennifer Four had awakened as a more complex being. He had begun having it review encyclopedias on DVD, keep track of the day's news Netcast, and keep him abreast of what was happening.

Gild didn't know when he'd started thinking of Jennifer Four as a *she*, rather than an *it*, but his changed perspective had been cast in sharp relief as he neared orgasm one night, with her beautiful nude form, jutting, slim hips surging beneath him, and he had realized that she had cut her hair, choosing another, sleeker, shorter style. He had realized that the change had meant that she had begun making choices about herself, that she had become self-aware. And he wondered, raising a hand to caress her face as she looked up, watching him, watching him — if she were awake now, as aware as any flesh-and-blood woman — whether he were committing rape with a sex slave, not just soiling a sex toy.

He did not have sex with Jennifer Four again, and she became a sort of daughter surrogate to him instead.

But he missed her, missed having her in an intimate role. But what she was was no longer what she had been. Deep down inside, even knowing that their roles had changed, even knowing that he'd done no wrong to the old Jennifer Four, the domestic, even knowing that their relationship had changed precisely because she was not any longer the unfeeling automaton he had purchased, guilt over his actions, his sex with her, clung to him, gnawing at his conscience.

She began to interpret, not just read, the files she studied. And she learned about wars and the North American Trade Sector, which had brought a single currency to its signatory nation-partners; she learned of the Global Climate Shift and the rise of the Great Firewall of China, behind which the Communist Dragon had shielded itself from corrupting Western data, and of the Far Eastern Currency Collapse. And she had learned about the human slave trade.

When Gild had left for the market one gray day, she had let herself into his workshop, positioned an array of mirrors around her head, brushed back her hair, and flipped open her cranial access hatch, exposing a circuitry array. With newly acquired knowledge of her own design, she had deftly disconnected the physical component of her permanent link to StellarNet, replacing it with a digital online/offline switch that she could toggle at will.

They wouldn't be calling her, but perhaps she'd call them.

She had upped the contrast in her coloration, choosing a darker set of tones for her make-up accents, and a dark, deep, nearly brown red for her lips. She packed a utilitarian set of tools, supplies and clothes in her satchel — she didn't need much, didn't really need a place to sleep — and went street-level with an old tune she'd downloaded from a Netherlands bootleg .mod site running on playback through her head: Johnny Cash's "Ring of Fire."

In the weeks that followed, she realized that for whatever reason, Gild wasn't going to follow her, and she started looking for specialized, low-key work. Being very, very good with computer access and security — she'd downloaded every available resource on the subject, and she didn't forget things — she had taken a name to match her tech-savvy new line of employment: Jonny Cache.

She had established contacts around Old New York, sending word around that for the right price, she was the Netrunner who could get into and out of any system, secure or otherwise, undetected, caching whatever information her clients needed. And as guarantee of their confidentiality, she'd run a memory-burn app on any files she'd taken during a raid, leaving her in no position to offer the files to others.

seven

Effie brewed a mean cuppa.

Cage let the mug warm his hands as he inspected the external damage to the Olds, shaking his head: A few scrapes, but nothing serious.

"Built like a tank," he observed.

"You're not. You look a little bruised up. Thought you stopped driving like that in high school, Cage. You're damned lucky to be alive," she said, more relieved than scolding.

"I wiped her out in the drink," Cage told her. "Something's not right here. That little Huang-Sen shouldn't have been able to outrun the Olds. Someone put the little bastard on steroids," he said, taking a swallow of the hot java.

Back in the office, Effie started to read him the new file.

"Oliver Jaspin, age — uhmm — forty-eight. Hardware engineer for Chapterhouse Computing, liked Beaujolais so much he had a minor personal crisis when the nouveau got pricey and harder to come by in the French vineyards' collapse — "

"Minor?"

"Significant enough to be noted in his work file," she said. "Which is how we know about it. Let's see — company man with company coverage, no time for a family, spent his vacations on the Jersey shores before the sea level rose. No rivalries noted in his work records. Girlfriend says he wasn't a violent man, didn't have anything bad happening in his personal life. No leads. Police look like they're running the same play they did with Gild."

"Guess that's not surprising," Cage said.

"No? Jaspin lived on New Bombay at the time of his — uhmm — immolation."

"Different cop outfit, different force; smells of outside influence. Which island?"

"New Bombay One."

Cage draped his soaking-wet trenchcoat over the old coat tree in his back office, made his way to his desk, and started to review

28

the case files left by Janice Gild. Drawing a dirty tumbler from his desk drawer and dropping the boost sample chip into its case, Cage pulled a bottle of amber liquid from the bottom drawer and poured.

He pulled out a black and white glossy of the scene, the black-circle sore of scorch and ash he'd seen in James Gild's bedroom, two feet, cauterized just above the ankle, resting almost unharmed just at the edge of the circle of the crater.

Something's not right, he thought. *There's an assailant. People don't just blow up.*

As he began reviewing the official reports, exhaustion set in, given weight by the scotch in his tumbler, and Cage nodded out.

Effie tiptoed in, draped a blanket over the private detective, and drew the blinds on the windows separating his back office and her own workspace.

Effie Leichtkinde's was an old story, as in old money. She didn't need the paychecks that Cage — barely — provided. But she wasn't one to stay at home, her only interaction gleaned from clubs and taverns and VR chat.

And this made her a perfect employee for Cage's situation: One who didn't mind when business was slow, as it sometimes was, and Cage had to IOU her checks until the next case came along.

She had inherited young — her parents had both succumbed to cancers — but didn't spend much time at her uptown address. She'd thought, when her family's friends began to light out for Atlantis Five, Metropolis Nine, and the other synthetic island-cities, that that way lay boredom. White flight not from downtown, but from the continent.

She had wanted a little adventure in her life, so she'd stayed, answered a *Help Wanted* ad Cage had posted, and had found her-self employed in a weathered, beaten part of the Old Gotham Quarter she was grateful to be able to fly to. Ground traffic in the area was, she thought, unsavory at least and unsafe, certainly.

Over time, she'd developed a mild crush on the unshaven, not particularly muscular Cage. She didn't need to pursue it now. But maybe some day —

She knew he had no time for romance and no desire, yet, to become involved with anyone, knew from the shards and broken

29

pieces he'd shared with her about how his life had fallen apart when Expedite had had him removed from the force, how his perfect two-point-three children, ocean-city-going, beaming-little-wifey future had collapsed when he wouldn't leave well enough alone.

Cin — Hyacinth Merriam Vandervelde — had come from an upwardly mobile family that had known poverty in past generations and refused to allow it to seize them again. She'd been beautiful, Effie knew that from her description. But Cage didn't keep pictures of her.

She had ascribed to an economic philosophy that had gained momentum over the years and was quite in vogue in monied circles these days: Linear Climb. Linear Climb mandated that marriages be founded upon a sound economic base: old family money and/or a solid guarantee of new family money. The "and" version was preferable.

Cage had only a glimmer of a hope of new family money somewhere down the lines as it was. His ascent to detective with later promotions had been guaranteed in his contract, his retirement package promising a posh payout if he didn't fall to a bullet first.

But when Cage had lost his job, he'd no longer met the sound economic base mandate. Linear Climb advised that relationships that could not maintain these requirements should be disbanded, in order that poverty be avoided by the couple and, later, by the family.

Normally, Linear Climb involved a certain amount of old-money mating, rich families meeting and more or less arranging the marriages of their offspring, and Cin had already skirted that issue with her family. But when a push came to a shove and the Ennays had stopped flowing in, she tore up their prenuptial contract and left for New Chicago On Sea-Two.

Cage hadn't had much of an appetite for relationships after that.

eight

Jonny wasn't afraid she'd be lulled into stupefaction by a recall from Expedite; she'd rewritten the segment of her operating system that left her susceptible to the notice, adding her digital online/offline switch before she had left Gild; she'd still hear it, but the call wouldn't reduce her to a helpless automaton, as it was designed to.

After a close study of Gild's volumes on viruses, she had devised a delivery mechanism: A recombinant virus to feed to her OS to rewrite the recall segment. She'd passively uploaded the new code to a memory bubble she'd swiped from Gild, then downloaded it again into her own system, delivering the payload herself.

She'd waited, watching the reshaping of her OS through its completion, and, pausing briefly to wave her hand before her photo of James Gild and herself together, watched it play out, the sound muted against the constant *thump-thump-thump* rumbling through her place. She smiled, reflective for a moment.

With the software and hardware components of the company's recall system neutralized, she felt completely autonomous: Her own woman, at last. She headed streetside to find what the night had to offer her.

The hackers and NewSchool Grrls, Nouveau Gothics and røgue-bøyz and Z.Brites she knew mostly hung out at *Nine Circles*, a high-bandwidth, hardwired underground bar on Washington Crossing in Old East Village and her next-door neighbor in the massive, smudged old building; people didn't snoop in Nine Circles, and the club's owners didn't censor incoming or outgoing bandwidth. It was a strictly Free the Information-ascribing haunt.

An immense club, *Nine Circles* catered to conscientious street-smart folk; "Harm No Other Without Provocation," read a plank over the club's entryway, and the sentiment was enforced. The club provided a safe place to be, a good place to do business free of the usual owner insistence of a flat fee or two percent in-house tax on all deals done on premises. *Nine Circles* allowed no violence within the club, with deference to members first; people the owners knew, second; and regulars third in consideration of a waiver of the usual policy of handling such situations with brutality and eighty-sixing.

Designed at first with inspiration from a chip-tripping architect's troubled dreams following a sample-addled reading of Dante's "Inferno," the club was laid out with nine levels, meant by the designer to represent the nine descending circles of Hell. With a stage back and center on the bottom-most layer, the club was composed of concentric circles lining the club as they rose from the floor, each spire around the hollowed center supported by an elaborately carved, meticulously detailed, gothic-era-church-inspired set of columns — all black, their highlights lumined in a sonic-responsive paint that gave the entire club a pulse whenever music played within. Each layer was constructed with its homage to Dante.

On Caina — at level nine, representing the ice realm of Hell — temperatures were kept to a chill.

Most business was conducted on level eight, in the club's tribute to Dante's ten categories of thievery: The owners' little joke at their customers' expense.

The seventh circle was purely a bondage-fetish locale. NoGo S&M gear encouraged; cuffs, corsets and any of the myriad restraining devices welcome.

And so on, theme by theme, floor by floor, down to the Pit, the club's live-music core.

NoGo, a synthetic replacement for leather, had come into vogue when the wearing of dead animal skins and furs had become both unfashionable and — in an age of wild climatic change and firebomb attacks on the meat and fur industries — impossible. The fabric name was derived from the Sanskrit word for cow — *go* — and the word "no." After all, who held cows in higher esteem than the Hindus?

Booths had been installed with an eye to privacy on each of the *Nine Circles'* circles.

The dimly lit booths were fitted with just enough dampener that those within could conduct business, hold a conversation, even while a band played on stage, and expect that at the same time, their words wouldn't leak into adjoining booths.

The walls were coated with a flat, olive-drab primer, the bar itself boasting a collection of beers and liquors and a file of intoxicant sample chips for hourly or nightly rental.

In the old days, when they and their companion-part wetware readers had been introduced, the benefits to society had been much-ballyhooed: With the right chip, you could speak flawless German; or Italian; or whatever; you could even purchase your choice of accent.

A person with a reader installed could plug in a chip containing any sort of information he or she wished and access that data in a few moments.

But mass commerce had, as mass commerce will, other, less productive plans.

The sample chips most people came to know and demand, the sort available at the Nine Circles, delivered a chosen intoxicant to anyone who had gotten a reader installed. The chips carried a snippet of brainwave from someone who had actually done the mind-altering substance of choice, edited to an endless, seamless intoxication-pattern loop, which the reader could then read and impose on the brainwaves of the chip-tripper. The chips imparted the benefit of being ejectable; a removable high, low, trip.

In bars like Nine Circles, chip rental outpaced demand for alcoholic beverages, and people quietly zoned out to the music, happy to turn over their chips at night's end and avoid the hangover that accompanied actually ingesting the drugs.

Not that that mattered to Jonny.

Things people did to chase off their boredom held no draw for her. Not as she strolled past a doorman she knew by the handle Harshburger with a familiar nod, hearing Lysergic Precipitation conjuring its insistent, rhythmic movements, filling the club with wave after wave of pervasive, shifting, multi-layered sonic assault.

Jonny found her way to one of a hundred identical booths in the bar, a booth with two long, dim, black duraplex seats and a table, one green-hooded wall-mounted lamp at the innermost end of the booth, with plugs for any uplinking that customers might wish to do while conducting their usual business at Nine Circles.

A curvy Nouveau Gothic waitress stopped. The server's expression suggested a vague amusement with the world, an amusement accented by laser-precise black lipstick over broad lips, heavy

33

eyeliner and graduated-screen eye-shadow over far-eastern eyes, all like deep gravity wells in the ocean of her stark, white make-up base. The waitress's hair swung in loose spikes, a weeping willow scorched black, still swaying dead in the wind, but with an expensive, light-reflective, neo-metallic sheen. She dressed down very carefully: An expensive interpretation of pennilessness done up in black lace, an all-too-vital poise and attentiveness to the tinting choices of the undead.

Her server looked Jonny over, allowing a flick of a smile to corrupt her inexpression, and leaned into the sonic-dampened region of Jonny's booth.

"How ya doin', sexy lady?" she asked.

Jonny broke into a broad, full smile, grabbed the waitress, and dragged her into the booth. "Yin-Angelique! How are your other regulars treating you tonight?" Jonny asked, still hugging the server.

Quickly returning the hug, Yin-Angelique freed herself.

"Not bad, Jonny. You know the cops practically ignore anyone with an obvious source of income down here."

"Where's your inverted better half?" asked Jonny.

"She's working bar," replied Yin-Angelique with a conspiratorial arch of her left eyebrow.

Jonny smirked and, bending toward the lamp, flipped a switch.

As the prompt light outside the booth lit, she said: " Glenlivet straight, please."

A voice like Yin-Angelique's done over in a tinny AM-radio transmission replied: "Directly."

Motioning Yin-Angelique further into the booth, the two waited for the drink to arrive.

A curvy Nouveau Gothic waitress stopped. The server's expression suggested a vague amusement with the world, an amusement accented by laser-precise white lipstick over broad lips, heavy white eyeliner and graduated-screen eye shadow over far-eastern eyes, all like pools of light in the ocean of her dark, black makeup base. The waitress's hair swung in loose spikes, a weeping willow blanched white, still swaying dead in the wind, but with an expensive, light-reflective, neo-metallic sheen. She dressed down very carefully: An expensive interpretation of pennilessness done up in white lace, an all-too-vital poise and attentiveness to the tinting choices of the undead.

The new waitress looked Jonny over, allowing a flick of a smile to corrupt her inexpression, and leaned into the sonic-dampened region of Jonny's booth.

"How ya doin', sexy lady?" she asked.

Jonny and Yin-Angelique seized and dragged Yang-Angelique into their booth, sloshing the drink and chaser.

The Nouveau Gothics had arisen from an asynchronous anachronistic yearning embracing the glamorous, erotic, lavish style of Shakespeare, of medieval royal courts, of Rice and Brite and bondage, much as the Z.Brites had; but the Nouveau Gothics had branched off from their literary Z.Brites kindred with a sophisticated taste for technoculture, for hardwired upgrades and spiked biochemistry.

At once retro and futuristic, in their own way tributes to Bela Legosi, Buck Rogers, William S. Burroughs, Frank Lloyd Wright, the Nouveau Gothics embraced hypertext (and its ancestor, cut-up) and black-and-white celluloid; purely biological fuck-drive and purely technological means of sharing it; a fashion sense begun in earlier movements with Joy Division, Bauhaus, the Velvet Underground, Siouxie and the Banshees.

But their music was something evolved from the mating of the technology and that passion: Something akin to Sarah MacLachlan laying down vocals to the soundtrack of a *Survival Research Laboratories* performance, the passion and the synthesis all part of the final product.

From the ashes of the past, the true forefathers still cited today were the likes of Skinny Puppy and Lustmord, whose unintentional copulation, decades later, in the minds of a troupe of young friends tripping on mescaline (rather than a mesc-sample chip) for the first time resulted in the hatching of *Lysergic Precipitation*.

The real ones — the committed Nouveau Gothics, at least; the lifers, the ones who lived it, not just the bored rich kids in heavy rouge and white pancake — were hardwired on some level, the least being a chip reader. The most? No one really knew. Some added a data-transfer node at a major sensory receptor — an eardrum, an eye, some perceptory organ that handled a lot of data — somewhere where the nervous system was used to dealing with wide-bandwidth input. Most people have pairs of such wide-band-width-capable organs.

For some who had wished for a guaranteed academic career thirty years ago, for example, the loss of one eye's sight or the hearing in one ear might not be too high a price to pay for the resultant direct-input/output interface. Today it was the only chance, the only way to really take in and store enough. Better have a good piggy-back processor to help you sort it all while you were doing other things, too, or you were just another Ph.D. janitor who was too well-equipped to be allowed into the building. (Who knows what you could download?)

How far to take the biomechanics? Who knew, really?

The Nouveau Gothics had adopted the technology for them-selves, not in the pursuit of a career.

The binary Angeliques sat beside one another, a perfectly matched matter-antimatter duo. Every polished drop of makeup, every loose, spiky hair, every scrap of lace, tight or flowing, on Yang-Angelique mirroring that of Yin-Angelique viewed through a film negative, mirrored.

Yang-Angelique arched her right eyebrow conspiratorially.

"Scotch is an odd drink for you, Jonny," said the Angelique on the right.

"You certainly won't get anything out of scotch, Jonny," said the other.

"Camouflage," said Jonny. "Gotta do the organic-life-form thang."

Yin-Angelique and Yang-Angelique were a binary pair unlike any other: They'd been hardware-enhanced, and shared their love for one another via the most intimate of connections: Each had hard-ware permanently embedded into their skulls, allowing them the most intimate, honest transmission of thought, word, feeling and sensation; they swore by their sex, and their friends did not chal-lenge them.

On a lesser level, they were always connected. Their choice. The two could establish an uplink to their bar and handle the biz better than any Donatelli.

The link they'd installed let their brainwaves commingle; the commingling of their brainwaves made them more understanding of one another, more adoring of one another. More alike. They could shut down their link, but they had never done so. Mostly they lived the Eros of being always-on, even if only a little trickle of commingling flowed across their link to one another.

It kept them piqued.

After hours, they enjoyed letting themselves get lost in the wash of intermingling thoughts, feelings, perceptions, like two stones dropped in opposite ends of a still pool, the resulting pattern an orderly chaos, a harmonious collision and assimilation of the separate waves.

They were more alike than any two non-androids Jonny had ever met.

"How did your little reconnaissance run fare?" they asked.

"I'm not sure. I set up in the old Montgomery office building across the street. To make sure there were no police watching the old place, you know. I spotted someone there, obviously looking for something. I don't know what yet, but I got a still of his plates."

The Angeliques nodded in simultaneous concurrence, watching intently. How connected were they right now? Jonny couldn't tell.

Theirs was a secure, private network.

"Then he left. So I was packing my gear, waiting a bit, getting ready to go run the security at the condos, when light spilled in from the hallway — someone came through the door, into James' apartment.

"I watch him look around, too, only now I'm really curious, so I go back to the window, watch him store a few images, and then, bing: He sees me."

Mirrored, opposite, excited smiles.

"So I bolted, got myself roofside *schnellste*, and lifted off. He tried to stick with me, but you guys know I'm good with machinery. You know pretty damned well, Yes?"

The Yin-Yang smiles widened a bit.

"I pushed the car for all she was worth, got out ahead of him a bit — not so much that he had a comfortable margin for navigation — and led him along until the right obstacle came up. I dived under the old train bridge on Evans, and he couldn't clear it."

"A fatal pursuit?" asked the Angelique on the right excitedly.

"Yes," perked up the other, "was your pursuer killed?"

37

"No, but he couldn't follow me, either. Still. I don't know who the two intruders were."

The Angeliques stood, smiling, and Yin-Angelique said: "You may always come to roost here, sister."

Yang-Angelique nodded as Yin Angelique spoke. Yin-Angelique added, "But we do have a business to run, dear one. And I must watch my bar."

They've broadened the bandwidth on their link since Yang-Angelique got to the booth, thought Jonny; she waited for them to notice their transposition.

Yang-Angelique spoke up, "Yes, we have — oh!" The two flashed quick smiles at one another. "*I* have a bar to watch," said Yang-Angelique. "*She* has customers to attend to."

A patter of pizzicato laughter passed happily between them.

Transposition amused the Angeliques — a brainwave sharer's error that seemed at once an inside joke and subtly erotic to the Angeliques when it happened.

With a tiny giggle at her friends and a smirk, Jonny began an enhancement regimen on the stills she had taken of the license numbering from the auto of the first man at James Gild's apartment the other night.

"Stay as long as you like, Jonny. We're up all night. You know."

nine

Cage felt like he'd been up all night.

Outside, it rained black again.

Outside it was still dark, the dirty gray near-night of the best-lit days of Old New York.

Cage wrapped the blanket around himself and walked groggily to the window with a newly-poured cup of java.

He watched traffic fly by several stories up, cops' Sedans ascending from an emergency call somewhere down the block, blazing as they made hotrod-lateral liftoffs — cops were supposed to lift off vertically to the traffic altitude like everyone else, but who could penalize them? — their glaring red and blue lights burning so brightly in the cloudy, hazy night that they momentarily caused the windows in Cage's old office building to shade over. Cage watched, sipping the coffee, as the window tint righted itself.

He sat before his desktop, drawing the blanket about him, and double-tapped the voice-recognition alias.

"Sound file: Bennie Green, 'We wanna cook.' Start at track 'That's all.'"

Green's slow, contemplative jazz trombone piece sauntered into the room via Cage's desktop.

"Open file: James Gild," he said.

The desktop emitted a stutter of low-volume clicks, a machine-gun stapler sound turned down. On his desktop display field, with projection screens below and behind, Cage watched the familiar cycle as a folder-envelope flew forward from a small alias on the flat back screen, growing to a three-dimensional image hovering in the air before him, several inches across; the protective top flap of the hologram-envelope opened itself and Cage's Personal stills from that afternoon hovered like an armada in the air before him, the earliest-taken images to the rear, the last-taken appearing in the air before him, the depth of the interface emphasized by a spiral-staircase effect from the back to the front.

"Personal files, too," he said.

Rapid-fire clicks responded; on screen, a series of documents opened and arrayed themselves to the right in the air before him.

He looked over Gild's health, finding no particularly egregious flaws — certainly nothing potentially fatal. He knew this was no attack of some disease, but he needed to find out whether something odd might be there, buried somewhere in the past, he didn't know what: A nuclear energy experiment? Treatment with some heat-producing compound? He didn't know.

And he didn't find anything.

James Gild was as plain-vanilla and socially and politically clueless as anyone Cage had ever met. His parents had done well enough for themselves to keep him out of the helter-skelter public school system, so he'd only known about that second- and third-hand, by news reports, probably. He knew he'd had it easier, but he had no idea what it was to fear rape or knife attack just trying to get from class period three to period four, as most children of his generation had.

His folks had paid his way through school and died young, in asylums, victims of the prion epidemic that had taken most of Britain's cattle, then spread to North America, infecting mink, sheep, and deer, never fazing the market-dollar-driven wall of denial that never really admitted the possibility of livestock succumbing to the brain-dissolving plague, the general populace never dreaming that when prions — the little proteins that caused mad cow disease — leapt to pigs and cows, the logical next step would be up the consumption chain, as it had been in the old UK.

Hundreds of thousands of everyday Americans, complaining about smoking bans in restaurants were asking, "What'll they take away next, red meat?" one day, drooling and biting at nursing attendants the next, reduced from professors and street musicians and presidents of corporations to incontinent beasts too dangerous to be allowed to live out their final days among other humans.

What an ugly, demoralized way to go, Cage thought: *To watch while the essence of you is sucked away, pieces of who you are dissolved with the parts of the brain that dissolve, until what's left is a kicking, screaming shell that shits itself regularly and can no longer stand.*

How much horror did the victims feel, Cage wondered, *when they felt what they were being robbed of them, memory by memory, chunk by chunk?*

He shivered involuntarily.

After his gated private-school life, Gild had attended the Ivy League virtual campus, Kellingsworth University.

Kellingsworth had become the first upper-crust university to hit the old, low-speed World Wide Web, and the first to buy into the little patches of virtual real estate that were offered at public auction, becoming a permanent part of StellarNet.

Kellingsworth hosted classes using a new CIVRML, or Consensual Interactive Virtual Reality Markup Language, protocol that allowed students to login and attend classes, actually experience the classroom and the interaction with professors and teaching assistants and other students — or their professionally crafted avatars, at any rate — to earn undergraduate and graduate degrees.

Kellingsworth cut down on overhead significantly, while still charging students an ivy league price for an ivy league degree.

Gild had been good, Cage read; he'd graduated nearly top of his class in programming theory. He'd never had a reader installed — said he didn't need one, and had proven himself right. He had had a gift for computer languages, and had learned a good deal of the hardware, as well.

He didn't date. Ever, apparently.

That explained the domestic he'd purchased. But where had it gone? There were no records of sale. Had it just broken down and been tossed out? No clues.

James and sister Janice met regularly — about once a month — to dine and catch up with one another. They had no set restaurant or meeting place, but clearly James Gild hadn't brought his sister home; otherwise, she would have known about the domestic.

Nothing so far.

James Gild had been a hot property graduating from Kellingsworth, and he knew it. He hired an agent to find him the best corporate offer and the job that suited his interests the best.

The agent brought the brilliant young Gild to *The Lightwave Garden* Inc., a government-subsidized search for ways to efficiently and profitably collect something that most took for granted in those days: solar power. Because the government wanted no part of any permanent subsidy, it had looked to *The Lightwave Garden* to find its way, eventually, into the free market. Accordingly, Gild and a team of co-workers were awarded generous salaries and benefits with hefty, if potentially worthless, stock option packages.

With Gild aboard, the team behind *The Lightwave Garden* had developed a successful orbiting solar-energy-gathering system, Cage read.

About eight years along, as Janice Gild told it, *The Lightwave Garden* Inc., riding high into the stock exchanges on its first public offerings, had allowed some of its top minds to move on. Gild had been one of those top minds and, at thirty-seven, he had happily cashed in his stock options and found himself financially comfortable enough for an early retirement, and completely removed of any influence he may have had over the company. No more punching time clocks for Gild. And just in time.

Her brother had told Janice Gild that *The Lightwave Garden* had been a success, but that bureaucracy and fossil-fuel dollars had kept it from expanding beyond supplying power to a few test communities.

Still, its stock had held steady as investors had smelled in the project the Next Big Thing in the energy supply business.

The humidity had started a charge toward hell about eleven years into the endeavor, well past James Gild's time with the project, as the world's oceans had begun to heat up, and the oceans' new, steamy fog banks had begun gathering around places with smog problems — Los Angeles, New York, Mexico City, London, Bonn, Hong Kong, many of the big cities — and staying for longer and longer periods.

As the clouds had gathered, the development team at the project had encountered technical difficulties of a nature ruled *classified* by the corporate interests guiding *The Lightwave Garden* .

In time, the smogs no longer left. And they had begun to spread, and darken, and strengthen under the constant addition of water vapor from the warming seas and air pollution from a public that would not, at any cost, have its vehicles taken, industries that would not, at any cost, have restrictions placed on their smoke stacks' output.

The Lightwave Garden 's solar energy endeavor had become

completely stalled not long thereafter.

Although funding and operations continued for a few more months, the project had been shut down, and the government had ceased funding it, its private-venture side collapsing when the power flowed no more.

After his retirement, Gild's file showed only paychecks from the occasional independently contracted job, probably just small duties he'd sought to keep himself from going stir crazy in the pre-middle-age retirement.

The checks ranged from a few months after his departure from *The Lightwave Garden* to a silence in his freelance efforts six months before his death.

The bank accounts all appeared to be quite healthy; no one had been cleaning him out *post-mortem* between the time of his death and the time of Janice Gild's inheritance of the estate. Regular injections of interest payments kept the inheritance aloft.

Nothing. Nothing, at least, that Cage could see on the surface.

He sipped his cold coffee, turning his attention to the information he'd gathered concerning James Gild's death.

There were problems. James Gild had no enemies, and no one with a motive to kill him, save Janice Gild, for whom inheritance might be a motive, but for whom money was also no issue.

She also had an inheritance: a portion of their parents' estate.

The facts: The police recorded no signs of forcible entry into James Gild's condominium. The windows were sealed-environment duraplex, and had been undisturbed.

Weird.

Then the facts took a turn down Bizarre Street:

At 1500 degrees Fahrenheit a room, house, apartment, condo, whatever, explodes and burns like a furnace. Not much before, certainly.

But the temperature required for the cremation of a human body was closer to 2200 degrees. And Gild's conflagration had done little damage outside a tight, obviously controlled circle. No smoke damage to the ceiling overhead, where there should have been. No spread of a fire obviously hot enough to send the place up.

It didn't add up.

Cage hefted his mug to take another pull and, finding it dry, made his way out to the front office coffee-maker, pausing to wrap the blanket around his sleeping Girl Friday.

He poured himself a cuppa, rubbed his eyes, and poured the hot black liquid back into the carafe.

"Effie," he said gently, nudging her. "It's quittin' time, kid. Give you a lift home?"

Stretching, Effie looked blearily up from her desk, an imprint of the wire binder of her calendar across her cheek. "S'OK, Cage. Mine's on the roof."

"OK, Effie," he said, pulling on his coat and a black, non-react coated NoGo fedora she'd left on the coat tree for him, watching her drift off again.

He typed in a memo to have the Olds checked out and refueled in the morning; he'd be out of town for a bit. He made sure to transmit it to her desktop.

He was going to catch the Bullet to New Bombay One.

He was going to find out about Oliver Jaspin's burn.

With a kiss on the cheek from a sleepy Effie, he made his way upstairs to the Olds, fired the ignition, and tapped in the liftoff sequence.

As his Olds lofted to the traffic altitude, Cage leaned forward, pushing in the button at the base of his long, slender dashboard mic. "Home, James," he said, the voxcode activating his autodrive, reading in the preferred route home.

Cage sat back, watching the lights of the city unfurl below him, spreading out into the distance, like faint stars in the dark ink of the night air, immense ads on vidboards covering the sides of buildings, lighting the haze like garish, animated constellations.

ten

Jonny's best efforts only cleared up a partial license number from the intruder's car. But androids have time. All the time in the world. They can afford to be patient.

She let herself sink into the music while she worked, at once relaxed and feverishly active: multitasking.

The voice of one of the Angeliques spoke up from the lamp in her booth: "Jonny, we have someone here who inquires after your services. Are you entertaining guests?"

She reallocated the amount of processor time she was devoting to the partial-number search. "Yes, Angelique, and thank you. Please show the inquiring party to my booth."

A tall, too-slim man in a close-tailored, ash-gray suit and what appeared to be a constricting black tie appeared with Yin-Angelique outside the booth. His hair was clipped to the merest fraction of an inch all the way around.

"I shall leave you to your own devices," said Yin-Angelique with a wry little smile, and she disappeared back into the bar.

"Baldisari. Winston Baldisari," said the man, his voice quiet, but sounding forced, as though it took a certain effort to produce an even, conversational tone from his vocal cords.

Jonny gestured to him, indicating that he should take a seat, and the too-slim man did so.

"My benefactor dislikes public attention in matters such as these," he said in that weird forced-voice monotone.

Uncomfortable, Jonny thought.

"Matters such as what, Mr. Baldisari?"

"Matters of — how shall I put this? — importance to my employer. Someone has been tapping into our classified files, strictly not-for-public-consumption material. We would like to have that someone stopped. And we have it on the authority of the owners of this establishment that you would be the right sort of person for our needs in this matter."

"I don't do contract kills, Mr. Baldisari. I'm strictly a systems

45

lady."

Raising his hands before him so that both were pointed with palms toward her, about chest height, Baldisari said, "No, Ms. Cache, you mustn't think that that is what is asked of you here! We want their path tracked, our data burned, and their attack software and hardware disabled. Nothing so crude as the elimination of human life, Ms. Cache. We need a Netrunner."

A smile flicked at the edges of her mouth; Jonny was amused at the too-slim man's exaggerated actions, his tight-but-well-fitting suit, his mousy, monotonous voice.

Fighting down the smile, pondering the irony of someone seeking retribution through her for illicitly-gathered data, she said, "My services are not cheap, Mr. Baldisari."

"My benefactor is not one to be concerned with such matters. Name your price and method of transaction, and we shall enact our agreement," he said.

Within twenty minutes, Jonny Cache was on the job, online, looking around the server hosting the URL that the too-slim man, Baldisari, had given her.

She began a file-recovery sweep, searching for any digital scraps their hacker might have left behind, not erased well enough, forgotten about.

From the information on the server she learned that it was Day-Windham that had hired her, an investment firm dealing primarily in retirement accounts, individual and otherwise. Day-Windham did a lot of business for employees of Expedite, she learned, handled most of their people's accounts.

The trail was sketchy — she could see why they needed someone with expertise: Whoever had hit them had done so with a certain enthusiast's polish, probably sporting some code even Day-Windham's system-admin wonks couldn't deal with.

She found no names, of course, and did not expect to, but over the course of the next few hours, she did manage to piece together another partial number set, this time a referring URL. She could begin tracking the interloper based on this data.

But what would help her would be if she knew why whoever it was had hit the Day-Windham server. The obvious answer was that they were information thieves, Netrunners like herself, looking for account numbers, wire-transaction codes, and the like.

Her preliminary take on the scenario looked like this: Someone with a little expertise, more expertise than Day-Windham's system administrators had, had broken into their server, copied some cash-appropriating numbers, and run a burn on the server's login records.

Not bad. But Jonny Cache was better.

As far as she knew — and she'd researched the matter — no one could cozy up to data like she could.

It was getting late now, though, and it seemed appropriate for her to head around to the side-alley entrance to her part of the building, the part she called home. She wasn't tired, but in public, generally, she tried to make certain that she only appeared to be doing what was humanly possible.

With a warm smile and a wink to the Angeliques, she made her way to the door and started for home, pulling on her slick, black NoGo leatherlook coat, trying for Harshburger, the door man, to look a little weary.

What, she wondered, *is it like to feel weary?*

eleven

Cage wearily made his way down the steel-grate stairwell; generally he took this route rather than the elevator, but he'd spent nearly twenty-four hours on his feet, except for a brief nap, and was fantasizing about shut-eye the way some fantasize about lost loves and pin-up girls.

As he rounded the corner, striding through the roof-access door, Cage spotted her: a woman in red stood before his apartment door, blonde, about five-foot-four. Janice Gild.

"Miss Gild, what the hell are you doing here?" Cage asked firmly, wearily.

"Effie told me you nearly lost your life investigating James' death," she said, obviously worried. "I wanted to check up on you. Make certain you were all right."

Cage stepped toward the apartment door, sizing her up.

"Miss Gild — "

"Janice, Mr. Cage. Please call me Janice."

"Janice … would you like to step in for a drink?"

Once inside, Janice Gild, with directions to Cage's bar, began pouring them each a Laphroaig.

Cage gave her the details of the encounter at her brother's former dwelling, and, with a shudder, Janice Gild began to weep.

"What — what is it, Ms Gild?" he asked.

"I was — I was thinking of when we were younger, how close we were. And how we haven't really been close in more than a decade. And. I don't know," she said, her eyes tearing, downcast.

Cage went into the bathroom, returning with a box of tissues.

"We all grow apart from family, sooner or later. It's human nature," Cage said. "It just happens." She moved closer, buried her face in his shoulder, and Cage reached around her, embracing her, hoping to comfort her.

Then it began. It began with a kiss. The kiss of a person desperately alone, a professional with no time for life away from work, met by a man who almost — almost — thought he'd forgotten how to be attracted to someone.

These weren't days that inspired yearning; no beautiful season of rebirth arrived to infect every living thing with the spawn-lust of Spring Fever; but even in the midst of ruin, even amid slow erosion and decay, there was desire, however instinctive, cautiously loosening buttons, tugging back clothes, in an endless night.

They fell together on Cage's couch, carefully progressing, fear in each advance, fear that a touch or a kiss might send the other away.

Cage had felt an attraction, a desire for her in his office when she had hired him, and, despite an almost overpowering weariness, he felt it again.

They searched one another as though mapping for later expeditions, two people no longer familiar with these rituals, feeling erect nipples, a steely, earnest male response, an inviting, warm wetness, guiding, shaking hands.

Cage awoke alone to a tinny, synthesized voice, a man's voice with a snappy tone straight out of a black-and-white flick from the 1940s: "Mail call!"

Janice Gild was nowhere around.

His interface had lit up, stirred from its slumber by the Netmail arrival, casting an eerie phosphorescence from its screens. Clearing his throat, Cage said, "Display new mail."

In the holofield between the screens, with Effie's signature file registered in the first few lines, was an enhanced image from the on-board cameras of Cage's Olds: A readable license number from the figure he'd seen observing him in the building across from Gild's place.

Cage set a trace on the number into motion, while he roamed to the bathroom. He returned to his desktop, a hand-held shaver buzzing at his beard, and waited.

In a moment a new document stood suspended in the air before Effie's mail; he had the information: The Huang-Sen that had outmaneuvered him was registered to James Gild.

Cage scowled at his screen, making his way back into the apartment to check his alarm; he had trouble telling the time of day through

49

the barely discernible differences in light outside.

5:47 a.m., it read, the alarm still set for 6.

Cursing, he decided to shower and prepare for the trip.

As he stepped out of the shower and pulled on a pair of trousers, suspenders dangling at his sides before the sink in the cramped bathroom, Cage heard something at the door, a faint rustling.

He grabbed his gun, checked its clip, and stepped to the door to listen:

Nothing. Whoever or whatever it was, it had gone. Cage took down his security, keeping the gun in hand, and thumbed the door control. As the reinforced barrier slid upward, a flat, plain-brown envelope fell inward. Cage brought the gun up and stepped cautiously into the hall; whoever left him the envelope might still be around.

But the envelope's deliverer was nowhere to be seen, even after Cage scouted around the floor a bit.

Returning to the apartment, Cage picked up the parcel and examined it: No external marking; too small to be rigged with a bomb.

Inside he found a few papers and a photo of Gild's immolation — no — not Gild; the bed, the sheets were different. The remains of the feet ajar from the position of Gild's after he'd gone up.

Whose burn was this?

"Secure," he said into a panel near the doorway, and the metal gate slid back down into place with a crash and locked.

Cage looked over the papers that accompanied the photo, carefully inventorying the prints he found.

The documents accompanying the photo were a case file of some sort: "Alaina Quinn, age 38, Hackensack, Old New Jersey, taught at a private school for children called Jyoti Institute. Cause of death: immolation."

Not ones to be entangled in the sentimentality with which New Yorkers had added "Old" to their city's name when New York2 was launched — a reference to a passage in the Sinatra classic — the people of the state declared Old New Jersey upon the inauguration of the commercial New Jersey2 simply called their state what they had always called it: Jersey.

50

There was more personal information, employment history in the form of a Fax copy of Quinn's résumé, an uneven bit of white space — something blotted out before the Fax had been sent? — on the grainy copy; the address she had lived at in Hackensack; he didn't learn much from the packet. Only A) that there were more of these unexplained burns than he'd realized, at least one more, and B) That someone wanted him to know about them.

But who? The man he'd chased in Gild's Huang-Sen? Janice Gild?

There was no clear connection yet, Cage knew; he only found himself with more questions.

He dropped into the chair at his desktop, examining the image on the screen for a moment before sending the unit back into sleep mode.

He had a Bullet to catch if he was going to look into the death of Oliver Jaspin.

twelve

In the messy rain outside the Giuliani Launchport, Cage could hear the throaty, deep, alien bellowing of the Morlock laborers shouting directions to one another.

The Bullet was the fastest way to make long-distance journeys, Cage knew, but by no means the cheapest. Plume Aerospace had introduced the low-orbit, booster-aided flights about seven years back amid much pomp and circumstance, and for all their speed, the Bullet flights were still a new mode of travel. The first flights — shuttle service from New York$_2$ to London, Chicago to Tokyo — were frequented by businesspeople taking advantage of a progressively open world market.

As far as Cage knew, only the Great Dragon of the East, communist China, remained outside the competing multinational free-trade zones, its data locked away behind the Great Firewall of China (although, as it sealed its country in, the ruling party had argued that it was protecting the Chinese people from the corrupt and tainted information feeds of the Western world).

As the well-to-do had gained more disposable income, the less fiscally fortunate had found, as Cage had found, a middle class quickly eroding to nothing. The era of freer trade spawned classes of new rich, but created had far more vast numbers of new poor.

Business didn't cater much to the poor.

But the new rich found that they could live in a Chicago suburb, say, and commute to that Nikkei office in Tokyo or that Envirochemie workspace in Berlin, to the jobs that still required their physical presence, thanks to the speed of the new low-orbit flights.

In the distance, through the haze, hundreds of yards from the launchport, Cage could just make out the long tubes covered in gray, heat-resistant tile, their sturdy wings designed to handle the stress and friction of re-entry and winds at speeds well above the sound barrier; the low-orbital planes were dubbed "Bullets" for their shape and speed, as much as for a marketing-trained mindset that craves a name that was sleek and sexy, not technical.

Marketing 101: *Technical talk doesn't sell.*

The Bullet was wired with permanent, high-bandwidth links to StellarNet, allowing a businessperson to work on the way to work, or wish a child a happy birthday while en route to London.

Virtual Being There, a pop psychologist had dubbed that: The emerging syndrome among the new rich of so-called virtual parenting, parenting by remote contact over StellarNet while the hired help did the dirty work of child rearing.

In the space of only a few years, communications companies had managed to convince adult corporate professionals that they could have the sixty-five-hour work week and be responsible parents as well: They just needed to make lots of long-distance conference uplinks to home.

Daddy works at Nikkei, Mommy at a brokerage in Bonn? No problem! Just phone home to say good-night as the nanny tucks junior into bed. Living in different time zones making it difficult to keep up with junior's bedtime? No problem! Record a data playback of your good-night wish and Expedite Communications, a division of Expedite Corp., will Netmail the message to junior after a specific time delay, or, if you're very, very, dedicated to your job and can't spare the time, the message can be scheduled to be sent at the same time each day.

A generation of children was growing up detached, more bonded to au pairs and nannies than parents.

But it was good business.

Cage still had a debit account from Janice Gild for expenses related to the investigation, and as she had told him about Jaspin's burn, he was going to check it out on the Gild account.

He hadn't been on a Bullet since his once-prospective father-in-law had sent for him over the holidays to spend a Christmas in the Alps one year: A place to vacation so elevated and removed from human society that he had hardly ever had to wear his filtermask.

The terminal was crowded with three distinct social classes: The suits and Climbers bustling off to the next big deal, looking down their noses at the other classes; the rare, once-in-a-blue-moon travelers like Cage; and the blue-collar class of workers who cleaned, sold concessions and magazines, and staffed the bars at the Giuliani

Launchport.

Of the three, Cage found himself most fascinated with and, he admitted to himself, disturbed by the workers. Not all of them; only the ones who never went back.

He could trace his fascination with them back to the influence of a rather radical professor, Sarasvati Narayan, from Kellingsworth University, who'd taught a North American anthropology night course he'd taken early on in his career on the force, when he had still been trying for advancement to detective.

The blue-collar staff, he recalled, came in all shades and races and spoke a peculiar polyglot of English, Japanese, Spanish, German — the languages of the places served by the Bullet. They, however, were divided into two subclasses: regular humans, who worked inside the launchport; and Morlocks. And the Morlocks were the closest thing to frightening alien life that humankind had encountered as it had begun to colonize the friendlier moons of Jupiter; the only other alien life in the solar system had turned out to be non-threatening new species of fish found in the oceans of the Jovian moon Europa, and subterranean microbes on Mars. Not smart microbes. Nothing miraculous. Just single-celled life forms thought to be all that was left from a Mars once teeming with life, long before the rise of Earth's life forms.

Those who dealt with operations outdoors were prone to deafness and diminished eyesight from the thunderous, blazing takeoffs if they did not submit to recombinant DNA engineering to protect themselves. With a set of recombinant DNA viruses owned by Plume, the outdoors workers grew a protective husk over their ears and a specially designed, birdlike, third, inner eyelid to close during liftoff, which allowed them to keep their original eyelids open while shielding their eyes from the piercing brilliance of the boosters flaring at liftoff.

The recombination also produced side effects. Those who underwent this sort of protective recombination also became more stout, their bones and musculature growing, slabbing on mass, and this imparted a stooped posture and the illusion of shortness in the Morlocks, when they were not short at all. They became hairy, an unexpected result of the recombination yielding a thin coverage of black hair from head to toe.

54

These workers — who chose the name Morlocks for themselves, after the underground monsters invented by H.G. Wells — signed on for a five-year stint in monsterhood. Plume's surgeons and DNA engineers claimed a high restorative success rate for the Morlocks who had served their contractually agreed upon time. Some required extensive plastic surgery.

There was no call for Morlocks away from the terminals, save for service as bodyguards, and regular people often did not wish to see them elsewhere. With their hearing-protecting husks and their excessive size, strength, and hairiness, the Morlocks generally could not mingle comfortably with regular humans, either; their deep, booming, brutish voices, raised to the painful volume that would allow them to communicate with one another despite the husks, combined with their hulking, hairy stature, tended to make them seem harsh and imposing to other, unengineered people. In a public place, Morlocks seen together were regarded as not merely an imposing presence, but often as threatening.

So the altered workers retained the status of freaks in most of society., and that status kept most of them uninterested in learning to communicate with streetsign. But they were well-compensated freaks, if they made it through their five-year contracts and didn't wind up dead by terminal accident or dead by their own hands.

But a peculiar contingent arose that seemed to thrive on the life led by the Morlock. When Cage was sixteen, he had heard the first report of a Morlock who had died of old age, and who had never tried to go back to his old genetic code.

Sprayed and starched news Netcasters had hardly even tried to contain their disgust with the idea of becoming and remaining monstrous voluntarily.

These Morlocks reached other Morlocks, spreading their word as they were transferred from terminal to terminal, striving to organize the disparate trollish workers into a labor force with which management would have to bargain.

The problem was, management had the recombinant viruses that could — usually — reverse their transformation. Most Morlocks didn't sign up to be hirsute alien giants for the rest of their lives. But over time, as the Netcasters had openly loathed them, as they had bristled against the regulations that kept them from using the areas of the launchports where the unaltered public might see them, some began to see strength in embracing the life of the Morlock.

A hard-hided pride had arisen, prizing commitment to honest labor and to fair treatment of the laborers. And, over time, their alienation from the rest of humanity had begun to grow.

The intellectualized labor movements of the previous century had seen the proletariat as a sort of sleeping giant. They had described the proletariat as the great mass of blue-collar workers whose sheer numbers could give them the strength to buoy the labor movement and raise living standards for the workers through organization, contract negotiations, and strikes against employers who would not hear their laborers' demands. In the Morlocks' case, though, as with the intellectualized labor movements, the proletariat tended not to recognize itself for its own power.

Despite work conditions that were both inhumane and inhuman, most Morlocks were only along for their five-year stint, and did not identify with the effort to organize the great mass of the re-engineered laborers. The Morlocks became just another unmotivated part of labor's sleeping giant.

The Morlocks of Cage's adult life were only loosely organized, though the organizers and the Morlocks For Life movement persisted in their efforts. The majority retained every intention of returning to as regular and human a life as they could following their tenure, and this limited the more radical Morlocks' progress.

Cage found that he had to actually push his way through the crowd of suits and Climbers. In a flurry of thousand-Ennay business *ensembles*, it had become fashionable to be seen conducting one's business on the go. Suits and Climbers jostled one another indifferently, their eyes locked on their conferencing Personals, actively trying, and failing, to do business while navigating the masses of travelers.

The Aerial Traffic Authority had become so infuriated with the growing number of auto crashes caused by people posturing with their Personals, not paying attention to traffic, that they had instituted mandatory autopilot regulations for anyone conferencing while driving.

Not that it helped.

But with cars streaking to a fiery crash at street level, with the danger not just to those causing the problem, but to those around and on the ground and in the buildings below them, the ATA had had to do something.

Business types tended to be the ones who sought the speed and exclusiveness of the Bullet for getting around; vacationing working-class Joes couldn't usually swing the exorbitance of airfare on a Bullet.

Cage arrived an hour ahead of schedule, as the ticket counter attendant, a petite, cross-dressing redhead with a hint of five o'clock shadow and pert little breasts that were just a little too picture-perfect, had instructed him. Finding little to do to use up the extra time, he made his way to another indicator of the affluence of Bullet travel: the launchport's only public bar.

Although plenty of traffic passed through the launchport, as plenty of business-on-the-go demanded the speeding Bullet, social jockeying demanded that Climbers purchase memberships in the pricey airport clubs that rented real estate from the terminals.

Searching for a watering hole that would let him buy a drink, Cage passed a Red Carpet Club, a Sky's The Limit, a Platinum Wings, a Stratford, even a Shi Kai Far East — all exclusive social-club chains.

Cage was allowed into Lucky's, a neon-decor throwback to the glitzy Netshow revival of an old television cop show set in Miami.

Donatelli Three was tending bar, the model's usually subdued wardrobe abandoned in favor of a giant-flower-print Hawaiian shirt and baggy summer shorts.

After a disappointing scan of Lucky's top shelf, Cage called for a Depth Charge: a house java with a shot of espresso.

"Sharpens me up," he'd once told Effie.

When pre-boarding for his Bullet was announced, he remembered the routine: Multiple-mode scan for weapons at check-in, as he waited in the too-warm terminal, the smells of sweat and perfume and scorched rocket fuel swarming in a foul *melange* about the place; one small carry-on bag; the long, cramped, claustrophobia-threatening tube to the Bullet itself; taking a seat and strapping in; the tilt of the Bullet being raised to a vertical launch position.

Then — *boom* — the explosion that sounded far away through all the shielding, the compression that brought passengers a flattening, two-dimensional-threatening sensation.

The flight to the Tom Bradley Launchport at New City of Angels on the West Coast took about seventy minutes, Cage touching down earlier, once he'd adjusted for the time-zone difference, than when he'd boarded.

Outside the launchport, Cage contracted a taxi for the flight out to New Bombay One, located about three hundred and fifty miles off shore, paying half in advance, half promised for a safe landing; taxis operated in international waters, where regional and corporate laws got much less specific about what sorts of actions amount to what sorts of crimes; about who, exactly, was supposed to be keeping law and order out away from sovereign states and facilities.

Best not to pay up-front.

The taxi was a freelance operation piloted by a man with a thick-tongued German accent whose ID plaque announced him as Dieter Schneider. Herr Schneider affected the mode of dress of a pilot of a small, sea-going vessel: A dark Navy captain's hat; navy-blue overcoat; glossy, black, near-knee-high boots. He took long drags on a black fiberglass cigarette holder, bringing a glow to the coals of a small, elegant cigar, the smell of which Cage was not familiar with, but which reminded him vaguely of a library.

The synthetic islands had become much the same as the suburbs of major cities had before the Global Climate Shift: Safe, guarded runways where those in white flight from the inner city could land.

No small undertaking, the island groups were each corporate ventures; support pistons drilled deep into the ocean floor, designed to be raised by as much as fifteen meters in the event of more polar icecap melting and the sea-level rise that would accompany it. The feature was built into the New Bombays in the hopes that they would not be caught in pants-down indecision, as had Old New York.

New Horizons Ltd., the corporation that governed NB1, elected, as had others, to charge corporate tariffs. As corporations, rather than true regional governments, they were exempted, after forceful, high-dollar negotiations, by a loophole from free-trade zones, and thus had local-taxation options usually *verboten* by trade authori-

58

ties.

About twenty minutes into the flight, Schneider looked into his rearview cam and spoke up.

"Zo, Herr Cage," said a small, monochrome image on screen before Cage. "Vat brinks du to New Bhompay?"

German accent, Cage noted: Rolled Rs, hard consonants, tough time with the English *th*.

"Business. Gotta look in on the estate of an old friend," Cage replied, weighing how much to tell a cabbie he'd never met, in a freelance taxi, alone over the Pacific, chugging through the smog of the cities of the new West Coast, East of the San Andreas fault.

Cage tugged his Personal from its holster and ran a check on Dieter Schneider, finding that, as far as online databases were concerned, he was who he said he was. Charged with small-time graft, Cage read as an ad for the Expedite Jennifer models scrolled across his screen, but that charge had been mysteriously dropped. Caught occasionally smuggling in liquor and other contraband without paying corporate tariffs.

Nothing threatening, really. Schneider was probably just criminally inclined enough to be of some help in a pinch. Cage folded down the screen on his Personal and sat back a bit.

The taxi came in over NB1, joining a computer-choreographed hornet's-nest swarm of traffic over the commercial-grade island. Below, waves slapping against staggered duraplex barriers, walls spaced to take the strength out of the waves before they arrived at one of NB1's manufactured beaches.

"Herr Schneider, I need you to set down in the Graceline enclave once we've gotten clearance."

As they drifted down past the traffic altitude and toward Graceline, they passed something Cage had never seen before: Huge boxlike devices, perhaps twelve yards tall and wide and perhaps two meters deep, hummed a quiet, deep-bass tone from building rooftops every few blocks, massive propellers whirling within.

"Schneider — what are those?" Cage asked, peering out.

"Air scrubbers," Schneider said, donning a pair of shades that covered over his eyes entirely. "To keep de air clear, Ja? To clean it. Push smog out to sea."

Cage blinked in disbelief; he hadn't seen anyone wearing shades

59

to protect against the sun's brilliance, either, since the Alps. And now the sun struck him with a painful glare, reminding him that he had left the N.A. region under Nightfall's siege.

"Mind tinting the windows some back here?"

thirteen

Jonny didn't dream because she didn't sleep. But she day-dreamed, and thought that that must be something like the experience of dreaming.

She daydreamed of Gild, her owner-turned-father-figure, of how much more she had become once Gild had added to her software and hardware. She kept the photo of the two of them together that she had taken from its place on Gild's old wood-tone duraplex stand. The dresser upon which it now rested was already in the ballroom when the Angeliques had befriended her, offering her a place to call her own in exchange for the occasional juicy data run.

The converted ballroom she called home was lit differently from the club, differently from Gild's condominium: She had stationed wall-mounted lamps about the place, far enough apart to keep the hall only faintly illuminated. They cast islands of light in an otherwise dark expanse of room.

Outside, it rained cold sheets in the near night of an early day. But Jonny rejoiced in the rain in a way that her human counterparts at the *Nine Circles* did not: With the exception of imperiling clothing that had not been properly treated, its caustic wash posed no danger to her at all.

She waved her hand before the photo again, watching it replay.

She missed him. There hadn't been anyone else in her life like James Gild, and she doubted that there ever could be. Her status — that of artificial sentient gone underground — didn't lend itself to social situations of the sort that got people together.

When Jennifer Four had first begun to read up on the human slave trade of the past, she had shared a kindred sense with those shackled people. But later, when Jonny had visited other clubs with the Angeliques, she had realized how truly alone she was: The Donatelli units were more or less what she had been before. Not before she'd read up on slavery, but before Gild had taken her down to his workshop and started improving upon her design.

Somewhere along the line, he'd brought her across; somewhere along the way, she had ceased to be a high-tech appliance with complicated interactive protocols and became, instead, an autonomous mind in a high-tech shell, not merely capable of original thought and self-awareness, but contemplatively self-aware and always thinking new thoughts.

She guided her internal processes, certainly, but she guided them consciously.

Born of silicon and steel, simskin and sensors, Jonny Cache was the first and only one of her kind.

She needed to make another journey to Gild's domicile, as quietly as possible. No sense being caught corrupting the scene of a police investigation.

Jonny ascended to the rooftop parking, pulled open the hatch of the little Huang-Sen, and began her ascent into traffic.

She set the souped-up Huang-Sen down on the old Montgomery Building, trying to be gentle with her unauthorized landing. The Montgomery had been built before the advent of low-aerial traffic in the cities. Its roof had no landing plate, but the lightweight superpolymer shell of the Huang-Sen didn't apply much stress.

Jonny worked her way into the building, finding an unoccupied office space with a view across the street to Gild's — her — old home.

The condominium was dark; it appeared to be unoccupied. So she took the Huang-Sen back up, backtracked a bit so as not to arouse the attention of the condo's Aerial Traffic Authority post, and landed, the car's transponder signal still identifying it as one belonging to a resident.

She wrapped a black, lacy scarf about her head and pulled on an overcoat before stepping out of the car and making her way toward the old chambers.

It wasn't likely that anyone would recognize her — Gild had pretty much kept to himself, and she had never gone outside the apartment before she left Gild — but she could take no chances that some early bird who'd gotten up and about for a jog on the condo's track or a swim in the condo's pool might see her in the building and recognize her.

She gently tugged aside the police tape before Gild's door, passed her copy of his cardkey through the lock, and let herself in, carefully replacing the tape behind her.

She surveyed the apartment with a small, infrared flashlight, avoiding activating the main lighting for fear of drawing attention.

Jonny had loved Gild, but she had also come to need to be away from an existence in which she had been owned. Gild had known she would grow out of her role as daughter-surrogate as she had her earlier function, and although he never knew exactly how it would happen, exactly what changes would come, he did know that in time, she would metamorphose entirely.

She played back a few of the pictures, smiling, wondering whether what she was feeling would bring tears in an organism with tear ducts.

She packed a few more of the pictures into her satchel, then started back for Gild's workshop, when she heard scraping and shuffling outside the apartment door, sounds she heard whenever Gild had returned from some errand.

Not that anyone would see the light from her infrared lamp, but to be safe, she turned it off and willed herself to be absolutely motionless.

After a few more moments of scraping, the door swung open; whoever it was, they'd breached Gild's cardkey lock.

Light spilled in from the hallway, casting a trenchcoat-clad man in silhouette. As he reached for the lighting access panel, Jonny sprang from her position faster than any human could, faster than the man could have, a deftly placed kick folding him, coughing, at the waist.

Too late, though, she realized he had something in his hand. Too late her ears filled with a high-pitched feedback scream and her sight began to fade to the snow of a dead television channel.

She got one look at her assailant as her vision flickered: not tall, really, not as tall as her. Paunchy. A bald dome rimmed by feisty, unruly, graying hair.

Then he was clutching his stomach, lurching toward the roof-access lift. She figured that he must be gasping, but she couldn't hear anything above the scrambled-sound din.

That pudgy little bastard! she thought. He's getting away. *What did he shoot me with?*

As she lay, toppled and twitching on the floor, she wondered whether she had identified the murder weapon used to kill James Gild.

But she couldn't follow the intruder. She cursed, willing her limbs to action to pursue him, but her body responded only with harsh, static-discharge twitches. She reached out across the 'Net and opened a conference channel to the Angeliques.

Within a few minutes, the Angeliques arrived in all their beautiful binary splendor, even so early in the day, hefting their friend and her satchel, Yin-Angelique taking Jonny aloft in the Nouveau Gothics' black Takei, Yang-Angelique retrieving the Huang-Sen.

"OK, girlfriend," said Yang-Angelique, gazing languidly over a bank of monitors and readouts. "As far as I can tell, you're fine. But you would know better than I."

Jonny felt ridiculous. Her own internal diagnostics told her she was fine.

"What the hell did that paunchy misfit hit me with?!" she demanded, punching a dent into the metal plating of her workshop table.

"Temper," said Yang-Angelique.

"Temper, dear" said Yin-Angelique. "It would appear that he had some form of neural stunner — a little palm-sized unit, judging from your description."

"Not designed for you, dear Jonny," cooed Yang-Angelique with reassurance. "The sort of bolt that he shot you with would have put down any organic for hours. You just wound up with a little trouble with internal transmissions."

"Why was I able to reach you?"

"*Internal* transmissions, dear Jonny," cooed Yin-Angelique with reassurance. "I doubt that either your original designers or James Gild thought to shield you against such a concentrated burst along your neural network."

Jonny was pacing now, angry that she'd been put down, been put down by anyone, let alone an out-of-shape, middle-aged human male.

"Was that weapon capable of the incineration that killed Gild?" Jonny asked

"We do not know for certain. It looks as though it was meant to stun a human," said Yin-Angelique.

"It does not look as though it was meant to unleash enough heat to induce cremation," said Yang-Angelique. "But we do not know for certain."

"I got a clean look at his face before his little shock-gun blew out my visual relay. If I get lucky, I'll be able to find out who and where he is with that alone."

"Careful, Jonny," said Yin-Angelique.

"Careful, dear sister," said Yang-Angelique, "With so many automated searches gobbling up processor real estate, we wonder whether you might get a little distracted."

Jonny considered the binaries' warning.

"I'll watch it, girls. I'll keep the searches running lean and low-bandwidth. I'll be OK."

fourteen

Schneider received landing clearance for the Graceline enclave and piloted the taxi down to street level, bringing Cage back to an age he had forgotten: The age of ground traffic. Sort of.

It wasn't real ground traffic, not like the speeding, manual-control, heart-quickening race he had read that the *Autobahn* had been. No, on NB1 the streets were fastidiously blacktopped, and there were regulations for ground traffic. You couldn't just cruise around, but you could, for example, land your car and drive for a block or so before parking on the street. A perk afforded by the controlling corporation.

Oliver Jaspin lived in Graceline Domicile 65, one of an expanse of homes with outer shells made of Duraplex molded and painted in pastels to resemble the dwelling of 1950s America: The Good Old Days that no one in this day and age had ever lived through. Not that this was any obstacle to enterprising developers looking for ways to instill a sense of rightness in their islands, that soft-focus "Leave it to Beaver"-themed feel of a world of well-starched and well-manicured white people, where crime and the poor did not intrude.

A pseudo-suburban setting based on a soft-focus daydream, a Norman Rockwell *Saturday Evening Post* portrait of an America that never quite had been.

Identical houses spanned Graceline for block upon block in every direction in a light-blue pastel; from the air, the six-block-by-six-block enclaves, each in its own pastel shade, looked like a baby's blanket patched with neighborhoods.

Duraturf plastic lawns stayed well-maintained, NB1 management liked to remind tenants, freeing residents of yard-tending duties.

The Good Old Days, die cast in Duraplex.

The perfect landing strip for rich white flight.

Cage climbed from the taxi, making certain that Schneider understood his services would still be needed, and that he shouldn't go anywhere.

He walked up the perfect, textured, hard-plastic sidewalk to Graceline Domicile 65 and tugged aside the yellow plastic police tape strung across the threshold.

A quick dusting revealed the same smudgeover of prints — cop prints, he was reasonably sure — that he'd encountered at Gild's condominium.

Inside, Cage found the layout he knew he'd find in any of the other homes in this dwelling zone on NB1: A modest, but accommodating living room, two bedrooms, a den for the man of the house, kitchen, and a bathroom of generous enough proportions to serve the entire family.

In the second bedroom, Jaspin had a minor wine cellar: twelve shelves against one wall, some of the slots still occupied — quite an accomplishment if they were the real thing, and not some of the synthetic wines, or the still-immature vintages from newer winemakers that hit the market after the French vineyards' collapse.

Enough bottles had been recently disturbed that Cage could see the hand of the island's corporate constabulary in the investigation.

Among the synthetics, Cage found a few dusty bottles of Beaujolais, but most of the real wines Jaspin had left were from Australian vineyards — a sampling of Shiraz, Syrrah, Cabernet.

The gentleman had preferred red.

Cage found Jaspin's bar intact, and though Glenlevit was a fainter scotch than he preferred, he poured himself a single just the same.

He tugged his Personal from its holster and began shooting stills as he made his way through the house.

Jaspin's bed was intact, as had been the bed of James Gild, an angry black crater of cinder and spent heat in the middle. Cage shook his head and took a few stills. *Nothing new here*, he thought.

In the den, Cage looked over Jaspin's desktop, hoping to find a file near the surface that could tell him whether the dead man had had any enemies among the quick.

But he found nothing. Rather, he found nothing of use. Hundreds of old family photos had been scanned into his album. Work-related documents were there, near the top level of his filing system.

Cage fed scans of the prints he'd lifted into his Personal, transmitting them, along with copies of the documents aboard the desktop, to his office on the mainland.

On a bulletin board in the prefabricated kitchen, Cage found three small promotional fliers from a place called *The Electric Cafe*, in downtown New Bombay 1.

Then he heard something he did not expect: A knock on the door.

Folding one of the fliers and slipping it into his breast coat pocket, Cage made his way back to the door.

Through the door's peephole, he spied Schneider, shifting nervously. Schneider knocked again.

Cage tugged his brown, texture-woven vest forward and opened Jaspin's door.

"We had better go, Herr Cage," said Schneider. "Police. I hear it on die emergency band. Dey haff dispatched a car to see who iss poking around here."

Schneider was OK.

fifteen

NB1 was, as the other NBs were, a self-contained city, mostly prefab — that is, the prefabricated units were more affordable.

For a small fortune, an individual, family, corporation, or government with an interest and the proper combination of references and clout could have a custom design added to one of the islands of New Bombay.

Also for a price, businesses could buy a piece of post-American pie by purchasing rights to set up in the downtown districts of the islands. Corporate tariffs weren't cheap, but keeping current with taxes from New Horizons Ltd. meant keeping access to a population that always had a debit card ready.

The Kennedys had purchased a permanent piece of the man-made real estate, having a chateau blueprinted, its molds lavishly planned and executed, with private access by a small waterway they negotiated into the design. Old money that had managed to survive the upheavals of the early twenty-first century. They had even shipped in furniture constructed of real wood.

Newer money made on the rising star of Expedite Corp. had been held by Tobias Steag early in the century. The Steag family compound on NB1 was actually larger than that of the Kennedys, with the Steags having come later to the island and finding a challenge in the arena of prestige.

When the first Steag had encountered resistance to the scale of his planned New Bombay estate, the economic juggernaut that Expedite Corp. had become had simply purchased New Horizons and ordered the blueprints for the Steag compound approved.

The expansive property was now under the control of Tobias Steag III, a clone of StellarNet's founder and chief architect, who jealously retained his hold on the reins of power even as his own clone/son, Tobias Steag IV, languished in Expedite's chief executive position, a post rendered largely symbolic by Steag number three.

There had been some sort of strife between the two, Cage had read at the rogue Internet 'zine *W@v?£?ngth$*, but details about the dispute had been hard to come by on the old network, and completely absent on StellarNet.

Tobias Steag IV made it clear that he did not care for the company of his forebear, Tobias III. Not that this was generally an issue on the island; Tobias III simply forbade the younger Tobias from setting foot in the family's island compound.

With a friendly, corporate version of martial law in effect, most of the islands were relatively low on crime, at least in their brochures and in reports to the public.

That meant — on a newer island such as NB1, anyway — that the club-and-bar district had a surreal, Hollywood-set feel about it.

It was too clean. The patrons' hair and style and makeup and jewelry and clothing and shoes and eyewear were too picture-perfect. The night life was cookie-cuttered from the pages of the important fashion 'Netzines.

The streets, buildings, benches, everything was washed down at night with a detergent that wouldn't harm their black Duraplex composition, the dirty runoff rinsed into molded gutters, channeling black waters out into the sea. The architectural engineers and designers of NB1 had a vision for this business district — separated into a distinct region of the island, as were residential, restaurant, New Horizons Ltd. governmental, and other commercial and non-commercial zones — a vision that looked nostalgically to Paris before the Global Climate Shift: The tough Duraplex was cast and painted as wrought iron, brickfaced buildings, cobbled streets. With no automobile ground traffic, save for taxis, the club-and-bar district looked for all the world like the set of a movie scene set in a Paris street cafe.

Schneider and Cage pulled up, rare traffic traveling more than a few blocks on the ground, but they turned every few blocks to avoid raising suspicion among the residents.

There was ample taxi-stall parking on the simulated blacktop.

A sign projected out at a right angle to the building housing *The Electric Cafe*: A lighted blue-neon coffee cup, six wavy blue tubes extending up over the cup to simulate steam rising. First three waves lit, every other one, then, with a harsh sizzle, the other three. A low, wrought-iron-look fence and gate, in black, surrounded an open-air sidewalk serving area which was separated entirely from the cafe by the sidewalk. The little die-cast tables included permanent buckets for chilling bottles or carafes of wine, real or synthetic.

Cage and Schneider made their way into the cafe together. Inside, the decor was spare; a strong scent of coffee suffused the air of the club, whose only lighting emanated from behind a row of blue glasses on white glass shelves behind the bar. Couches, coffee tables, and booths were scattered throughout *The Electric Cafe*, the works of lesser-known and local artists gracing its matte-gray-colored Duraplex walls. The few patrons who sought refuge from a harsh afternoon sun looked up, glancing at Cage and Schneider as the two entered the coffeehouse. They took seats at the bar.

The barkeep, Donatelli Three, strode easily along the bar and took up its station before them. "Gentlemen. I do not recall your ever visiting the cafe. You must be in dire need of a drink to be out during ozone alert hours."

Cage realized his gaff: He'd gotten so used to perpetual rainfall that he'd forgotten about the precautions taken in these floating cities during the sunnier hours.

"I'm a tourist," Cage said. "Forgot."

"No matter," said Donatelli Three. "It would take more than one day out in this to contract one of those nasty melanomas."

"What may I serve you gentlemen?"

"Depth Charge for me. Tall," said Cage.

"'Depth Charge,' sir?" asked Donatelli Three, puzzled.

"Yeah, Donatelli. I'd like a house coffee with a shot of espresso," said Cage. "Tall."

"Ah," said Donatelli Three. "A Midnight Special."

"A glass of Shiraz, Mein Herr," Schneider told the bartender, fixing a small, brown-leaf-wrapped cigarillo to his cigarette holder.

He produced a rectangular silver Zippo from the double-breasted coat, flicking his facial features into sharp black and white under the brim of his pilot's hat for a moment as he ignited the smoke.

"Hydroponic number twenty-nine forty-two," said Schneider admiringly, smoke wafting from his mouth and nose as he spoke. "A fine feat of crop re-engineering science."

A silence passed between the two as they sampled, then enjoyed their drinks.

Schneider broke the silence: "Did you find anything at the Jaspin residence, Herr Cage?"

Cage gazed thoughtfully into his Midnight Special. He had hoped to find something more at Jaspin's domicile. When nothing earth-shattering turned up there, he had hoped for a lucky break here, at the coffeehouse/bar where Jaspin had spent idle hours. But here they were, with no island contacts and little new to go on. And a Donatelli minding the bar meant no indiscretions would pass from its lips to Cage's ears, no matter how much cash or cajoling he might try.

Cage sipped his coffee. "More dead ends, Schneider. More dead — "

Cage stopped and looked up, eliciting a puzzled stare from Schneider. ·

He felt a tremor along his leg. Tugging the Personal from its holster, Cage flipped up the screen hatch and enabled its conference mode.

"Cage," said a tinny, am-radio voice as a pixelated Effie took form on the screen, an ad for Puritex tapwater filters scrolling across the bottom, "those prints you lifted at Jaspin's — mostly partial sets and corporate flatfeet — easy to trace at the New Horizons Human Resources server. But one set you got came up with an in-house match."

"In house?" Cage asked, arching his eyebrows hopefully. "What are you telling me here, kid?"

"I mean a match with some prints you already collected. Cage, whoever those non-cop prints from Jaspin's house came from, that person has also been to the apartment of the late James Gild."

sixteen

Jonny Cache flipped down the cranial hatch at the rear of her head with a solid snap and laid an instrument on the dented steel workshop table with a metallic clank that echoed off the polished tile flooring and walls and ceiling in the deep, high-vaulted and disused ballroom she called home. She glanced up toward the huge, backlit clock she'd resurrected from the old Grand Central Station. Its ghostly white glow permeating her otherwise unlit living space.

It had taken hours, but she had had hours. Androids do.

The scent of solder, of cooked metal, drifted along on the cool, lazy current of air in the cavernous room. She'd been adding insulation to her neural network.

The day had moved on to evening, and as she looked out into the drizzle, Jonny studied how the rains outside took their toll on the cathedral across the road from the *Nine Circles*, acidic wash slowly wearing away at the cut-stone architecture, once-phallic spires now rendered impotent, stubby projections.

And the Angeliques dreamt.

Yin-Angelique had been born Beautiful Angel Singer — an inspiration on the part of her parents for which she never quite forgave them — the daughter of middle-class career people squeezed out as the middle class was whittled to insignificance in the age of open trade zones.

In the private schools of her youth, she'd developed an aptitude for working with machinery and circuitry, a consuming gift that sometimes interfered with teachers' efforts to instruct her in other subjects, but that, nonetheless, had them employing her, rather than Yellow Pages freelancers, to fix wiring and computer problems at home.

When her parents' raises had become something that their business forms industry employer felt its employees could forbear on a regular basis, they had slowly began to slip financially, gradually giving up the extras they had come to enjoy one by one: A private water-filtration service to clean up the public-tap offering; the mail-order club that shipped three-bottle cases of selected wines each month; the second car. In time, and unhappily, her parents came to realize that Angel's private-school tuition expenses were threatening their ability to feed, clothe, and shelter the family.

She was forced into a bankrupted, inadequate public school system looted by generation upon generation of lawmakers complaining about how much it cost to take care of the citizenry; arguing that the poor should pull themselves up, not count on federal handouts, cutting education expenditures year-in and year-out.

The schools went the way of untended gardens, of abandoned buildings: Gangs of thugs grew like weeds in the cracked foundations, bringing weapons to school regularly enough to force other students to do the same, simply to match firepower with firepower.

Angel had been pampered, by comparison. She had attended institutions where learning was the principal goal, once tuition was paid, and where the atmosphere had been conducive to the pursuit of knowledge. Now, in high school in the public schools, she was just another rich kid to hold in contempt, a naïve little girl who didn't know enough to keep off the floors controlled by gangs. Practically a snack.

When she had needed a friend the most, Veronique had been there. But not in a particularly friendly way.

Veronique Bentham had done her time in the public schools and allied herself with a gang of røgue-bøyz to keep from being kidnapped, raped, and killed, her body dumped into the river or out in the rain in some alleyway to erode and decompose.

Veronique Bentham had studied a Brazilian fighting system called Capoeira under the tutelage of an old *mestre* who lived in her family's apartment complex and who taught kids he thought had potential in an abandoned building six blocks from home. When she had used the style's powerful kicks and fluid, agile aversions to save herself from an attack on the way to school in junior high, she had left two of her attackers broken and unconscious, the third unable to right himself and walk. But she had seen flaws in her fighting ability in the black eye and bruised ribs she had taken away from the fight, and decided she needed to learn more.

The old *mestre* helped her learn Western-style boxing to complement the kick-fighting prowess of Capoeira, and she found herself able to walk away without a scratch after the next attempt by schoolmates to take her.

Veronique had been down the hall when she'd heard Angel scream out as she was being dragged into a bathroom on a minor gang's corner of fourth floor West. With a staccato set of taps on a pocket transmitter, she summoned a contingent of young røgue-bøyz whose counterfeited adrenaline samples made them much stronger and more dangerous hand-to-hand fighters than the cowering crew that had jumped Angel.

Veronique spotted something in Angel's beauty that called to her, but not loudly enough to keep high-school-tough arrogance in check; instead of comforting Angel, she lectured her for her naïveté, for barely escaping the situation with her life, and then only with the help of strangers.

Veronique stalked off with her røgue-bøyz allies, dragging Angel along until they could find a reasonably safe part of the school in which to deposit her.

Angel hated Veronique for looking down on her, for lecturing her and belittling her when she'd thought she was about to lose her life.

But time changes people; they grow. And in time, the two began to run into one another more in classes, finding themselves at the same movies, or hanging out at the same coffee shops.

Once they spoke again over twin cups of Kona, their friendship was sealed, and Angel became a røgue-bøyz member with Veronique.

røgue-bøyz typically banded loosely on the streets, finding safe, stable, abandoned places to hold their meets, places they could tap into a local fiber-optic line for their better Netrunners to utilize for an unauthorized uplink. They tend toward their own take on the Robin Hood philosophy, making runs against large, ponderous, unwieldy companies' sites in exchange for monies for their own purposes.

They liked to keep their technology compact and efficient: A sub-subcompact Personal for business on StellarNet; the occasional surgical modification, say, a set of talons to extend from the ends of fingers, or a set of overlapping subcutaneous plates to protect vital organs from physical attacks — a kick, a bullet, whatever — and readers.

Readers were the key, and although none of them could install one at first, their shared approach to hot technologies — tech that they'd lifted — meant that once the first few had had their readers installed professionally, they could bootleg samples of the know-how for the procedure from rogue sites out on the 'Net, have a shopping list ready, and have their røgue-bøyz *Kameraden* pick up a few extras while out on raids.

Slowly, all of the røgue-bøyz got the readers. Slowly, after Veronique cut a sample of her fighting sessions with *mestre*, the members of the røgue-bøyz cell she was allied with learned fighting expertise. Slowly, they all improved upon their designs, some spiking their biochemistry for youth, or strength, speed or intelligence, some angling more toward technological enhancements.

And although they never lost touch with the røgue-bøyz they'd been allied with — røgue-bøyz still frequent the *Nine Circles* — Veronique and Angel became more of a couple, more together with one another than with the rest of the group. And they went the way of the technofetish: Their interests began to lean more toward the Z.Brites and gothic culture, or what was left of it, and technological enhancements.

They drifted from the røgue-bøyz, not intentionally, and toward a movement called Nouveau Gothic. They fell in love with it as they fell in love with one another, becoming more and more together, becoming closer emotionally and philosophically, becoming more unified.

The stylistic affectations of the binaries caught their eye, and as Veronique and Angel evolved over time, they became deeply interested in these people: Couples who intentionally, for reasons of aesthetic, style, pose, philosophy, whatever motivations, sought similarity and unity with their mates.

When Angel and Veronique decided on the binary lifestyle, they wanted more out of it than fashion: They wanted to truly unite, at least some of the time; to truly become one. Money they had stashed along the way from raids on Expedite, Aerospace Ventures, Plume, and others financed the installation of unique, fixed, channel-sharing hardware of Angel's design into the skulls of the two.

And while their tech-savvy røgue-bøyz friends, augmented with chips containing twenty-seven years of surgical experience from a retired physician, performed the installations and watched over them as they recovered, they found within themselves emerging, new personalities: Veronique and Angel were their given identities, names from a life now past, with its naïvetés and despair at the world around them and lack of direction.

They chose a solution that suited them: a blend of their names, a moniker that would reflect to them the swirl of personae they had become. They arrived at Angelique — part Angel, part Veronique. Their makeup and fashion choices were a nod to both Nouveau Gothic culture and their binary philosophy, but taken further than any binary had gone before.

The Angeliques embraced the Yin and Yang of Eastern philosophy in their lives and their names, and endeavored to mirror one another in reversed coloration: Two identical, opposite pieces of the same puzzle.

The Angeliques had stirred and begun an afternoon wakeup routine of setting their coffeemaker into motion and activating their large, round whirlpool for an early-morning (relatively speaking) romp amongst the suds.

Jonny wanted to test her new installation, but the Angeliques were clearly occupied in their master bedroom.

Yin-Angelique and Yang-Angelique broadened the bandwidth on their sharing connection, splashing down in the hot, bubbling tub surrounded by lit red and black candles. The only way to wake up, both thought with a broad simultaneous grin: With a machine-gun stutter of orgasms amid the bubbles.

With their sharing hardware, the boundaries between masturbation and sex with another person became blurred, but in exchange, both knew with perfect honesty which flicks of the tongue, which caresses, which of their toys brought the other — and, via the sharing link, them both — the greatest pleasure.

And in a soundproofed environment the sort of which the Angeliques had constructed, they felt no need for suppressing cries of pleasure.

Through the link, Yin-Angelique became lost in the stimulus from her counterpart, and Yang-Angelique did as well.

The apartment filled with the scent of fresh-brewed Hawaiian

Kona and the sounds of exuberant, euphoric, life-loving fucking.

Jonny checked their kitchen drawer by drawer until she found their stunners.

As the bleary-eyed binaries walked their befuddled, orgasm-quaking walk out of the master bedroom, arms wrapped around one another, Jonny stood, strode to Yang-Angelique, and handed her the stunner.

"I've been in the shop all day. I owe you some raw materials, ladies, hope you don't mind," she said.

"Jonny, what — " started Yang-Angelique.

"What's all this, Jonny," asked Yin-Angelique.

"Shielding. For my neural net. I've been working while you two slept and fucked," said Jonny, amused at her technologically joined friends. "I need you to hit me with a bolt from that stunner."

For a moment, the Angeliques both looked doubtful, each beginning to shake her head, but some silent evaluation took place over their link, and they acquiesced.

Yang-Angelique approached Jonny, placing an arm on her shoulder. "You can't take shots like the one you took this morning very often, Jonny," she said. "You're strong, but you're no soldier unit."

"Careful, Jonny," said Yin-Angelique. "When's the last time you tried a backup?" she asked, knowing that Jonny didn't have anywhere to store a backup: Storage facilities like that didn't grow on the few remaining trees, and she hadn't had time yet to find the proper convergence of cash on hand, motivation, and time to arrange the inconspicuous purchase of something so unusual. "Careful," whispered Yin-Angelique.

Jonny nodded, indicating that she understood her friends' warnings and wasn't going to reconsider.

Yin-Angelique took Jonny by the hand and led her into the master bedroom, over to the Angeliques' VR facility. It looked for all the world like a footlocker cast in plastic the purple-black color of a bruise, the Expedite logo that once graced its side carefully scraped away.

While the binaries poured themselves hot cups of coffee, Jonny established a link with the little storage facility, took a snapshot of her files as of that moment, and backed them up. If the stunner disrupted her software somehow, she could reload her memories and OS; she wouldn't remember being hit with the stunner, but the Angeliques could let her know about it.

Jonny walked out and gave Yang-Angelique a determined, prepared look.

With a simultaneous sigh, both Angeliques sulked momentarily, looking toward the floor. Then the two sharpened their attention as Yang-Angelique raised the stunner, leveling its aim at Jonny Cache.

With a sizzle, the stunner fired an arcing energy trail into Jonny. The impact shoved her back a step, but she was unharmed, save for a small, smoldering circle about the size of a quarter in her shirt, where Yang-Angelique's stunner had hit her.

She patted out the blaze, and smiled. She could always buy another shirt, but the upgraded defenses brightened her long, dark day.

seventeen

Cage hated to leave New Bombay One behind with so little to go on, hated to leave with so little of an investigation completed, but he knew that he'd had no luck at Jaspin's little slice of post-Americana, and he knew that NB1 security would be watching the Jaspin domicile now. He had little choice but to head back to the mainland, back to his office in Old New York.

"Mr. Schneider?" Cage asked, snapping the Personal into its holster.

"Herr Cage?"

"Let's finish our drinks. I need to get back."

Schneider's little taxi lofted toward the traffic altitude and left the crazed, racing ballet mechanique of cars awaiting landing clearance over New Bombay One. Left it and arced out over the ocean toward California's New West Coast.

Cage had spent the entire day on travel, looking over Jaspin's place, and finding and looking over *The Electric Cafe*, he realized: As the headed East, he saw that they were again headed into the night, into California's smogs, and he knew that awaiting him at home would be the nearly perpetual black rainfall. Looking out the taxi's rear window, he saw the black smoke plumes rising from the smokestacks of NB1 against the sunset.

When the Bullet touched down at Giuliani, Cage found Effie in a non-react raincoat waiting for him at the launchport, manila envelope bulging with documents in one hand, a cup of hot, black java in the other.

"Made it back with no new holes shot through ya, huh, Cage?" she said, smirking.

"Only just, Effie," Cage laughed, hugging her. "Only just."

She handed him the java.

"A house java with a shot of espresso," she said; she'd remembered.

Cage took the coffee gratefully.

"Whadda they call it again?" she asked.

"In New City of Angels, Effie, Donatelli Three says that's a Red Eye. On New Bombay One, it calls the drink a Midnight Special. Around here, it's a Depth Charge," Cage said, a shrug to show that he didn't follow the linguistic drift in the name.

Outside, she handed Cage the matched print set and an analysis.

"You drive, Effie," he said. "I wanna look these over."

In the foggy, black, rainy night, Cage flicked on the passenger-side lamp in the Olds to read the documents.

The prints were a match — no question there. One person had turned up at both of these recent burns: Jaspin's and Gild's.

The analysis software also reported that this bearer of the prints was a male, someone who hadn't committed even the most minor crime in the past, apparently, because he hadn't turned up in the police database Cage had accessed to run these checks.

Police stored the prints of everyone they ever booked, that storage eventually becoming part of a global fingerprint image database that Expedite said was meant to make tracking known criminals easier. It also gave Expedite full access to those files, of course, and, coupled with the corporation's larger database of prints of all of the employees of Expedite and its subsidiaries, the most powerful corporation on the planet was also leaps and bounds ahead of law-enforcement authorities on such matters.

The same was true for the global DNA database: Law-enforcement agencies could access it, but Expedite had images of its employees — even the temps, the custodians, the programmers, the food servers — everyone.

If you worked for Expedite or any company Expedite acquired along the way, best not to ever get in their way again, because they'd know all about it.

Cage knew he'd have to try to get into one of Expedite's servers if he wanted to get a match on the prints. And he wasn't interested.

As Effie set the Olds down at Cage's office building, he realized he hadn't eaten. He and Effie agreed on Hong Kong Charlie's, a streetside vendor who ran a clean enough operation and slung a mean lo mein.

As Cage sifted through the documents, he began to wonder what it was that had been blotted out of the résumé of the earlier burn victim, Alaina Quinn.

He pulled out the Fax of her résumé and looked it over: No chance to scrape off the whited-over entry here, with a copy of the document. He'd need an original.

Cage found himself standing before his desktop, deep in thought. The only place to run prints on someone who had no criminal record was Expedite. Period. And he didn't really want to raise the ire of them — Steag, any of him — again.

His meditation was broken by a buzz from the street-level entrance. Cage looked out of his window and down to the street. One of Hong Kong Charlie's trademark delivery tricycles, the ones with the insulated baskets just behind the cyclist's seat, was parked by the ground-floor door.

Effie called into the back office: "Cage, chow's here."

"I'm not good enough to run the Expedite central server and not get caught, Effie," Cage said. "I'm going to need some help."

"Who can do it, Cage?" she asked.

"Maybe K^a£$_i$."

"The head NewSchool Grrl, Cage?"

Cage scowled a bit; he didn't like the idea that he needed help from anyone but Effie; and the NewSchool Grrls were a little too erratic for his liking, their motivations a little too inscrutable. But they took Ennays in hard currency, distrusting e-commerce, and they had a code of professional silence on shadier jobs.

And for what little it was worth, Cage at least knew this NewSchool Grrl.

The NewSchool Grrls movement had built up over the course of decades in response to a philosophy of alienation from the well-to-do, from Expedite-owned firms, and, as its potency waned against the global conglomerates, the government: If you had the assets, your government would deal with you. if not, you were just grist for the mill. A free market at its most untamed.

These weren't thugs running the streets — although they did run the streets; nor were they the petty weapons runners who eked out an existence by supplying guns, knives, stunners, whatever, to those looking for an edge at street level — although they did have occasion to arm themselves.

The NewSchool Grrls tended a rogue garden of the brightest, those who had promise that the world of commerce would not see because neither they nor their families had the monetary resources to pay for their educations. While not everyone could gain entrance into a university's curriculum, not everyone could be a NewSchool Grrl, either: A strict policy against the sorts of thuggery that made mere gangs thrive was part of their code of NewSchool, its own set of requirements for becoming part of the thorn in the side of a world dominated by one company and its subsidiaries.

Kᵃ£¡ — she pronounced it "Kah-lee," after the Hindu goddess of death — had opted out of Kellingsworth University's Ivy League refuge from the market-driven world when money had become more of an issue than the education. Of course, in some ways, this had always been the case at universities: In the past, if a student couldn't pay a tuition bill, that student's education would halt abruptly at any institution. So in a way, the market had long since strong-armed institutions of higher learning into behaving like competing businesses, well before family desirability and social-class rankings became part of the admissions recipe.

The NewSchool Grrls were a product of the rebellion of Professor Sarasvati Narayan, rather a rogue element in her own departments: She held a joint professorship in the departments of philosophy and software engineering at Kellingsworth. Her status as a woman of strong opinions, an Indian philosopher in the programmers' realm, and a chiphead in a philosophy department primarily concerned with aesthetics, Narayan was an outsider wherever and whatever she taught on campus. Her students loved it, loved her rebellious attitude and disregard for the sneering derision of others in her departments, loved her *fuck off* attitude toward her detractors.

When Professor Narayan quit Kellingsworth, she didn't go out quietly: She sent out a set of interlocking viruses one at a time to the university's servers; as the servers exchanged information, over the course of about a week, the viruses found one another, docked to form a single program, and decompressed, rewriting

83

Kellingsworth's greetings pages with a manifesto on what had gone awry in education and, by extension, in the world around her.

In it, Narayan had laid out a series of protocols that should be observed in fighting the power in a world of rigged elections that allowed Expedite-promoted candidates to win the top governing offices, and how to self-govern in this day in what she described outright as a state of siege: A siege on the governments of the developed world by Expedite.

She had designed the viruses to take over Kellingsworth's servers simultaneously, but with a delay, so that her Trojan horse could storm past the gates without time for the university to set up a defense against it, and so that she could complete a disappearing act. She had emptied her accounts, and purchased whatever mode of travel she used to get out with hard currency only, and bailed.

Among her recommendations were a withdrawal from the sectors of society that embraced a market-governed world; a dedication to improving the world through guerrilla instruction; and an active, if radical, resistance to the forms of racism spread in corporate propaganda that allowed Expedite to distract the people of the world from the company's expanding grasp on power and toward differences between the peoples.

And in the tradition of Martin Luther nailing his thesis to the church door, she had signed her name to the manifesto. Then, with a bit of animation, a line struck through the graphic display of her name, and $K^a£_i$ had appeared beneath it. She arranged for it to be the only thing that anyone could pull up at Kellingsworth University's computers for seven days and nights. Then the program erased itself, disappearing as thoroughly as Narayan herself had.

Her manifesto had become the foundation for the NewSchool Grrls' movement, its bylaws. And although NewSchool cells are only loosely affiliated, each adheres to $K^a£_i$'s code.

$K^a£_i$ taught that the information should be freed and distributed, and that, as visionaries past had said, information was power. Not just any information, but education.

The first NewSchool cell comprised $K^a£_i$ and a few of her most loyal students, and together they had set up an anarchistic university of sorts in Old Manhattan, in a business development that was far enough above sea level to have avoided destruction in polar

84

thaw, but that had also been abandoned by its builders because Old NYC itself was being abandoned by the business community.

The infrastructure of high-bandwidth fiber-optic wiring and sturdy new architecture was in place; the invading NewSchool Grrls rigged a dependable power supply for their new home and began finding the equipment that they needed.

The NewSchool Grrls specialized in runs against Expedite — not that this was any surprise; K^a£¡ found that she could easily work around the company's defenses and get out without leaving a trail, and she certainly viewed the monolithic corporation as the main enemy of the people. Expedite couldn't keep up with her, and a bogus ID generator made the NewSchool central server appear to all traces to be set up on one of the synthetic islands off the West Coast, or in Norway, or (a favorite) from an uninhabited island that had been razed in an Expedite weapons test.

They opened their arms to those who embraced their philosophy, instructing their charges in traditional organic and less traditional chip-reader lessons in their little office-cubicle-building-turned-schoolhouse.

Never had so many learned so much with no chance of earning an officially-sanctioned degree.

NewSchool Grrls tended toward biochemistry spiking, and sought a social identity unique unto the group, but consistent within it. Recombinant DNA made their re-engineering of the self possible, allowing them to reject the tension of their disparate races by electing to become one of a new, collective, self-selected race whose characteristics were chosen and engineered by the NewSchool Grrls.

They selected a deep, burnished-olive tone to their skin, tightly-curled hair modeled after the descendants of Africa, hair which they kept close-cropped; an intentionally athletic build, with small-ish, firm, breasts, utilitarian insofar as they would not get in the way during martial training; the wide, flat nose of the Indonesians; thin-slitted, far-eastern style eyelids; and a strangely reflective green pigment to their eyes that was modeled after the reflectiveness that some animals' eyes — cats, for example — exhibit when a light is shone upon them.

A NewSchool Grrl can tend to stand out.

85

Their reflexes reworked to be faster, their bodies reprogrammed for strength and intelligence, Kª£¡'s daughters became new tribes of Amazon, new leagues of augmented women rising up from the rubble and ruin of Old New York.

Cage knew it wouldn't do to try to fly directly to Kª£¡'s school, to try to just set the Olds down at her compound, even though, from months of talk at *Gotham George's*, he had come to know where the anarchists' answer to the Ivy league was housed.

Cage tugged his brown, texture-woven vest forward, straightening the double-Windsor of his plain, black tie. He pulled on his trench coat and fedora and made his way down to street level and, flipping up the coat's collar to ward off the drizzle, started toward Washington Crossing. The only NewSchool Grrls' hang out he knew of for sure was a streetwise Old East Village joint called *Nine Circles*.

eighteen

Cage made his way into the club, past a muscular, surly-looking doorman and up to the bar to spy one of the most strikingly beautiful Nouveau Gothics he had ever laid eyes on. But she was looking the other direction, talking with a group of NewSchool Grrls.

He'd never really gone for the heavily made-up, theatrically dramatic fashion favored by Z.Brites and Nouveau Gothics, but the bartender (a *human* bartender!) had a beauty that pushed aside his usual protests.

Then he saw another one of her appear near the end of the bar.

As the second bartender approached, the first straightened, never looking his way, but suddenly aware of Cage's presence. She turned from the group of lithe, dark NewSchool Grrls she was talking with at the end of the bar and made her way down to Cage.

"Ladies' night, tonight, tall, dark, and handsome," cooed Yang-Angelique. "I'm afraid I'll have to ask you to find a seat away from the bar. Perhaps one of the circles of Hell? We have an excellent complement of dominatrixes. Or perhaps a quiet, contemplative booth not so very far from the bar."

Cage sized her up, trying for all he was worth not to watch her breasts, criss-crossed in shiny black laces, bulging against them and the shiny black fabric of her dress.

"Just need a quick word with one of the ladies at the end of the bar first, if you don't mind," he said.

Yang-Angelique arched an eyebrow, amused. Men had such accessible weaknesses.

"Which one?"

"Doesn't matter," said Cage. He turned and pointed, indicating a booth. "Ask one of them to come over, if you don't mind. And I'd love a single Laphroaig, too."

Yang-Angelique gave a slight, smiling bow and returned to the bar to pour his order.

The scotch appeared at Cage's booth, borne by the second Nouveau Gothic he'd seen, and followed closely by a woman of deliberately athletic build, smallish breasts, an even, deep-burnished olive skin tone, and the animalistic, reflective green eyes that, all together, were the recombinant calling card of the NewSchool Grrls.

"You wished to see one of us? Fetish man?" She asked.

Cage smiled wryly, trying not to visualize.

"I'd like it if you could tell the professor that an old student by the name of Cage would like to speak with her."

The Grrl smiled, a little mockingly, and said, "Professor, sir?"

"No games. Just tell her. Please," Cage said. "Thanks."

The NewSchool Grrl gave a quick, short nod and returned to her party.

Cage had another Laphroaig; he wanted to give the message time to reach K^a£¡, lest his arrival ignite a defense that would get him blown out of the sky. He'd given the Olds enough bumps lately.

He stood to leave, noticing that the Grrls from the bar had gone, and that only the two Nouveau Gothics remained in this front section. He shrugged; it was still early.

Making his way down Washington Crossing, Cage passed from the district illuminated by the Nine Circles' lights and into the scattered, piecemeal streetlighting maintained by public works.

Along about the eighth block from the club, Cage heard an unfamiliar sound as he passed an old, bombed-out meat truck, the familiar "MEAT IS MURDER" slogan etched into its side by the Animal Liberation Front — he heard a sort of *boing*. He looked around, not seeing or hearing anything else; he started walking again.

This time he heard two boings: the original, and one a bit higher-pitched, like two notes being struck with a steel hammer on the strings of an old piano.

He stopped completely and looked around.

Looking back, he saw a handful of figures arise from the shadows of the old, bombed-out meat truck.

To his left, across the street, more figures emerged from an alley. Ahead of him, more, one holding something curved — a bow? — he wasn't waiting around to find out.

He ducked into an alley to his right, pounding down the unlit, oily-slick passage, realizing too late that the *boing* sounds had taken up a rhythm with a clear, plodding, repeating cadence. And that it wasn't getting any farther away: The rhythm was being broadcast into speakers located around the alley. He'd been herded here, between the disused buildings; this was an ambush.

88

nineteen

He knew that he couldn't backtrack; the people who had worked to corral him were there, and would be in pursuit; He looked around, finding nothing surprising, save for speakers mounted on some of the lower reaches of the fire escapes leading into the alley. He slowed to a cautious jog, assaying the position of a dumpster and its location beneath one of the fire escapes.

He picked up his pace, jumping toward the dumpster and pulling himself up. Slowly, too slowly, he recovered from a slip on the slick metal lid. Too slowly he swung his legs ungracefully up beside him. He heard a hollow, metallic, echoing thump on the dumpster lid. Too slowly, he got to his feet, reached for the fire escape, noticed a NewSchool Grrl spinning gracefully before him, a blur of a leg extending from the gossamer twirl of her form to caress his cheek with a deadly *armada* kick. He felt the right side of his face go numb under the cold, hard, grit-laden sole of her foot as it lashed out from her spin.

Cage's fall from the dumpster was cushioned by a bank of flimsy trash cans that crumpled as he came down on them. He fought his way free of the cheap aluminum and stood; the Grrl who'd struck him had been ahead of the rest.

And now she was gone.

Cage made his way down the alley as the cadence of the beaten string churned into something that sounded vaguely African to him.

Chuck chuck chuck chucka chuck chuck chuck chucka ~

Like a sound loop echoing in the oily wet cold of a forgotten alley in the black rain in the night.

He walked on to the end of the alley, seeing no other escape; waiting for him was a circle of the tough little NewSchool Grrls, eyes reflecting an animal green in the cold, unnatural white light of a single street lamp overhead, a Grrl at the far end holding the bow-thing he'd seen earlier, striking its string with what looked to be a shiny, slim, black fiberglass stick.

Chuck chuck chuck chucka chuck chuck chuck chucka ~

89

He stopped, but another Grrl, one of the group who'd herded him into the alley, gave him a shove forward into the middle of the circle, a surprisingly strong shove that pitched him headlong onto the floor of the alley, cold, coarse gravel and grit biting into his palms.

Cage stood slowly, wiping his scraped hands on the coat, the shallow new wounds stinging in the downpour, bits of gravel and dirt lodged in the ground skin. When he looked up, he noticed one of the Grrls kneeling before the leader — at least, he thought she must be the leader — holding the bow-instrument.

She touched the bow with one hand, reverently, tenderly, smiled, and started into a slow, lazy, easy single-handed flip into the center of the circle, just out of Cage's range, and began a swishing, fluid slide from side to side.

Cage stood his ground, not raising his defenses. Waiting.

When the Grrl began a spin toward the ground, Cage stepped back. As she spun, a kick flying up from the ground, Cage intercepted it, his ribs holding against the hard, certain impact of the Grrl's foot. Holding onto the foot, he kicked the supporting leg out from under her and watched her fall into the alley the way that he had, nearly, but she didn't fall as heavily, not as clumsily.

She launched into a slow roll from the ground, up onto her hands. From a stable sort of handstand, she loosed a kick to Cage's already bruised ribs. Wincing, Cage threw a kick with everything he had into her midsection, sending her over effortlessly onto her feet.

Except for the footprint, Cage had left no indication that she'd been hit.

Another NewSchool Grrl was kneeling now before the bow instrument, making the same sort of tribute his first opponent had. As the new Grrl flipped into the circle, the first playfully jogged out.

The new Grrl looked the same to Cage, less the dirt from her wipeout.

Cage watched, never looking away, and the Grrl still seemed to almost disappear in a spinning blur in the black rain in the white light in the night. She had slapped the ground hard with her hands as she started into the spin, a hard knot of agile, inertial power flinging out a spinning kick from the ground and, when Cage managed to dodge the first one, continuing in a dizzying pursuit, chasing him while still spinning, kicking, tagging him, setting off little bursts of white across his vision: his numbed jaw, white *burst*, his aching ribs, white *burst*, two kicks striking him, *burst, burst*, then three, *burstburstburst*, then the ground against his back, *burst*.

He hadn't realized he was falling.

He forced his eyes open against a field of swirling sparks and saw the second Grrl actually perched over him, her hands supporting her, her legs tucked to her body, waiting to strike.

"OK, Grrls," said another woman's voice.

His opponent extended a leg and ever-so-gently placed a steel-reinforced toe against Cage's forehead, letting him know for certain that he hadn't been in any position to save himself, to run, anything.

A Grrl wearing a bright little light fixture on some sort of headgear, the light aimed out into the circle at Cage, stepped forward. The NewSchool Grrl was wearing a zoomable camera of some sort wired to a Personal. Shaking his head, he sat up, leaning on his elbows.

"I didn't think you'd be able to stop them, Mr. Cage, but it's always good to give the Grrls field training — real hands-on stuff. Especially against a tough man like you."

Cage shook his head, trying to shake out the cobwebs.

The voice was coming from the speakers arrayed around the alley; the Grrl wearing the camera was not the one talking to him.

Ka£¡.

She was watching, but she wasn't there in the filthy alley with them.

His opponent offered him a hand, but Cage pushed himself up on his own, ignoring the pain of the rain washing into the scrapes in his hands, ignoring the burning, and standing unsurely, a bit awkwardly.

The Grrls were already coiling the cables and packing the speakers they'd placed throughout the alley.

"Grrls, bring Mr. Cage to the school."

Within a few moments he was blindfolded, being led to a car, lifting off and arcing away into the night.

twenty

Back in her apartment, Jonny Cache flipped to full-panoramic Netview, cruising the datastreams in search of the missing pieces of a puzzle: three digits in the middle of a partial URL she'd cobbled together from whoever had made the Netrun on the Day-Windham server.

Recent excitement aside, she had a job to do and a client awaiting results.

Out on the Net, transfer rates in terabits per second across multiple channels made the old dreams of a virtual environment a possibility. On the information backwater that the old World Wide Web had become, data transfers had been too slow for users to experience virtual reality in real time; it took time — often a long time — to download all of the textures laid out over shapes in a Virtual Reality Markup Language world. A digital line couldn't load a VRML world quickly enough, let alone the lower-speed connection afforded by commoners connecting with old-style telephones on the copper-wire POTS system.

But when StellarNet went online, everyone who could link up to it could access the data faster. Much faster.

Although VR worlds proliferated on StellarNet like bacteria on chicken meat in the sun, user groups began to form coalitions and pacts, agreeing to standards for the permanent VR worlds, the advantage being that a user could download a template of each of these worlds' main features and textures and sounds, meaning that only data that had been updated, changed somehow, had to be downloaded; a copy of the rest was stored on each user's own desktop.

A VR world wasn't a VR world at all, necessarily; it could be a VR room, or a dark, unsettling cathedral, or a city, the only limit being processor power and time needed to download and interpret the shapes and sounds and textures. But larger files, worlds containing more detail, took longer to download, so users tended to keep VR worlds compact.

Jonny was cruising Sixth Street, a VR world modeled by one of the online collectives after the famed nightlife district in Austin, Texas, North American Trade Sector. Here, the Longhorn Collective sold virtual real estate to those who wanted in; and savvy code-slingers could design an online bar like *Macbeth* — a virtual meeting place, really — or an online store, where patrons might have a look over the latest clothing styles or magazine offerings, place an order and have it shipped.

Jonny loved Sixth Street, loved how it spanned for miles, yet still seemed to reference the photos of the Sixth Street of old that she'd found in a historical booth on the world.

But this world was a street. Users could stroll or skulk or drift for miles up and down Sixth Street, but the world's boundaries were sharply limited to one block's virtual distance off Sixth street, and users couldn't actually access a Fourth or Fifth Street because the Longhorn Collective had never written them.

The coloration of this Sixth Street, setting it in opposition to the original, lit everything as though shone under a constant bath of black light. Inside the shops and stands set up along the street by members of the collective, everything could change, but out on Sixth Street, the color-palette protocol was set.

Jonny had an advantage over other users on Sixth Street, though: She could read the data beneath the rendered imagery. She could read the addresses of each referring URL.

Finding her way out to the worlds of the larger collectives had seemed a logical first step: The first numerical string of the URL address was a convention used to identify the larger commercial VR worlds. Whoever had raided Day-Windham had started in one of the big ones.

On Sixth Street, avatars of all shapes and sizes — within the limits of the collective's protocols — walked and loped and swam and flew past her, taking it all in.

As she strolled past the *Macbeth*, the Rain Forest, Reference House, and True Blue, she skimmed beneath the surface imagery, into the data, looking for a match. As she gazed up into the virtual night, she found the same, deep, dark, electric-blue glow in a sky with no sun or stars, massive advertisements drifting/scrolling overhead amid the rendered gaussian cloudcover.

She strolled her Plain-Jane avatar past a thumping virtual dance hall called the *Nuclear Nightclub*. The exterior was a light-absorbing black with flyers about upcoming shows and events posted on the walls along Sixth Street. Torture-Tech pounded out onto the digital byways of Sixth Street, a steady stream of avatars coming and going.

The Plain-Jane avatar Jonny had constructed, hoping not to attract attention, stepped aside as a radiant, glowing Halogen blonde bounded out of the club, a Jim Morrison avatar following close behind; off to a little cybersex, Jonny supposed.

Just down the block, Jonny watched as an eight-foot-tall, hair-covered hominid standing before a storefront noticed her glance, turned, and disappeared into the store, stooping with an oddly precise awkwardness to avoid the door frame.

Jonny paused her avatar outside the store's node. Its sign read: "Unknown Frontiers." An ephemeral avatar resembling a shifting cloud of tiny, glittering gold globes breezed past her on the walk.

The storefront didn't look like a space-movie club; its stern, black-marble tile, its window bearing images of purported UFOs and flying discs, the occasional sea monster movie, ancient Bigfoot and Yeti stills.

Just beneath the image, she dipped into the datastream and found what she was after. The storefront's referring URL matched her recovered partial sequence; they fit together like pieces of a jigsaw puzzle.

Time to learn about these Frontierspeople, she thought, a grotesque avatar resembling a giant angler fish, a glowing bait-worm dangling from its angling arm, swimming past, its pale green eyes glowing grimily, mouth gaping dully open.

Jonny walked her Plain-Jane avatar into the little virtual storefront. She'd never met a UFO enthusiast before. The inside of the little shop was much larger than the outside — a trick programmers can do that architects cannot: Store a large room within a space that's too small for it.

Inside the *Unknown Frontiers* shop, Jonny found row upon row of sometimes grainy, sometimes animated images suspended in the air, side by side, of the purportedly paranormal, including a copy of the famous, jumpy, hand-held footage shot by Roger Patterson

94

back in the twentieth century of a supposedly true encounter with a Sasquatch among the timbers in the American Northwest.

But the Frontierspeople had no avatars here now; none of them, apparently, was online.

Now that she had their name, though, their URL and a few keywords would lead her to the Unknown Frontiers' physical location. She'd still be running a little slow, some of her processor time involved in an on-again, off-again search for the partial license number she'd shot from the Montgomery Building while she was watching Gild's place, but the hard part of her paid mission, at least — reconstructing an erased URL — was done.

She moved to flip her link out of full-panoramic Netview mode, when she felt a long, low-pitched *thoom* shake the entire world.

In the distance, she heard a long, peeling mechanical cry that she recognized from old motion-picture 'Net sites.

She couldn't believe what she was hearing.

twenty-one

Cage winced as someone thumped a rock-hard cold pack to his aching jaw.

"Hold this," said a Grrl.

Cage didn't like all the hush-hush and security hoops he had to jump through to get to Kª£¡'s rogue school, all just so he didn't damage their much-prized sense of secrecy. But he'd already roused the ire of the Grrls by calling for an audience with their once-mainstream-academic leader, and it had been made plain to him that he was in no position to do anything except play by their rules.

He felt his weight shift as their carflight slowed, felt himself lighten a bit as the car began a vertical landing sequence, felt his weight return with a soft *thump* as the car set down.

Two of the NewSchool Grrls, one at each arm, lifted him out of the car, the suspended weight of his hips and legs stretching his bruised ribs, pulling in shearing sheets of pain at the damaged muscle groups overlaying the injuries, separating his ribs just enough to bring agony. He didn't dare to cough or huff in pain; that would worsen the effect.

When his feet struck the ground beneath him, he was surprised by his own sharp exhale of agony; he hadn't realized he'd been holding his breath, gritting his teeth.

They wordlessly led him inside, down a series of twists and turns, and through a door. Then one removed his blindfold, and he could see that she looked very much like the other.

"Well. Frank Cage," said a voice he recognized as his former professor, Sarasvati Narayan — Kª£¡ — from behind him. The voice had deepened somewhat over the years, but it had had such a severity to it when he'd known her that the difference seemed only slight.

He turned to face her and found her only minutely older by appearance than the two who had brought him, the two who had leveled him on the street, the one who'd kicked him down from the dumpster. But her accent was flavored with South Asian habits, a *masala* of her training in Hindi, Sanskrit, British English, and, lately, her company among Grrls from North America.

"Just Cage, professor," he said thickly, adjusting the cold pack. His tongue wasn't working as easily as before the Grrls had ambushed him.

"All right," she said with precise severity. She was sitting bolt-straight, her hands folded on her lap, a posture at once relaxed and alert: She didn't feel threatened, only put out by his intrusion into her schedule. "Just Kª£¡, Cage."

Cage could just make out the cheekbones of an instructor he'd known once, years ago, when he was taking night courses, trying for a promotion to detective on the force.

She eyed him intently, her expression flat, controlled, her eyes blinking so infrequently that Cage had to fight back sympathetic tearing in his own eyes.

"What the hell is this about, Cage?" she demanded.

"I don't get it," he said, ignoring her. "Why'd you set me up for a beating in that damned alley?"

"I don't like snoops, Cage. And I tend to trust men less. Particularly men who want to talk with me in person. You were disoriented and shaken down to ensure that you carried no tracers or bugs. When I ID'd you, I called off the Grrls.

"So again, Cage: What the hell is this about?"

Cage took a seat, looking around the drab office-turned-classroom, a blackboard behind Kª£¡, desk-chairs throughout the room, the harsh, white incandescents overhead.

"I need help. Your kind of help. From someone with your kind of expertise," Cage said finally. "Money's no problem. Cash, I mean, not transferred credits."

She allowed a small smile of approval to creep into her precise, controlled expression. "Smart boy. What's your task, Cage?"

Cage drew a deep breath, trying to relax after the roughing up he'd had, after being knocked around by one Grrl after another.

"I need to get some information from Expedite's corporate server."

"What sort of information, Cage? Some data are easier to find than others."

"I need to run a set of prints against their server. I tried law enforcement, but the man I'm after wasn't tracked there. I think he's stayed out of the law's way, mostly," said Cage.

"What's this man mean to you, Cage."

"That's business, K^a£$_i$. Case I'm working on. You understand."

She gazed at the rumpled, unshaven, and now, since his ambush, dirty detective for a long time, long enough that Cage began to think she couldn't — or wouldn't — make the run.

"The Grrls shook you down. Where's your cash, Cage?"

"No one carries that much cash at street level, K^a£$_i$," he said.

"No? You planned to meet with me, but you didn't bring your Ennays?" she said, a slight tone of — what? Ire? Ridicule? — in her voice. She was tolerating him. There was no old camaraderie here.

"No. Your Grrls swept in and thumped me easy, but there are less principled attackers down there who wouldn't just beat me to prove a point."

"What point do you think the Grrls and I were trying to prove, Cage?"

"That I was in your control from a few seconds after I sent out the call for you. That your tough little Amazons could trounce me whenever they felt like it."

The dark, slim woman regarded him with open amusement. He was right: This had been exactly their point in dragging him through these trials.

"OK, Cage. I'm interested."

After a brief negotiation, Cage was blindfolded again and ferried back to his office. He retrieved the Ennays from the wall safe he kept hidden behind a fading painting of what some starving artist thought a summer in full bloom might have looked like decades ago, before the rains that came and the night that never left. And then, his blindfold secured again, they returned.

The Grrls didn't say much to him.

twenty-two

Cage waited, watching through a heavy glass window from outside the room that housed K^a£¡'s imposing workstation. It looked like a preposterous snarl of steel and cables and adapters and peripheral bays and monitors. It looked like some sort of disemboweling of a desktop gone completely awry. It looked like a repair technician had taken apart four separate desktop units and accidentally begun interconstructing them. Duct tape and surge-suppressers and backup power supplies littered the floor.

K^a£¡'s hands caressed her souped-up desktop, fingers flicking over the top of the unit like the interaction was all sex and soma.

Cage had no such passion, but found himself stiffening as he watched her pore over the console. He found himself hoping none of the Grrls would notice and take offense.

While he watched, the desktop's representations hovered holographically before her, but she incorporated a VR helmet and leads that plugged directly into her suit: She went full-panoramic VR onto StellarNet. He could not see what she saw, but he was awed by the pure, animal sensuality with which she worked.

"Interesting," she said, tinges of sexual stimulus coloring the severity of her voice.

Cage saw a flat, two-dimensional image appear before her in the desktop's projection zone: A white male. Overweight, Cage could see, but Cage's perspective on her workstation left him seeing the image from the side, scarcely more than a glowing silver sliver of holography.

"What's — oh — I see — " she was saying, talking to herself as she slinked her way through the Net, into Expedite's central server, quietly sidestepping their security, mining for the data she needed.

Cage awoke to a shove on his shoulder. His neck felt like a stack of loosely associated chunks of concrete rubble, their sharp edges painfully pinching nerves.

Looking around, squinting at the pallid, death-white incandescence of office-building lighting, he cleared his throat.

"How long did that take?" he asked.

"Long enough for your eye to blacken over, Cage," said Kª£¡, her tone all business.

"Your man's name is Eliott Jovanovic. N.A. Trade Sector citizen, no criminal record. Heart problems. Works with a bunch of UFO nuts who call themselves 'Unknown Frontiers.'"

Cage rubbed a hand across his day-old stubble now, waking slowly. "I don't get it. Why would a UFO nut want a retired programmer burned to death?" Cage asked, talking more to himself than to Kª£¡.

"You're the private dick here, Cage," she said, flipping a silver disc into his lap. "You've got your information. And I've got my Ennays. Time for you to head home."

Cage nodded slowly, pondering the new information.

"*Latte*," said Kª£¡ to an assistant. One of the Grrls brought her a steaming cup of stiff, properly brewed coffee, its scent wafting to Cage, beckoning, its caramel color catching his eye.

"Milk?" he asked, disbelief in his voice. *Any treat for the tastes of the powerful*, he thought.

She eyed the bruised man coolly.

"Soy milk," said Kª£¡, emphasizing the *soy*. "Made from soy beans. Grown contraband, without the regulation prescription cocktail of herbicides, pesticides, and gene splices mandated by the Agriculture Authority. That's part of why this school — this movement — is so important, Cage. No one seems to have even noticed that they're swimming in their own shit."

Cage glowered back at her. "What are you talking about?" And, when she didn't respond immediately, "What, Kª£¡? What do you mean?"

"Think about the food, Cage! The world is one huge, decimated, polluted toilet. Animal life is so defeated by humankind's juggernaut advance that we had to construct a fake food chain to keep everyone from starving, and you don't even know enough not to think of milk from another animal species as something precious! Cage, it's one of the things we've killed and confined and drugged and beaten animals for for centuries, never caring about the damage we were doing to the world and the animals and ourselves!

100

"The food chain started to collapse with the death of plankton in the Atlantic in the early '90s, Cage, and we didn't — and still don't — even give a damn enough to notice. Didn't then, don't now. Remember, Cage? The ozone? We let it go, Cage, so the big companies wouldn't have to lose any profits? The increased solar radiation started killing plankton and frogs early in the '90s, but the corporations made it all look political: NASA was making it all up, they said, remember? No, Cage, of course you don't. Someone who just thought of milk as a luxury to be had wouldn't bother thinking about it.

"Cultured, steroid-boosted, antibiotics-laced nori is the cultivated food-base paste most of our food is made from, not because meat and milk are so good for you Cage, not because meat and milk are such a delicacy, but because we killed everything. We made it swim in our shit until it died off.

"But that's the sort of evil pigs our species are. The food chain has collapsed, in all natural terms, and so we get by by culturing nori — seaweed — using the same methods that killed everything before, because the corporations paid the lawmakers to make it illegal to do otherwise. We're still waging war on the world for our food Cage, we're just doing it all further down on the food chain. And almost no one fucking cares, Cage!

"When we were kids, Cage — remember? — and we got milk and meat cheap, no one gave a damn about the pain and aggravation and environmental ruin we caused, so long as we could be 'all-American,' and keep pretending those burgers weren't making half of the population die by heart attack, keep downing that milk, keep pretending cheese and milk weren't fat-heavy, clogging our veins, while at the same time we were paying people to hurt the animals producing that milk, paying them to make sure those cows were so tightly corralled that in their entire lives, they couldn't even turn around, never left their stalls, but we all kept these pastel-painted, idyllic images of cows at pasture that we knew — we *knew* — weren't true anymore in the age of the corporate megafarm."

Cage was looking away from her now, unprepared for this torrent.

"And the only reason we don't keep doing it is because we've done so much wrong and so much damage that we are no longer able to have it, Cage! We didn't stop because it was wrong, or because it was bad for us, or because it was so hard on the entire planet, but because we fucked the environment over so badly that we can't sustain animal agriculture anymore."

She glared at him. He still couldn't look her way.

"We shit in our environment, and ignore our shit, all the while knowing that we're the ones doing the shitting and that we can stop, and that the shit kills everything, and we still refuse to care."

She looked directly, harshly, into his eyes.

"*That* we find worth fighting against, Cage. You never learned a thing from me."

Shamed, silenced, Cage could think of no way to respond.

Kª£ị turned to the Grrls keeping watch over the detective.

"His business here is through," she said, sipping her latte. "Get him the hell out of here."

Cage let a pair of the professor's Grrls blindfold him.

He cast his head downward. He really hadn't ever thought about it. It had all seemed so distant, somehow. Like he wasn't even involved.

He wanted to drift back into sleep for the drive, but pain from his knotted neck and his bruised ribs kept sharply reminding him of the day's events. He was let out on the rooftop, next to his Olds. Back at the office.

The perpetual black rains rendered everything the slick color of molten lead. The taillights of the Grrls' car danced across the rain-slick black of the rooftop, fading into the distance.

Wearily, he made his way down the damp, musty stairwell, the stench of mildew hanging in the motionless air, patches of black mold spreading along the baseboards of the stairs, black ice sickles reaching out away from the main, blotchy colonies.

In the office, Effie gasped at the sight of him, battered and walking slowly, carefully, guarding his abused rib cage. She went to the office fridge unit and brought out an ice pack she'd started after he'd left to find Kª£ị.

"It's funny," Cage said exhaustedly to Effie. "The NewSchool Grrls have so much going for them. They really do hold the philosophical high ground on a lot of things. But they're a failure. Another failed attempt to answer people's problems."

"What do you mean, Cage?" asked Effie.

"I mean, for all their education-freeing, you still have to be one of them to do it. For their vaunted stances against racism, the best answer they could come up with was to invent their own, separate characteristics, then get an attitude of superiority about their new race. And they fight so hard against sexism only to hold men in open disdain. All men. They haven't solved the problems of the people they oppose; they've just become self-important reflections of them."

He plugged the new ROM he'd purchased from K^a£¡ into his desktop and began to pore over the file she'd raided on Jovanovic.

A 47-year-old businessman, Jovanovic was in dealings with a group of UFO enthusiasts whose interests also plumbed such murky folkloric depths as Sasquatch and sea monsters. Together, the group ran a hobby shop specializing in role-playing games, conspiracy theories, supposedly nonfiction books and magazines, and outlawed publications such as "The Anarchist's Cookbook."

Jovanovic and his clandestine comrades rented a piece of Sixth Street for a storefront called *Unknown Frontiers*.

Cage decanted two fingers of Laphroaig, wincing as the smoky seaweed and iodine flavors in the liquid scorched places in his mouth where the encounter with the Grrls had scored his cheeks and tongue against his teeth. The peaty potency of the drink replaced the coppery taste of blood he'd forgotten about until he'd washed it away.

He looked over the list of victims:

James Gild, age 42: middle-aged, retired computer programmer with Sumner's Syndrome; Oliver Jaspin, age 48: A hardware engineer for Chapterhouse Computing with a taste for Beaujolais; and Alaina Quinn, age 38: A teacher at a private school for children.

Why did a group of UFO nuts want these three, apparently harmless, apparently unaffiliated people dead?

In the dark, in his exhaustion, in his office, Cage had no answers.

Outside, the sky to the east had taken on a dull, red glow, backlit by a sun that could not get through, giving the only desperate, sickly color that would reach the denizens of Old New York today.

twenty-three

Thoom!

Jonny Cache bounded across the street to get a better view of the distance; virtual buildings obscured her vision of things far away. But she knew what she'd heard: She'd replayed samples of that peculiar metallic cry hundreds of times, trying to find the attraction that the Japanese could not seem to shake for a towering, nuclear-radiation-mutated dinosaur.

Sixth Street was under attack by a virus designed to look like an old movie monster.

Sixth Street was under attack by Godzilla.

Thoom!

Jonny watched as the tourists and denizens of Sixth Street, avatars by the hundreds, streamed out onto the thoroughfare to halt, mouths (of those avatars that had mouths) ajar, staring toward the west.

At the Western edge of the VR world, something enormous winked into existence, a cloud of digital dead-TV-channel snow filling a hulking reptilian frame, looking for all the world like the transporter strobe on the original "Star Trek" television series.

Someone had studied the science fiction of decades gone by and had chosen to dress a new, digitally viral technology in the cloak of old, cheesy science fiction special effects.

Jonny adjusted her perception of the monster, peering into its code, but she could only spy stream upon stream of gibberish within the monster.

The cry came again. Godzilla, his eyes an impossible gamut-warning, lightning-like color, the huge, preposterous, not at all natural-looking spines on his back glowing suddenly in a halogen halo, blasted the Dell Memorial Virtual Event Center with an uneven rush of fiery, gamut-warning-colored breath that corroded the code representing the Dell center, wore at its binary walls until the structure exploded, a vapor of alphanumerics rising from the building and blinking out, chunks of busted code slamming into other digital structures nearby, polluting and corrupting them, as well.

As Sixth Street's visitors and dwellers signed off, fleeing the virtual party central, avatars all over the boulevard began the quick collapse to a single point of light that marks a logoff from VR.

Jonny was reading up on Japanese *anime* as the monster advanced. A perfunctory analysis of forty-seven films featuring giant monsters showed a high probability that the appropriate response to a giant, attacking monster was a gigantic, anthropomorphic battle robot.

She crafted a new avatar on the fly, overriding the user preferences allotted visitors and resetting the height scale of her new creation to four hundred feet.

One second, Plain-Jane was gawking up beside everyone else on Sixth Street, the next — *thoom!* — the thunderous sound of another set of gargantuan footfalls arose from the east.

The avatars of Sixth Street turned to the east and found a gleaming, four hundred-foot-tall, silver samurai lumbering in from the distance, drawing a sword that flowed with blue flames. The battle robot's face was a polished, reflective grille worked into a vaguely malevolent grin. The grille was inset with two smoldering red pupils rimmed broadly in black, its polished silver helm flaring out low about its head; it struck an imposing martial posture.

Its chest was emblazoned with a red inset manga-influenced geometric shape that suggested swift cut with a sword.

Jonny leveled the tip of her sword at the Godzilla virus, loosing a column of blue flame which arced over the structures of Sixth Street, exploding on the hide of the digital monster.

With a metallic shriek, the beast returned fire, disrupting the data of more than a dozen avatars between itself and the samurai.

Jonny-Samurai advanced down the boulevard toward Japan's greatest nuclear horror, blasting again with the sword, the blue flames opening up flaws in the great mutant reptile's side, exposing a seething tumult of code, flickering a random cascade of harsh yellow on black, white on black, black on white.

Godzilla blasted Jonny-Samurai, but her gleaming armor held, the blast dissipating off hard custom code the likes of which only an artificial intelligence could have created.

She advanced on the monster, whose mode seemed to shift,

then. Abruptly, Godzilla turned from the attacking Samurai to face the virtual structure that housed *Unknown Frontiers*, firing a blast of viral attack code that demolished the online store, leaving a sputtering, flickering crater in the building.

Covering your masters' tracks, beastie? she thought. *Too late, Unknown Frontiers. I've got your URL.*

With the fluid ease of a ballerina, Jonny-Samurai spun gracefully on her left foot, the right whipping around to flick out and kick a hole through the dark-green, scale-covered abdomen of the virus.

Standing directly before the listing, malfunctioning virus-monster now, Jonny-Samurai raised her flaming blue sword, waited a moment as though a ceremonial pause were required out of some ancient, Far Eastern tradition, then brought the sword down hard, cleaving the virus-monster into two sparking, collapsing heaps of code, a hot, glowing vapor of alphanumeric characters rising from the monster's halved, scaly green hide.

A cheer went up from the avatars who'd stayed online for the fight and managed not to wind up corrupted.

Pivoting to face the masses, Jonny-Samurai bowed, and if she could have found a way to make the polished metallic face she'd programmed smile more sincerely without disparaging the entire genre of Japanese Giant Foam-Rubber Science Fiction, she would have. But just at the moment, she had the feeling she owed something to the genre.

While the Samurai avatar was bowed, she signed off, the gigantic Samurai winking in an instant down to a single glowing point, then to nothingness.

They'd have to reload Sixth Street from their backup.

Freed of the VR accouterments of the Sixth Street world, Jonny rode the wave of the data streams, looking for a little information on a group that called itself Unknown Frontiers, hoping to learn why they'd arranged to blast their own piece of virtual real estate rather than let her examine it more closely.

The conspiracy-theory nuts were definitely hiding something.

twenty-four

"Site Down," said the message, hovering in the air before Cage in his darkened apartment.

"'*Site Down*'?" asked Cage, incredulous, shaving. "Sixth Street never closes, I thought."

No luck following up on their virtual location, then, he said; *time to look them up.*

Cage launched a search engine to find the physical location of *Unknown Frontiers*, yawning as he slid his boost sample back into his reader.

As she signed off from Sixth Street, Jonny noticed that one of her searches had completed itself.

Her partial license sequence from the intruder at Gild's apartment had turned up a possible make/model match. She pulled up the datasheet her search had returned.

The North-American-made Oldsmobile she'd been pursued by was owned by a private detective named Cage, whose office, she learned, was in the Old Gotham Quarter, here in Old New York.

His file detailed his history — the lost engagement with the Climber named Hyacinth Merriam Vandervelde, who went by "Cin," his removal from his job as a police detective, his economically unimpressive foray into private investigation.

Her search also perfunctorily informed her of Cin's subsequent move to New Metropolis Three and a pending prenuptial contract with a thirty-something security manager on one of the synthetic islands.

The private detective hadn't been seriously injured when he'd chased Jonny across town, she noted; he hadn't sought medical attention anywhere, and he had logged onto StellarNet several times since the pursuit.

Who would be looking into James' affairs? She wondered. *We never really told anyone I was there — could Expedite have found out? Could they be after a rogue domestic unit after all this time?*

"But I've never received the recall signal," she found herself telling Yang-Angelique in the binaries' apartment.

"Perhaps," said the sultry Nouveau Gothic, "if they somehow learned that their signal wouldn't summon you, they would attempt to find and surprise you, hmm? Take you unawares?"

Jonny pondered the question.

"The detective, Cage, nosed into something they wanted kept quiet," she said. "They crushed him, destroyed his plans for his future."

"Money talks, Jonny," said Yin-Angelique from their apartment's breakfast nook. "Perhaps it spoke with this man."

"Well, Jonny," said Yang-Angelique, "what, then, can you do?"

Jonny Cache flashed the binaries a quick, clever smile.

"I'll shadow him. See if I can figure out what he's up to and why he was at the old place."

The binaries smiled. "Careful, Jonny," said one of them.

Cage flipped off the exterior lighting on his Olds, turned off the car's transponder (all very illegal), and dropped out of traffic altitude and into Old Greenwich, checking his scopes carefully to be certain her hadn't been pursued.

He landed the Olds vertically in an alleyway and climbed out. Turning, he leaned into the driver-side hatch, toward the mic, and said, "Run invisible park one."

He closed the hatch on the automobile and stepped back.

After a brief pause, the Olds, still dark within and without, lofted to an altitude of about twenty meters, staying close to the side of the building, and hovered, its jets all but silent against the white noise of the black rains.

Cage made his way down the street, searching building designations and markings for an office building called Warner Square that should be right around here somewhere, if the maps he'd downloaded were accurate.

Old Greenwich had blossomed and faded before Cage's time in Old New York, but old-timer regulars — hell, Gotham George himself — told him that it had been a bustling part of the city in decades past. Over time, as the sun and the people and the businesses fled, it had been mostly claimed by the hapless who couldn't afford to leave, and the homeless, who took up residence in the abandoned tenements. And troupes of would-be thugs who still called themselves gangs.

For all their territorial disputes, for all the petty drug peddling and traffic in contraband arms, though, the most dominant among them never seemed to realize that he only ruled a section of a junkyard abandoned by all who could get out.

Not that that made traversing Old Greenwich any more safe. Cage kept his gun at his side and kept as much as possible to the shadows. No need to draw unnecessary attention.

Cage found the run-down, and probably once-majestic building with a cast-bronze plaque identifying it as Warner Square. The building's marble face had endured insult, injury, and age. Its once window-covered entry was bricked over, having fallen to decades of bored kids with nothing better to do than smash whatever they could find. A single street-level door allowed access.

Cage cautiously let himself in; the halls on ground level were not lit, and stank of mildew and urine.

Cage rubbed his eyes. How long had it been since he'd slept more than a nap?

He didn't dare brave the elevators in this place; rather, he headed for a stairwell, twin floodlights fighting back the gloom at each floor.

Cage headed onto the building's fifth floor, through a door that emitted a screech of protest as he pushed it aside.

He paused outside the door, consulting his printout to double-check the number: 512. The door bore a small, plastic placard that read "Jovanovic/*Unknown Frontiers*."

Inside, he could hear the tinny chatter of someone's AV unit playing.

He cleared his throat and knocked.

There was a sudden flurry of rustling, followed by a hushed consultation of some kind; then came a timid voice, a male voice: "Who is it?"

"Name's Cage," he yelled into the door. "I need to speak with someone about *Unknown Frontiers*."

With another whispered consultation, the door opened, screeching with as much protest as had the stairwell entry.

109

A shortish, chubby man stood in the doorway holding a stunner, its nozzle leveled at Cage.

The man was red-faced, maybe even shaking a bit, Cage noticed. A coat of perspiration made his forehead and nose almost reflective.

"Who sent you?" asked the man uncomfortably.

Cage raised his hands, making certain they were in plain sight.

"I'm a private detective, sir," Cage mustered his most polite, professional tone. "Just looking into something for a client, and your group's name came up. I'd just like to ask a few questions."

"Cage, huh?" the man asked, suddenly sagging, relaxing a bit. He looked over his shoulder into a part of the apartment Cage couldn't see, paused, then nodded

"OK, Mr. Cage," he said. "You can come on in. 'Pologize for the state of the place an' all, y'know. Not much for housekeeping."

The man lowered his weapon and extended a hand. "Name's Eliott Jovanovic, Mr. Cage."

Cage took and shook Jovanovic's hand.

"And these are my associates."

twenty-five

Jonny Cache sifted the data, seeking the connection between the physical and virtual locations of the group of hackers who called themselves Unknown Frontiers.

And to one to whom the datastreams are simply songs, to whom security is transparent, such data cannot hide for long. One of the members of *Unknown Frontiers*, at some point, would have viewed a site that logged information about its visitors.

Within a few minutes, she tracked down the address out on StellarNet and, still online, ordered the Huang-Sen into ignition sequence.

She tapped into the central database for the Aerial Traffic Authority and cursed, finding a liftoff entry logged for the private detective she'd seen at the apartment of James Gild, realizing she should have been watching him more closely.

She dressed for travel and made her way up into the cool, drizzling early-morning night of Old East Village.

"Biplab Basu," said Jovanovic, introducing Cage to a stout South Asian man, who smiled broadly and shook his hand excitedly.

"Julian Ellis," he said, gesturing toward a man with his back toward Cage, seated in a wheelchair before a jury-rigged desktop, a tangle of messy, frayed, shoulder-length blond hair all Cage could make out. Ellis waved, once, toward the computer.

"And Aleksandr Korsikov," said Jovanovic, gesturing toward a tall, muscular Russian, his bulk emphasized by a heavy, drab synthwool sweater.

The Russian also shook his hand.

Cage rubbed a hand over his stubble. "My information was that you guys ran some sort of hobby store," he said, sizing up the four.

"Oh, yesyesyes," said Jovanovic. "We own a piece of the VR world called Sixth Street." He beamed proudly.

"Which is presently down," said Ellis, still faced away from Cage.

"I noticed that," said Cage. "How can Sixth Street go offline? I thought it never closed."

The *Unknown Frontiers* people exchanged glances.

"We're not sure. There was some kind of giant-Manga battle there, and it looks like the fight damaged today's build of the code."

"Build?" Cage asked.

"Update. Oll zoftvare is compilet from its contingent parts; de vinished zoftvare is callt a built," said Korsikov helpfully.

"Any idea what it was about?" Cage asked.

Jovanovic shook his head *No* nervously.

Cage looked them over; these four misfits were trying to pokerface him. Refugees from a convention for role-playing games.

"You guys ever heard of a woman named Quinn?"

No reaction.

"Alaina Quinn?"

Again, they gave no response.

Cage raised his eyebrows in disbelief.

"Alaina Quinn. Thirty-eight. School teacher from Hackensack?" he asked, beginning to show irritation with them.

"Oh, no, Mr. Cage," said Basu with a heavy, retroflexed Indian accent.

Turning back to stare squarely at Jovanovic, Cage said: "Then why did you give me information that may be related to the case I am investigating?"

Jovanovic swallowed.

"Mr. Cage, our store is a hobby store: Role playing games, comic books, old monster movies, stuff like that."

"Yes?"

"Uh, w-well," Jovanovic swallowed uneasily again. "We didn't expect you to come calling, Mr. Cage. We just wanted to give you a push in the right direction."

"The right direction?" Cage asked, his eyebrows raised again. "Which way might that be, Mr. Jovanovic?"

"We know how Mr. James Gild died, Mr. Cage," said Basu.

twenty-six

"I'm listening," said Cage.

Turning from the computer for the first time, Cage saw the be-spectacled face of Ellis. Behind him, on the screen, were some sort of hairy humanoid 3D model and a much larger dinosaur-like model with some sort of death-ray breath.

"Have a seat, Mr. Cage," he said, gesturing toward a chair.

Cage accepted the offer, the static noise of the rainfall outside distant, but ever present.

"*Unknown Frontiers* deals in off the beaten path materials, but we are acutely interested in the paranormal and unexplained phenomena."

"Unexplained?" Cage asked.

"Sea monsters, Sasquatch ... " Ellis began.

"Demonic possession," added Basu, "poltergeists ... "

"Zombies," said Korsikov, "Abominable snowmen ... "

" ... UFOs," said Jovanovic, watching Cage hopefully, seeking some glimmer of interest.

"UFOs?" asked Cage skeptically.

"We have footage from all over the globe, proof of all of the phenomena we mentioned," he said reassuringly, waving a hand in the air as if to dismiss Cage's resistance to the subjects.

"Watch, Mr. Cage," said Ellis, a weird smirk on his face as he began replaying the most famous sighting of a so-called Bigfoot: jumpy, hand-held footage shot by Roger Patterson back in the 1970s. He followed this with aerial footage of the African dinosaur Mokele Mbembe, remote video of crop circles forming, hundreds of Unidentified Flying Objects ...

"I ... I don't get it, Ellis. The only extra-terran life we've verified so far have been some passive fish on Europa, right? And some Martian germs. So why all this interest in supposed UFO sightings?"

"Because they're there, Cage," said Jovanovic, his enthusiasm growing as he spoke. "Because it's all there, every one of the things we're showing you. Loch Ness Monster — several of them; Lake

Champlain's lake monster Champ. Bigfoot/Sasquatch/Skunk Ape/ Yeti. Alien abductions ... "

As Jovanovic railed, Cage saw a familiar image pass on the screen behind Ellis.

Cage raised a hand. "Hold it, hold it, Jovanovic. Ellis, can you back up that thing you're playing?'

Clearly pleased, Ellis turned and began to slowly backtrack through the presentation. On Ellis' presentation screen, a familiar image faded back into view: A harsh, black crater, about four feet in diameter, a pair of cauterized limbs resting just at the edge of the circle — a burn.

"Hold it," said Cage. "Right there. Look. That's the photo you sent me. Alaina Quinn."

"No, Mr. Cage," said Jovanovic, suddenly dropping his excited delivery in favor of a more serious tone. "That's a photo of one Keye Mtumbo."

"Who's Keye Mtumbo?"

"A member of our group," said Jovanovic. "Former, I should say. It was his spontaneous combustion that interested us in the — er — phenomenon." He straightened his messy button-up shirt hurriedly, aware, suddenly, of how involved he'd gotten in his presentation to the private detective.

"Like a drink, Mr. Cage?" asked Ellis, the weird smirk returning to his face.

"This is how you disposed of a former member of your group?!" demanded Cage, folding his arms, feeling the reassuring duraplex and steel of his sidearm through his trenchcoat.

Jovanovic gave Cage a look of genuine, bald-faced stupefaction. Ellis clutched his side, suddenly peeling laughter. Basu looked uncertainly to Korsikov, who intoned: "In no vay shape or manner dit ve do ziss to Mr. Mtumbo."

Cage kept his hand near the gun, but, when Ellis dropped to floor with a loud thump, complaining through his laughter of cramps, he let his hand fall away from the shoulder holster.

"Mr. Cage, you're onto a string not merely of cases of unsolved deaths, but of unexplained phenomena," said Jovanovic.

Cage shot a puzzled, somewhat annoyed look at the four, particularly at the ridiculous Ellis, who now pounded the floor with a fist and begged breathlessly through his guffawing: "Makehimstop! Makehimstop!"

"Right. Unsolved murders, I guess, are unexplained phenomena," said Cage, irritation and confusion in his voice.

"Oh, certainly," said Jovanovic. "But we mean *unexplained* such as what we've been telling you, not *unexplained* as in some murder mystery."

Cage threw his hands in the air.

"Jovanovic, what exactly the hell are you talking about?!"

Jovanovic, looking genuinely apologetic and a bit confused, replied: "Why … why spontaneous human combustion, of course."

" … " Cage tried to say. He looked at them, finding deadly serious expressions on the faces of all save Ellis, who was pulling himself up from the floor and back into his wheelchair, before his console.

"What?!" Cage managed, barely containing his contempt.

"Spontaneous human combustion. Doesn't happen all the time, but it has happened for long enough and frequently enough for us to know about it and for us and others to have identified and classified it," insisted Jovanovic.

"Jesus, Mohammed, Rama!" muttered Cage. *Freaks*, he thought. *They've got the clues and* this *is their solution?!*

"What's the problem, Mr. Cage?" asked Jovanovic.

"You — your group — how can you have hard evidence and only see little green men?" Cage asked.

Ellis chuckled softly to himself, in the corner. "Toldja," he said. "Five bucks, Korsikov." He chuckled again, returning to work at his desktop.

Cage rubbed his eyes, longing for sleep.

"You gave me information … "

"Yes, yes," said Jovanovic, nodding hurriedly.

"A tip … "

"Oh yes!"

"On the case I'm investigating … "

"The Gild immolation, yes," said Jovanovic.

"Because you thought … " Cage waited.

"Because we thought we'd like to help you find out what was

behind spontaneous human combustion," said Jovanovic, beaming. Basu and Korsikov nodded, smiling. Ellis stared at the screen, his back to the rest.

Cage dropped into the chair, speechless, and sat stunned. He'd hoped for a tip, hoped that the informant who provided him with the files on the burn of Alaina Quinn knew something more, something useful about the Gild case, something he could use.

"Then why did you blot out an entry on the copy of Quinn's resume you sent me?" Cage asked.

The four exchanged glances.

"Something was blotted out?" asked Jovanovic, straightening his shirt uncomfortably.

Then the aged wooden door to the office used by *Unknown Frontiers* exploded inward in a torrent of splinters and chunks.

A slim, sleek twentysomething woman with short, dark hair stood in the doorway, a wet NoGo leatherlook coat dropping behind her to reveal a flexible, close-fitting suit, a stunner in her hand aimed forward. She was, Cage thought as he went for his sidearm, beautiful. Truly beautiful.

A look of recognition crossed Jovanovic's face, followed by one of outright panic.

"Ohmygod!" he managed. "You're the one from the apartment!"

Recognizing first Cage, then Jovanovic, she smiled a truly malevolent smile, and said huskily: "How convenient."

twenty-seven

Jovanovic made a lunge for the counter, where Cage saw the man's stunner resting. But Jovanovic was neither lithe nor fast; he was not built for lunging.

As Cage watched, the beautiful woman seemed to disappear in a blur. Then Jovanovic hit the far wall of the office, crumpling into unconsciousness. She seemed familiar, somehow, but Cage couldn't place her.

Cage stepped forward, "Wait ..." he managed, as the massive Russian, Korsikov, charged for her.

She spun deftly, easily out of the way, as though the big man were moving in slow motion. Somehow she brought the heel of her foot down on top of the Russian's head, and he also fell to the ground, motionless.

"Hey!" Cage yelled now, trying to get the attention of the woman he already knew he could not match physically. She ignored him, whipping her fingertips into the throat of Basu, who made a strangled gasp as he collapsed.

Ellis spun around, wielding a stunner, and fired it at the impossibly fast intruder. But much to his disliking, the stunner's blast merely sparked off the attacking woman's stomach, not slowing her.

And Ellis was down.

Then she — this beautiful, deadly attacker — turned to face Cage.

And his gun. In the time it had taken her to stop the four from *Unknown Frontiers*, he'd just managed to yank his gun from its holster. The tiny red L.E.D. next to its sight that told him he had a target lock flicked on.

"Hey!" he yelled again. "Wait a minute! What's your trouble with them?"

"I know about you, Cage," she said, seething, not even breathing hard. She took a step toward him. "I know about you and Expedite."

"What?" Cage asked; what did this woman know about him? And why did she care about Expedite crushing him? "No farther," he yelled, doing his best not to show the intimidation he felt after watching her fight, keeping the gun aimed directly at her midsection.

She stopped, examining his face for some sign. She'd shown that she could take out any of them, but he seemed genuine in his confusion over her accusation.

"Frank Cage ..." she began.

"Just ... Cage ... please ..."

"Private detective. Your life was turned upside down by Expedite, and now you're trying to regain favor with them by hunting me down and returning me to them."

That was where he knew her from. He recognized her from the photo at James Gild's apartment, now, only she had had longer hair.

T*he domestic.*

But she was behaving like some sort of bodyguard android gone rogue.

"Look, lady, I don't like Expedite, they don't like me. If I dealt with them again in this lifetime I'd just end up dead. What the hell makes you think I'd work for them?"

She straightened her posture up, out of attack mode.

"Why did your pudgy little partner there," she pointed at Jovanovic, "hit me with stunner, then."

"Look, I've been trying to find this guy since he gave me an anonymous tip on my case."

"What case? What are you investigating?" she demanded.

"The death of James Gild."

She fell silent, looking into the distance. *Of course*, she thought. *That explains his presence at the condominium.*

"Why was Jovanovic at Gild's domicile?" she asked.

Cage studied her. "When did Jovanovic go to Gild's place?"

"Not that long after you did, Cage," she said. "When I interrupted his break-in, he fired on me with a stunner."

"Stunners didn't seem much of a problem for you today."

"I've since taken precautions," she said, allowing herself a small, confident smile.

"So you were here because Jovanovic fired on you?" Cage asked.

"No," she said evenly. "I am on a contract. I did not anticipate violence until I found Jovanovic. Then it only seemed appropriate."

"A contract for who?" Cage asked.

"Privileged information, Mr. Cage," she said, studying him.

"You are the domestic aren't you? Jennifer Four? But how could you be?"

"Not anymore. And not for some time," she replied, watching him. "I'm Jonny."

"But why do you care? How can you care? Where did you learn how to fight? Androids aren't supposed to be able to learn much of anything."

She just watched him. Coolly.

"So … neither of us is any closer to what we wanted to know?"

"On the contrary, Mr. Cage," she replied, again presenting the small, confident smile. "I have found the men my client sought. Now, before I finish my contractual obligations, I wish to know why they intruded upon my client's domain."

"Because," grunted Jovanovic. He groggily pushed himself up onto an elbow. "The central server at Day-Windham had information on the spontaneous human combustion victim we wished to tip Mr. Cage about."

twenty-eight

Jonny Cache looked squarely into the face of a retreating Eliott Jovanovic.

"You uncovered information on a death like that of James Gild at Day-Windham?"

"Yes," said Jovanovic, nodding, then shaking his head, "No. Not the way you mean, I think. Someone who died like Gild died — by spontaneous human combustion," he asserted again, "whose case we hoped Cage could use information on."

"Did you find information on Gild, or Jaspin?" asked Cage.

"No, no," said Jovanovic, struggling to his feet, straightening his shirt again. "Which is to say, we didn't look for them."

Cage's brow furrowed in annoyance.

"Why not, Jovanovic?!"

Eliott Jovanovic shrank back.

"Well — ah — because we knew Quinn had a Day-Windham entry on her resume. So they'd have a file on her," he said haltingly, uncertainly. "You see?"

Cage rubbed his eyes with his left hand, holstering his gun with the right.

"OK," he said after a pause. "Can you get back into the Day-Windham server?"

"Oh. Sure," said Jovanovic.

"You'll be traced again, Jovanovic," said Jonny Cache. "How do you suppose I found you?"

Jovanovic straightened his shirt and fidgeted with his hands, looking down.

A dismissive expression found its way onto her face. *Where'd she learn that?* Cage wondered. *How?*

"These guys can't hit Day-Windham again, but I can," she said.

"And your contract?" asked Cage, eyeing the android.

"Killers of family members come before other considerations," she replied. "The contract is on hold. For now."

Family? Cage thought. *An Android who thinks of people as family?*

twenty-nine

"I think maybe we should pool our resources," Jonny said to Cage.

"Oh. Agreed," said Jovanovic.

She turned sharply to face him again.

"No, Jovanovic. Not *us* as in you and me. *Us* as in Cage and me. You're hopeless. Do you even know why you shot me at James Gild's domicile?"

"Er — because you startled me? As I performed an illegal act?" he asked.

She turned from him, satisfied that her case had been made. "You think people are burning to death because of some otherworldly phenomenon, Jovanovic. But I think there's a reason."

"You say puh-tay-toe," Jovanovic said, carefully pronouncing each syllable. "Call it what you want."

"You guys are gonna have to lay low," Cage said. "If we run into trouble — no offense, but you'd just slow us down."

"What kind of trouble can we run into if she's making a 'Net run?" asked a plaintive Jovanovic.

"This isn't a discussion," she said. "We're not asking your opinion here. Those are the terms. That's how it's going to work."

And Cage, supporting her decision, knew that inside, he wasn't so sure. How good an ally could the domestic be?

He'd watched her fight, take out four men before he'd managed to draw his weapon. But a domestic? They were less than sheep — at least that was the idea. They were automata with recreational interaction — and little else — programmed in.

He watched her, though, seething with her own emotions, her own anger. What was it he was seeing? The first intelligent alien life?

But he had weighed in with her, and now …

And now, he realized, he was on the verge of physical collapse. He left them, left the four beaten believers in sea monsters and UFOs, left the strangely alive and aware domestic, left it all behind and staggered out into the hall, pulling his Personal from its holster.

I'm investigating the death of a man with Sumner's Syndrome, and my allies in the case are his sex machine and four deluded UFO chasers, he thought, shaking his head. *What the hell am I doing here?!*

Jonny Cache stared in disbelief as Cage turned his back on them and wandered out of the *Unknown Frontiers* office and into the dingy hall, looking small and spent. *How was it, again, that men became dominant?* She wondered.

"Vhud happenet?" asked Korsikov groggily.

Cage sat down in the hall, holding his head, wondering how he'd gotten himself so deeply enmired in such a mess, and how he could get out, and whether he could afford to, and Jonny came padding up beside him.

"What's *your* problem, detective?" she asked.

"Where do I start?"

She looked him over.

"How'd you get here, anyway?"

"I drove."

She looked him over. "You need sleep, Cage. Badly."

"Yeah," he said gruffly. "But I'll bet I have the same problems when I wake up."

He climbed to his feet, dusting off his trench coat, and started toward the stairwell, while she stared, again, in disbelief.

The rains ran through Warner Square, bringing a ringing, splashing cacophony, miniature waterfalls spilling through breaches in the roof to the stairwell's dilapidated tile flooring. It cut courses through sand and sediment that had built up on the floor and stairs over the years.

Cage started down the stairs.

"Hold it!" Now she was yelling at him.

He stopped, turned.

Looked her way.

"We work together on this, Cage!"

"I'm going to bed."

"You can catch a nap here."

"No," he said flatly. "I can't. I've been running on twenty minutes' sleep and a boost sample for three days. Now all this ... this ..." He made a quick street-sign flurry, a combination of irritation and exhaustion. "I rest, or I start hallucinating. That's how it works."

She stared after him as he began to descend. He stopped.

"Look," he said wearily. "Please contact me tonight, OK?"

Then he continued down the stairs.

At ground level, he punched a sequence into his Personal and waited; while she watched, the Olds that had pursued her coasted in silently, unlit, halting when he punched in another command.

Then, with a gust from its thrusters, the Olds lofted quietly toward traffic altitude, its exterior lighting flickering on in the darkness.

thirty

Cage made his way down the rooftop-access stairwell and toward his apartment, shaking his boost sample around in his hand like he wanted to shoot craps with it. Still rubbing his eyes, he rounded the corner onto his floor.

Turning down the hall, out of the corner of a bleary, tired eye, he spotted a figure standing before his front door.

His gun immediately in his hand, the tiny target-lock L.E.D. flicking on, Cage demanded: "Hold it!"

The figure turned, smiling, and Cage felt a smile, a mix of relief and happiness flood his face.

"Murph?" he asked in disbelief. "Corbin Murphy?"

The man turned, outstretching his arms in an exaggerated gesture, his trench coat flaring a bit at the base, and said: "Who else, pal?"

"Thought a company man like you'd have smarts enough to stay away from me, Murphy. I'm not good company for an Expedite-backed cop to be seen with."

"It's ancient history, pal. Think a juggernaut like that even remembers?"

In *Gotham George's*, soaking in the familiar bouquet of cigar smoke and hydroponic tobacco 2942 and spilled imports, Cage laughed, clapping his old partner on the shoulder. "I gotta take care of something, Murphy," he said. "Order two fingers for me, OK?"

In the bathroom of *Gotham George's*, Cage pretended to straighten his hair until the woman in the first stall was finished.

As the door swung first open, then sprang back past closed, then open again, Cage pulled the boost sample out and loaded it into his reader again.

Murphy was waiting with twin tumblers of a familiar amber fluid.

As Cage approached the bar, his old partner handed him one, lifting the other for himself.

"To old partners," he said.

"To old friends," Cage corrected him, and they clinked the tumblers together.

Cage made an oddly curious face, still holding the liquor in his mouth, then up to the light to examine it. He eyed Murphy suspiciously.

"You never liked scotch with enough peat in it, Murph," he said.

Murphy shrugged. "Why you like that briny swill is beyond me, Cage," he said, laughing and clapping him on the shoulder.

Cage felt the sample beginning to lose influence. Not enough sleep, he knew, not enough basic nutrition, lots of stress. But here was his old partner; how long had it been?

"Seven years, Murphy," Cage said, smiling amiably at his old friend. "Man, I thought I'd never see anyone from back then again."

"Back then," said Murphy, sipping his scotch, "was a long time ago."

Cage nodded, smiling, but the memories hurt. "Old wounds, Murphy," he said. "Old wounds. We were good cops."

Murphy ran a hand back through a dark, curly mess of hair. "Not anymore, pal," he said.

"Besides," he continued, pausing for a sip, "*you* were good cops. I ran. Remember?"

Cage waved a hand dismissively. "You did what you had to," he said. "You saved my ass enough times; you didn't need to do it again."

Murphy raised both hands, waving two fingers on each at Donatelli Three.

"Coming right up," said a familiar, smooth, flat voice, from the bartender.

"Still," Murphy picked up where he left off, "You did it right. You wanted to know why that man was killed. A Climber? Didn't bother you." Murphy took a pull. "Macallan," he said, savoring the scotch. "Not so peaty, but too smoky for your palate," he said, smiling sadly. "I don't even remember the stiff's name anymore."

"Fuhlber," said Cage. "I couldn't forget it without surgery."

Cage shook his head over and over, long enough that he realized he was getting old-fashioned drunk on old-fashioned drink, and there was nothing his boost sample could do to hold it off.

"The company looked in, told you to tone it down," Murphy said.

"Didn't matter."

"It should've," Cage said.

"No," Murphy insisted. "You did it right, Cage."

Cage was still shaking his head.

"You did it right," Murphy said again, putting back his Macallan, holding it, lost in thought.

Cage was watching him, now, wavering a bit.

"OK, Murphy. But say I had to do it again. If I knew it would all be over, I'd lose my marriage and job and future …"

"Your job, *then* your marriage," said Murphy. "Remember that. This is your future. From then, anyway. No one said she had to give up on you." He was looking into the smoke-hazed depths of the mirror behind the bar, behinds its liquors now.

"I don't wanna talk about her."

"She wasn't forced to leave, Cage," Murphy ventured on. "She left. You weren't Climber material."

Cage looked away.

"C'mon, Cage, who d'you think you're talking to, here? You and Cin see each other as enemies in a war neither is proud of, neither wanted to talk about. You never even saw each other again, did you?"

Cage shook his head.

"I'm tellin' ya, pal: American GI and Vietnamese after their war," Murphy said. "Same thing with you two."

He took a drink.

Cage wasn't looking at him. Murphy was right: He wasn't Climber material. He wasn't smart enough to shut up and play the game when the time came.

Cage took a long drink of the Macallan, wishing for peat and smoke and penitence.

"What are you doing with yourself, Cage?"

The lights in the bar softened themselves into little spheres of light. Cage realized his focus was slipping.

He reached down to find his magically full tumbler and drank.

He told Murphy of how he fell back on detective work for hire when corporate police work didn't pan out. About his office, not far from here, and about how weird his night had been.

"Weird?" Murphy asked after a drink. "Whaddaya mean?"

"Strange partners, strange case, no evidence that makes any sense," Cage said.

"Strange partners, huh Cage?" Murphy prodded him. "Who's stranger than me, huh?" His arms were exaggeratedly extended in question, now, Cage noticed slowly.

"'Member me talkin' that PCP-samplin' rough boy off the ledge?" Murphy demanded, grinning maniacally.

Cage remembered.

An almost freakishly stormy night had risen late in October, late enough that some were already in costume, already celebrating All Hallow's Eve.

The storms inland had been the dwarf spawns of a hurricane that had rolled up the East Coast, slowly losing steam as it headed northward, becoming a mere tropical storm once it struck Old New York.

In the middle of all of it, sooty rain, 150 kph winds tearing through the city, flinging wet newspapers and trash everywhere, the call had gone out.

An intoxicated perp had hefted a parked Chang Gaijin, unassisted, and thrown it, flaming, to the street below.

It was a cop's nightmare, back then: Violent criminal, superhumanly strong, had probably booted up a PCP sample.

Cage and Murphy hadn't been far away, they'd told dispatch, and they'd wound up being first on the scene.

The perp they had been after had been naked on a ledge, howling through the storm about the mother of all battles, how Thor was gonna show Gaia his hammer Mjolnir this time, when they had cruised in for as gentle a rooftop landing as they could manage, lights and sirens off, the propellers of the engine set for stealth.

Cage had begun to conference their location in to dispatch, and he and Murphy had climbed from the car and out into the rain.

As Cage had sized up the situation for corporate, squad cars had begun to arrive. Murphy had walked out, started to approach the perp. Cage had watched, following at a careful distance, trying not to alarm the perp.

Then the unlit, unmarked, black squad cars had begun to arrive – the company's version of a S.W.A.T. team.

Murphy had stepped up his pace, started talking to the naked perp.

"Murphy," Cage said, trying to yell and whisper at the same time. "Murph, what the hell's wrong with you?!"

But Murphy was approaching the man, and Cage saw why now: The man was naked, sure, but he was worried. He saw the squad cars and S.W.A.T. carriers, and he was worried now.

He thought he'd been putting on his own private show. For himself. He didn't know why the cops had been called.

He'd been ecstatic, Cage realized, not on the verge of jumping. He had been one of the New Pagans; probably nothing more dangerous in his reader than an ecstasy sample.

But the S.W.A.T. team was closing.

Cage had lunged back into his squad car, began trying to let corporate central know what he'd seen. But across the company band, he heard the launch sequence from the local 'Net news node.

Company-owned 'Net news node.

"Murphy!" he'd yelled, but the winds wouldn't carry it.

Murphy was talking to the perp now, though, and wouldn't have heard anything Cage had to say, anyway.

Gesturing and waving his hands every way he could think of to show the perp he was OK, on a level with him, he didn't seem to be making much headway. But he had managed to get himself close enough to breach company radius-of-fire protocols, so the S.W.A.T. team watched, waiting, adding precision to their aim.

And Cage could do nothing but watch.

As the naked man edged desperately away.

Toward a shrinking edge.

But he was watching Murphy, watching while Murphy talked, every gesture friendly, understanding, brotherly. Then, as the camera crews arrived, the winds dropped long enough for Cage to hear Murphy talking Gaian theory with the naked man.

And while Cage watched, while the news crew's cameras digitized and streamed it all, while he knew that the S.W.A.T. troops were itching for a kill for the public, Murphy suddenly stood straight, nodded with certainty to Cage, and stripped.

Then he walked with equal certainty out onto the ledge with the naked man to enjoy the storm.

For a while, anyway.

After a few minutes, with the trust of the naked New Pagan well-won, the two walked back to Cage's and Murphy's car, Murphy with his arm draped protectively around the man.

The P.R. division hated missing the opportunity for a live-streamed bad-guy kill, but with a lack of communication, the news was following Murphy, naming him the hero, and the company had little choice but to think up some sort of award for bravery and award it to him.

"They never bothered you, Murph," Cage said, feeling vertigo as he looked toward the floor.

"Dumb luck, pal," Murphy said solemnly.

Cage watched as his old partner sipped Macallan. Murphy, he knew, had gone against the company and come out squeaky clean.

"No, Murph," he said. "You did it right."

They sat silently for awhile as the deep gray outside faded toward black.

"Jesus, Murph, what happened?"

Murphy waved both hands at the bartender.

"Whaddaya mean, Cage?"

"I mean, you did it right, Murph. You played 'em and walked out without a scratch," said Cage. "Naked as a babe out in that … that shit, too."

"Yeah, yeah, Cage," Murphy was shaking his head. "Just dumb luck. It wasn't important to 'em, Cage. That's all."

"Yeah," said Cage. "Yeah."

"I'm tellin' you, Cage: You didn't back off. *That's* heroic, not getting naked on a roof."

"My 'heroic' got me working with nerds and sex toys, Murphy," Cage said sullenly.

Murphy raised his eyebrows. "Excuse me?"

"Sex toys," said Cage, his head swimming. "And diz … dismal nerds."

"Tell me about it," he said.

"Cage," said Murphy, shaking him on the rooftop. "C'mon Cage, tell your car how to take you home."

Cage thought: *The car? When did I drop?*

"Kh … hh … home, James," he managed.

"Good old Murph," he said, as the car lifted off and drove him toward home.

In the distance, in the neo-sleep realm Cage seemed trapped in, unable to collapse completely while the boost sample was still running, he dreamt.

In his dream, good old Murph tugged his Personal free as he loaded Cage into the Olds, and placed a conference.

In his dream, as Cage's Olds headed upward, Murph said: "Sir? He's not onto you yet, but he's close. I don't think it'll take him long."

thirty-one

Jonny Cache turned and walked back toward the unit occupied by *Unknown Frontiers.*

Pushing the door aside, she located Jovanovic and began advancing. As the worried Frontiersman backed slowly away, one advancing step from her, one retreating step from him, she asked icily: "So. Jovanovic. Why did you guys make the big lizard attack me?"

Jovanovic's fingers busied themselves with his tie.

"Oh," he said.

She advanced. He retreated.

"Oh. Well," he said, fumbling with the tie. "Because you might find out."

"Find out?"

"Oh yes."

"Jo. Van. Oh. Vitch," she said, stressing each syllable.

He looked uncomfortably toward her, raised his eyebrows in query.

"Find out what?"

"Oh," he said, clutching at the tails of his shirt, straightening it uncomfortably. "That I was the one who shot you."

She could no longer tolerate this silly troupe of clowns. For all her analyses, she realized, she had yoked a larger, more paranoiac conspiracy about the necks of *Unknown Frontiers* than they were capable of.

She left. She made her way out of Warner Square and headed toward home. She'd solved pieces, but not the puzzle, she knew.

She wandered into the streets of Old Gotham Quarter, working to put the pieces together. She had her client's trespassers, but no idea how to respond to their motivations.

They were hopelessly misguided, searching the world's devastated forests for Sasquatch and polluted waterways for extinct sea dinosaurs.

So she could argue that they were harmless.

131

She was contractually bound to demolish their technology, destroy their equipment, leave them powerless even to conduct their odd pursuits. But she knew that in their own way they were trying to help Cage learn how James had died.

No, she knew. She couldn't. The lost fee would be no great disappointment to her, but she had a reputation. And a customer who'd begin wondering soon enough when she did not report back with results.

Considering the problem, she lost track of time, walked around Old New York for hours.

She'd always wondered about the old Sinatra song about the city she called home: Was it some sort of booze-addled prediction, his dubbing the city "Old New York," decades before New York$_2$ was launched? Had he a had problem with his first name, like Cage did? Did he insist that friends call him only "Sinatra"?

As she arrived, she knew the Angeliques would be going through the motions of their early-afternoon morning, beginning to prepare for a night at N*ine Circles.*

She announced herself to their security system, which clicked and whirred for a moment before allowing her entry. She greeted Yin- and Yang-Angelique, blowing each a kiss good-morning.

"That too-slim man came calling for you at the club, Jonny," said Yang-Angelique, her white highlights peering up from a steaming cup. "He seemed anxious."

"He seemed anxious the first time," she replied.

"More so this time," purred Yang-Angelique. "What goes on, Jonny?"

"With him? I don't know what cards he has, but he's holding something," said Jonny.

"Why do you say that?"

"It's just a feeling."

"Jonny," said Yin-Angelique, her face edged in sharp, dark highlights, peering out from under a towel turbined about her wet hair, "Hasn't your Netrun for this man taken longer than for the usual customer?"

Jonny turned to face her friend.

"I've hit a snag, Yin-Angelique," Jonny replied.

"Snag?" the binaries asked.

"Snag," confirmed Jonny with a short nod. "As in: Family matter."

The Angeliques arched their eyebrows, their interest piqued.

"The people the too-slim man is looking for may be of some help in learning who killed James," she said.

"James … " Yin-Angelique purred quietly, pouring herself a mug of coffee.

"James … " said Yang-Angelique quietly. "We had hoped … well … "

She looked up, meeting Jonny's gaze, not speaking.

"We've had trouble understanding your attachment," finished Yin-Angelique.

Jonny looked from one binary to the other.

"I've never had any other," she paused, weighing her thoughts. "Family. Not before you two. He raised me. He's what I remember from when he awakened me."

The Angeliques regarded their coffee, communicating within.

"Of course he was," said Yang-Angelique, but the smile she attempted to force was not convincing.

Jonny made her way to the black, cavernous converted ballroom she had made her home, the ghostly white glow of the great recovered subway clock lighting the far end of the place, the *steady click-click, click-click* of her footsteps echoing off polished floors and sparsely adorned walls, the colliding sound chattering down to a faint matchstick chorus against the tall, cylindrical pillars lining the main floor.

James.

All she could think about, now that he was gone, was how fully, how wholly she missed him.

She strode to stand before her dresser, passing her hand before her photo, her purloined memory of the two of them together, activating it.

"I love you, Jennifer," came the tiny, tinny audio signal. In the past, in the photo, she turned her head, her long, dark hair spilling across her shoulder.

The playback stopped.

"I love you, too," said Jonny Cache.

Against economics, against her break with her past, and against her usual business practices, she decided that this detective, Cage, had the best chance of being able to help her learn how her estranged lover-owner-turned-father-figure had died.

She brought herself online, onto StellarNet, and sought out Cage's office — its physical address.

Cage awoke to the cold patter of November rain on the sill in his bedroom, rain that made a low, deep background hiss against the apartment building. A background hiss that was so even, so regular that he no longer really heard it, was only vaguely aware of its presence. A background hiss that mingled with his automatic coffeemaker pushing hot water through the grounds.

Looking down, Cage saw that he'd fallen asleep in yesterday's clothes.

He peeled off the soiled garments, tossed them into his overflowing hamper, and ordered his desktop to boot up.

Distantly, he remembered Murphy, a twinge in his stomach reminding him of far too much scotch after far, far too long without rest.

Good old Murph.

He showered, shaved, wrapped a towel about his waist, and logged onto the 'Net to check his mail.

Walking first down from the roof, then down the hall toward his office, Cage was relieved to find the lights on at his agency.

Entering the office, Cage expected to see Effie.

Instead, on her desk, was a note informing him that she'd be late.

Drawing his gun, Cage stepped cautiously back toward his office.

In the circle of light cast by his overhead lamp, black-boot-clad feet on his desk, Cage found the domestic.

"Cage," she greeted him.

"Nearly got yourself shot," he replied. "I'd appreciate it if as a courtesy you'd just wait outside, not break into my office and make

134

yourself at home."

She leaned into the soft circle of light from his lamp, looking up at him as he holstered the gun.

"You did tell me to contact you tonight," she said. She snapped her fingers and made an expression of mock-surprise.

"Tonight's the night," she said, looking intently his way.

He watched her suspiciously.

Sex toy, he thought.

"I don't get it, Jonny," he said. "I don't get it at all. I mean, I watched you fight. But I saw you in Gild's photo, too. Whatever you are now, you weren't then."

"No," she said.

"Explain it to me," Cage said.

"Explain what, Cage? Why you didn't find me hot and ready to map your sex habits and fuck you when you checked out the condo?"

Cage eyed her evenly.

"Yeah. For starters," he said. "Why aren't you Jennifer Four?"

"You know that I'm not."

"Yeah. I do," he said. "But I'm having trouble with Jennifer Four: the product, and Jennifer Four: what Jonny used to be."

"Fortunately, Cage, you don't really need to know," she said. "It's enough that I'm not what you thought I was."

"Enough for who?"

"Enough for you, Cage," she said, pressing on. "You don't need to know the why, you just need to know the fact that that's the way things are."

He threw up his hands, turning from her and starting toward the front office.

Hanging up his trenchcoat, Cage made his way to the coffee press and activated it.

"I don't know how you work, Jennifer … "

"Jonny," she corrected.

" … Jonny. I don't understand you. Never could figure out how AIs think about things, if you can call what your processors do thinking. You busted up the *Unknown Frontiers* guys. You could've busted me up. I couldn't've stopped you."

She watched. He poured himself a cuppa, offering her one, then pretending surprise when she refused. He was goading her, and

135

she didn't appreciate it.

"I seek files for my clients …"

"Files?"

"Yes."

"What kind of files?"

"Whatever my clients are after."

"What, illegal stuff?"

"Generally. Personal files. Security breaches. Incriminating information. That sort of thing. Generally."

"How do they know they can trust you?"

"When I've given my clients the files they sought, I assure their privacy," she said.

"How's that? They know you have their prize files."

"I burn them."

"'Burn'?"

"A multiple-pass memory overwrite and erase program. It's called *burning* a file. It leaves me without access to the clients' data — not even with a resurrection app. I assure their privacy."

Cage watched her, wondering. There was so much about her that was processor-driven. Had she ever really been the vacant-eyed domestic from the photo in Gild's apartment?

"You know the reputation, right?" he said.

She just watched him.

"Jennifer Four. Virtual Veronique. The old Digital Daphne model," he said, still not looking her way. "Products. Sex toys, Jonny. But somehow, you're telling me, you're showing me, there's something else going on in there," he said, tapping his forehead.

She tilted her head the slightest bit.

"What I'd like to know is: Why should I trust you with my life?" he said.

"Because you aren't dead," she said.

He watched her, sipping from his cup.

"Neither," he said, "are those *Unknown Frontiers* gents."

"Luck," she said, "and purpose."

"Purpose?"

"I'm also interested in James' death," she said, leaning forward. "In who killed him."

"In who killed him?" he asked. "What makes you think he was

136

killed?"

"The way he was killed, Cage," she said. "The fact that you're investigating his death."

"Then," said Cage, "I take it you don't buy the spontaneous human combustion argument?"

Cage eyed her, wondering. She gave no response.

"Jonny," Cage started, scratching his scalp through short, clipped hair, "why do you care?"

Her expression frosted over.

"*What?*"

"I mean, you're a domestic — " he caught a glare from her. " — *were* a domestic. Right?"

She gave him no response, so he continued.

"I mean, you were a sex slave, weren't you? Why do you care about this guy?"

"There was more to it than that," she said.

"Then why weren't you still with him?"

"That," she said taking on a tone of warning, "is no concern of yours, Cage."

He raised his hands before him, signaling her to be calm.

"OK, Jonny, OK. It's not a matter of *why* you care, it's a matter of *how*. And I don't know."

She looked suddenly away from him, as though a conference prompt had chimed, but Cage hadn't heard anything.

"Just a second, Cage," she said. "I have a call."

While he waited, the domestic-turned-Netrunner sat quietly, intent.

Cage sipped his cuppa joe.

After a few moments, abruptly, she looked up.

"Well?" Cage asked. "You look concerned."

"That was my client, Cage," she said. "The one who wants me to knock *Unknown Frontiers* on their asses and offline."

Cage watched her, sipping his java.

"What does your client want?"

"He wants a meeting, Cage. He wants to know what's taking so long."

thirty-two

Nightfall came as little more than a change in the hour, a later number on dashboard and wrist chronometers, another foggy, black, caustic rain pelting the streets of Old New York.

Cage stood at the huge, old bay window in his office, looking out into the night, first streetward, then to the barely visible cars in the traffic altitude above, their lights casting an eerie beauty through the smog layer.

"Whaddaya do, Jonny?" Cage asked. When he asked again — "Whaddaya do?" — shaking his head and looking floorward, she realized he was asking rhetorically, seeing her side, her difficulty.

He heard her stand, heard the *click-click, click-click* of her heel-to-toe stride and hard black soles on the polished hardwood of his office floor. She rested a hand on his shoulder, startling him; she'd crossed into personal space. And Cage found himself wondering, once again, how it was that she wasn't Jennifer Four.

She looked up into the Christmas-light whiz of traffic, backlighting the haze, beams of light passing overhead like ships passing a lighthouse in a pea-soup fog in the night.

"What do *we* do, Cage?" she corrected him. "Like ships in the night, huh?"

"Or strangers, Jonny," he said. "Or strangers in the night."

Cage turned his head to look at her; even in this light, even with his uncertainty as to how to define her, she was beautiful. And she was leaning toward him. And she was kissing him.

He turned toward her, pulling her closer, reaching out to touch her face, touch skin so real, feeling his uncertainty slip away, as if she were answering his unspoken question about what it was, exactly, that she had become.

Everything about her told him what he did not expect: That she was real, not just some thing that pretended to be real; that it was possible to want her; that it was possible, even, to need her. And that it was possible for her to want, maybe even need him.

Cage basked in her beauty, in her passion, her vigor, her

humanity. Together, they flowed with the hunger with which he pushed into her, and with which she responded, drew him in.

And their sex was not perfect, Cage slowly realized — it lacked the guaranteed one-sided perfection advertised for sex with a domestic. They were not simultaneous. But, passionately, they worked together to catch up with one another, to fulfill one another.

He realized how much they were interacting, communicating physically and verbally. Whatever she was, she was not simply satisfying him; she was guiding him, directing him in pleasing her as much as he was guiding her.

In the taste of her, in the scent of her, in her peaks and in her shortcomings, he knew.

Whether she'd outgrown the programming of Jennifer Four or whether she had shut down the first personality completely, he was certain: Jonny Cache was not Jennifer Four. Not at all.

She had shared with him more intimately and honestly, even, than had Janice Gild.

"Looks like I meet with my client, Cage," she said as they sat together, lights from passing traffic playing across her breasts, in Cage's dark back office.

"And me?"

"And you show up at the club ten minutes behind me," she said, handing him a small, curved device of molded plastic.

"Earclip," she said. "Listen in. But first, tell me what you know."

"OK, Jonny," he said. "Here's how I think it went down at Gild's place that night."

thirty-three

"It was raining that night, like it always is, so there was a background of white noise in the domicile. Judging from his photo collection and the general isolation, the loneliness in his life, I'm guessing that he was missing you. I don't know exactly what he was wearing, but I do know he wasn't ready to call it a night; he was wearing shoes and slacks when he died. And he kept it cool in the place, so he was probably wearing a sweater or something.

"He made his way to his small, immaculately kept and generously stocked bar in search of a drink to ward off the cold. He decided on a brandy."

"He paid too much for that bar," said Jonny, smiling. She was looking out the window of Cage's office, into the night. "An estate auction. Four floors down. Anyway ... "

Cage paused to make certain she was finished.

"Anyway," he said, "the cops contaminated the scene with fingerprints, but everything I found suggests he was there alone that night. A stain — water ring from his glass near the photos — suggests that he paused before the mirror, the one on the stand. I think he was being nostalgic that night, playing back old photos, stuff like that.

"He'd seen a specialist — a psychiatrist — about his difficulties coping with women. But as his specialist was a woman, he might have had trouble opening up to her.

"So. He spent his nights alone. He took his filled brandy snifter into the bedroom and placed it on the nightstand. Maybe he had a drink or two from it. Maybe not. Looks like he was going to read, but either hadn't yet or had finished for the time being: A book on his nightstand had a page near the beginning dog-eared.

"But then, maybe he started to sweat, maybe he felt that weird itch you do in your pores when you suddenly realize that the room you're in is uncomfortably hot. I don't know.

"Then," Cage paused. "Boom."

"'Boom'?" asked Jonny.

140

"Yeah. 'Boom.' Whatever hit him hit him there and then. He probably only knew for a few seconds that he was going to die. It was over pretty fast; didn't scorch the ceiling overhead, didn't ignite the room around him, didn't even set off the fire alarm.

"That's all I've got."

Quietly, still looking into the night, Jonny nodded.

thirty-four

A small group of NewSchool Grrls stood in a pack at the far end of the long, dark bar, chatting with Yang-Angelique as Jonny strode in from the weather, taking in *Nine Circles* with quick sweep. The Grrls' filter masks were set uniformly before them on the bar, parked in a way that reminded her of an image she'd seen digitized in an online museum: an old snapshot of a row of antique motorcycles.

She made her way through the thick early-evening crowd, catching a glimpse of throngs in VR contact lenses (the ones that silver the eyes over with that Etch-a-Sketch effect) and unisuits (the flexicircuit kind that look like black, lacy body stockings), the band Torture-Technique lashing at the crowd in the pit with virtual medieval armaments.

To Jonny, the group — three males with instruments, two women with microphones, all in NoGo bondage gear and black, vinyl masks with zipper-closable eyes, nose and mouth — did little more than swing steely, black batons toward the crowd.

Tuning to the Circles' VR frequency, Jonny could see band members' whips, the two lead singers swinging more elaborate cat-o'-nine-tales analogues that splashed day-glow laser sparks on contact with audience members, drawing a delighted response from them.

Jonny paused to smile at the group at the end of the bar, giving Yang-Angelique a quick wave as she made her way to her usual front-bar business booth.

She leaned toward the lamp and said, "Glenlivet."

Yang-Angelique appeared a moment later at the edge of the booth's sound-dampening field and leaned in.

"Jonny," she said, her smile curling her lips at the sides.

"Hello, Yang-Angelique," she said.

"You're early."

"Business."

"Oh?"

Jonny concentrated for a moment, then turned to the bartender.

"Check your Netmail; you've got my key," said Jonny. Her mail, Yang-Angelique now knew, would be encrypted.

Still smiling, the binary nodded and took her leave of Jonny, disappearing into the depths behind the bar.

While Jonny waited, Cage made his way in from the rains, past Harshburger, and toward the bar, but pointedly not toward the end where the NewSchool Grrls stood.

He took a seat at the bar, fumbling with the little earclip, unable to fit it on. He leaned forward, speaking into the lamp: "Laphroaig."

The Nouveau Gothic he'd seen tending bar before made her way down the long, marble bar, the white, willow-spikes of her hair swaying as she sashayed toward him, her hips defining her ankle-length NoGo skirt, her right leg flashing out through a high slit in the shiny white fabric. Weren't there two of her?

"Dick," she said confidently, her bottle touching the top of his tumbler with a sharp *clank*, decanting amber fluid into a glass before him.

Cage felt the little earclip snap into two pieces, rolled the two fragments into his hand and closed it. He stared at her, speechless, incredulous.

And, after a brief pause, "*Private* dick," she said. "It seems Jonny's adopted you."

"Yeah," Cage said, a little surprised. "Seems she has. Thanks for the scotch."

Yang-Angelique smiled wryly, scooting the tumbler across the bar toward the detective.

"Enjoy," she said with a mischievous flip of her eyebrows.

"Right," said Cage. "Right. You too."

As he sipped the smooth liquor, wondering what, exactly, he'd gotten himself into, someone clapped his shoulder. Hard.

"Cage!" yelled Murphy. "Man, back for more so soon?"

"Not that diet scotch you drink, Murph," Cage said, a smile growing on his face, then dissipating. "What are you doing here?"

"Buying an old friend a drink," he said, making a streetsign gesture to Yang-Angelique. She gave a quick, sharp nod under the white, weeping-willow hair.

The too-slim man appeared at the edge of Jonny's booth, ghosted by a towering, spare-Y-cell-looking homunculus: Hired muscle.

Jonny felt right at home.

But hired muscle looked a little too bulky — like he'd had an I.V. of gamma-boosted synthetic steroids to help with his bodybuilding career.

Winston Baldisari stood in the shadow cast by the hired muscle, a long, dark, non-react-coated trenchoat dripping into a pool at his feet.

He said something, but from within the booth's dampening field, it was inaudible.

Jonny tapped her ear, then shook her head "No," waving him into the booth.

In what looked to be the most uneasy manner, Baldisari bent, contorted, and squeezed himself into the booth, opposite her.

Uncomfortable, Jonny thought. Just like our first meeting.

Hired muscle didn't try to fit into the booth, but on closer inspection, now, she could see why he'd seemed overly bulky. He was a Morlock. He was massive; her modeling algorithm estimated his weight at four hundred and fifty seven pounds, but that was based on averages for people whose bones hadn't undergone the mass-gain mutations programmed into the bones of Morlocks to make them sturdier.

She'd never seen one up close, and didn't know how strong he might be.

The Morlock was also clad in a dark, non-react-coated trenchcoat, from which sludgy rain also pooled.

He wore a black fedora and wide, preposterous sunglasses, a single, molded piece of black, apparently opaque apparently metal.

"No use having him step in, Ms. Cache," said Baldisari, tapping his own ear, reminding her of the Morlocks' ear-protecting growths.

The Morlock stood stonily.

Jonny didn't take an eye off the too-slim Baldisari. She stopped blinking, locked eyes with her customer.

"What's this all about, Mr. Baldisari?" she asked. "I'm a busy woman."

"Yes, yes," he replied, raising both hands before him so that both palms pointed toward her, about chest height. "It's just that we expected expediency. You have taken *days* longer than expected."

144

Jonny watched the two. The Morlock didn't move. At all. His breath was wet and heavy, like a big hound who's just been out for a run. Baldisari was straightening his tie nervously, meticulously.

"I have other clients, Mr. Baldisari. You'll have your information. That was our agreement."

"Oh dear," said Baldisari, suddenly less uncomfortable. "No."

"No, Mr. Baldisari?"

"No, Ms. Cache. Our arrangement was that you track our intruders, find and burn our data, and disable their attack software and hardware," he said.

Jonny gazed evenly at him.

"In process," she said.

"Ah," he said. "But we have *other* information, Ms. Cache. Information which suggests that you have identified and, indeed had contact with them."

Her expression remained: an unshifting, unblinking stare.

Baldisari's eyes began to water sympathetically. He drew a handkerchief from his breast coat pocket and dabbed at them, struggling to retain some semblance of an imposing presence.

"Think of the damage to us, Ms. Cache, should it happen that you are forbearing completion of your contract with us for a better offer from our attackers."

Jonny straightened a bit.

"Your contract is still being executed, Mr. Baldisari," she said. "My methods are my own."

He cleared his throat.

"Indeed … "

The Morlock looked as though he'd been sculpted there. In stone.

" … your methods are unorthodox," said Baldisari.

Jonny stared with inhuman endurance, her face expressing nothing.

"And they involve a physical visit, as well. I understand."

Jonny Cache turned, judging the Morlock's center of gravity.

"So where is she?" Murphy asked.

"She?" Cage replied. *Oh*, he thought. *Oh yeah.*

"Your new partner," said Murphy, smiling. "Unless you're afraid of Sumner's, buddy — huh?"

Cage looked away from his old partner.

I told him everything, Cage thought. *At least it was Murphy.*

While they talked, Cage noticed an overly slim man who matched the description Jonny had given him entering *Nine Circles*, followed by a massive bodyguard.

"Listen, Murphy," said Cage, putting down his tumbler and pushing Murphy's drink gently to the bar. "There may be trouble."

Murphy followed Cage's gaze.

"She's over there, huh?"

"Afraid so, Murph."

Murphy paused, then asked: "What kind of trouble?"

"I don't know. But I have a feeling I should watch."

Murphy nodded, lifting his tumbler, then dropping it a few moments later as a slim, black-clad, female figure hit the hired muscle standing before one of the booths, folding him with a low, upward lunge that sent him flying across the bar and into the opposite wall.

Hired muscle fell slowly forward out of a new crater that began three feet up.

Cage cursed at having had to leave his gun secured in the car to gain entry into the club. "C'mon!" yelled Cage, sprinting down the bar as the big man lumbered to his feet. Cage threw his best right cross into the giant's midsection, but hired muscle only folded slightly.

Murphy, howling and swinging a chair, leapt off the top of the bar toward the huge bodyguard, but was caught by the neck, mid-air. Murphy brought the chair down hard on the head of the bodyguard, demolishing the fedora and revealing built-up cheekbones and husked-over ears.

"DU FLIEGT, BUT NOW DU HÄNGT, SI?!" bellowed hired muscle.

Jonny whipped an index finger forward into the forehead of Baldisari, who collapsed immediately.

Cage was faring badly with the Morlock, and a man she didn't recognize was suspended by his neck, trying for his life to kick free.

While she watched, Cage, after a fruitless attack on the Morlock, was also caught by the neck and lifted off the floor. The enforcers of *Nine Circles'* policy against violence in the house arrived, but

146

were quickly waved off by Yang-Angelique, who paused to concentrate, then retreated back down the bar.

Jonny leveled a Muay Thai kick to the knee of the Morlock, her shin slamming into the fragile joint, an action that sent it bellowing, crumpling to the ground and dropping the two former cops. Cage and Murphy covered their ears in pain as the Morlock cried out, his vocal cords, genetically readjusted for communications alongside launching craft outside a launchport, now capable of generating an incredible, high-decibel bellow.

Murphy gagged, propped on all fours on the floor, as Cage pulled himself up, cursing his inability to stop the mutant.

"Jonny!" came the voice of a woman somewhere behind him.

Appearing suddenly behind the bar, Yin-Angelique leveled a doctored multiphase automatic at the Morlock and fired a blinding white-noise high-energy round into the giant. The Morlock came crashing down into a table, sending a wave of splintered wood and glass across the floor.

"Wha-" gagged Murphy, "What the hell was that?"

"Morlock," said Cage.

"No," Murphy coughed. "Her gun!"

The Morlock was quickly surrounded and dragged back down a dark corridor, through a door Cage was certain hadn't been there before in the wall leading toward the men's room.

Looking around, Cage could not find either Yin-Angelique or the too-slim Baldisari.

"Jonny?" Cage asked, coughing a bit.

"No problem," she said. "Introduce me to your friend later; we're getting the hell out of here."

"Jonny — where the hell's Baldisari?" Cage asked.

Jonny grabbed the two ex-cops by an arm and hefted them along the same hallway Cage had seen Nine Circles staffers drag the Morlock down. No sign of the door they'd taken him through.

Looking back, Cage could see that the staff members who maintained order at the club had already erased all signs of the conflict; they did not like to attract official attention, and had quietly, quickly, and efficiently blotted out the disturbance.

Jonny led them through a wall that ended the hallway, and Cage's best guess was that it was a holoprojection meant to discourage patrons from going further. The hall twisted, running much, much deeper into the building than he had guessed; Jonny dragged the two men up a short flight of stairs and into an old, disused stairwell dank with stale, still air.

Releasing the two, she streetsigned for them to follow her up the stairs, up flight after flight until, Murphy and Cage winded, Cage realized that they must be making for the roof.

The door at the top of the stairs, its paint flaked and fading, read: "Roof Access. Authorized/Emergency only."

As the three rounded the last landing before the door, something thumped against it from the outside bringing them to a cautious, quiet halt, Murphy and Cage panting a bit.

With a second thump, the door swung open and Yin-Angelique hurried through, forcing the door closed and slamming its old, iron lock-bar down, her black, spiky willow hair collapsed around her head and shoulders.

"Cops!" She streetsigned at them. "Follow!"

"Cops?! How?!" asked Cage in a loud whisper. Jonny signed "QUIET!"

She turned gracefully over the railing and dropped to the flight below them, starting back down.

They followed, Jonny lithely, the two ex-cops more wearily.

They slowed after a few flights, Yin-Angelique looking cautiously through the hazy window at the base of a flight of stairs.

Outside, like a silent, black shark, his Olds drifted over to the window in stealth mode, all lights down, its propulsion on silent running.

Yin-Angelique forced open the ancient window, the roar of the rains filling the stairwell. As the passenger-side door opened, Cage saw Yang-Angelique climbing dexterously from behind the steering wheel, over the passenger seat, and, with a graceful, catlike leap, into the building beside them.

"Go! Go!" she said over the white noise of the black rain. Cage clambered in, followed easily by Jonny and uncertainly by Murphy.

Cage geared up the car and took it silently away from the building and out into the night.

"Cops?!" Cage said again, incredulous. "How'd they get here

so fast? How'd they even know — I'm sure no one inside the club told them."

"Baldisari," said Jonny. "Baldisari disappeared. Maybe he made the call."

"But so fast? It's like they knew we were there," Cage said. "Exactly like it."

Murphy groaned, sitting back in the rear of Cage's Olds, trying to massage out the pain in his throat without gagging himself.

"I think you should hear this, Cage," said Jonny, reaching out to tap the controls to the car's radio.

On the company police frequency, a squelching garble screeched into the car's cockpit.

"Scrambled," Cage said, looking at his watch. "See the program buttons on the screen? Hit *zero-four*," he told Jonny."

The transmissions cleared up a bit; Cage's encryption crack was good enough for the three to make out what was being said on the corporate police band. It cleaned up the signal enough for them to hear that the police knew that he was involved.

And if the police knew, Expedite knew.

Expedite.

Again.

His palms began to sweat. He'd been like a mosquito to them before. He didn't know how the company handled people who'd offended them twice; Cage had never met any.

And if Expedite had put two and two together, figured out that he was the same Frank Cage who'd earned their displeasure before, they'd find him eventually. Track down the physical address of his office.

Go there.

"Oh God," he whispered. "*Effie*."

thirty-five

Effie could hear someone hit the stairwell door hard enough for it to slam open, the metallic clang echoing against the unadorned walls, hear someone running down the hall leading to the agency for nearly twenty seconds before they appeared, out of breath, at the door.

Janice Gild was thoroughly disheveled: Errant strands of blond hair flew free from what looked to be an elaborately crafted hair knot; her red dress — one different from the first day she'd stepped into the office, Effie noticed, but the same shade of rose red — loosened by an all-out sprint; her eye make-up running.

"Effie! Is Cage having cop problems?!" she asked, distressed.

"What's the rumpus, Ms. Gild?" asked Effie.

"The rumpus," said Gild, panting, "is that," pant, "you've got," pant, pant, "about a dozen squad cars landing," pant, "unlit on your roof! They came in just after I did!"

Pant, pant.

Effie jumped up, ran into Cage's unlit office and looked up.

She could see the eerie, skygoing lighting of the cars, and between herself and the traffic altitude, the lights were disappearing behind something, obscured by black somethings hovering up above the building.

She punched a combination into Cage's filing cabinet, tugged at a door that just wouldn't open, kicked the side of the cabinet and pulled again, this time freeing the top drawer.

She wrested Cage's back-up weapon — his older gun — from under a pile of tardy tax forms and streams of crinkled thermal fax paper, fished around in the paperwork until she found the loaded clip, slotted it into the gun, and slammed the drawer shut, spinning the combination as she left the back office.

Effie paused in the front office to grab a dusty, disused, red cardigan from the coat tree. She jogged back into Cage's back office and draped the sweater over his chair, making certain that the shade was open.

150

Gild looked like a drowned rat done up for the ball.

"Ms. Gild," said Effie, waving her over.

No response.

"Damnit Janice, C'mon!" Effie ordered. "I don't know just what Cage's gotten himself into, but we can't be here when the cops show. Got it?"

Janice Gild shook her head as though coming out of a trance.

"Ms. Gild: Got it?" she asked again.

Janice Gild nodded, and Effie clutched her arms, leading her out into the hall, down four doors to the disused office of a travel agency. She produced a matte black cardkey the likes of which Gild had never seen, and slid it into the lock. After a moment, the lock's little access lights flickered from red to green.

Hearing footfalls in the stairwell, Effie opened the door, dragged Janice Gild into the office, and closed the door behind her as quietly as she could.

Effie hauled the stunned Gild through the old office, brushing through cobwebs and past ancient, dusty, discarded furniture and took her to a door at the back of the office.

"What's this?" asked Gild.

Effie kicked the door, to no effect, planted herself, and kicked again. And again.

"Fire escape access," she replied, between kicks.

On the fourth kick the door shuddered open, and the two peered out into the dense fog and rain.

"C'mon," she told Gild.

The two slipped and cursed their way down the ancient, rusted fire escape, supports and bolts creaking all the way. Effie cursed as her hands scraped raw against the corroded rail. The two dropped the last dozen feet onto a rain-slick dumpster, then to the ground.

Effie pulled a tube from her purse and fumbled over it with her thumb, eventually activating the telescoping mechanism of her umbrella.

She dragged the still-punchy-seeming Gild with her to a sidestreet pay phone, where she dialed a series of numbers; Gild lost count at forty-three.

"OK, Ms. Gild, let's go," said Effie, hanging up the phone.

"Go where?"

"We gotta lay low, Ms. Gild. Until Cage can catch up."

"Lay low where?"

"Cage has an arrangement with a barkeep. Won't be safe for long, but if we can get there, we can stay safe and sound for a few."

"A few what?"

Effie stepped into a shielded alley doorway, pulled out another unmarked cardkey, and tried to pass it through the lock. But the lock was corroded, encrusted in a hard, brown-black plaque after what must have been months of exposure; its access lights were no longer visible.

Effie pulled a set of duraplex knuckles from her purse, slid them over her right hand, and bashed away some of the crust. When she made another, shaking attempt, the cardkey slid into the reader slot, and with a shove, the door opened to reveal an unlit hallway, dim light and smoke and the stench of ancient, spilled beer drifting from a door near the end.

A tall male figure stepped, silhouetted, into the doorway at the lit end of the hall. A mass of bundled cable trailed down from his temple, disappearing behind his right shoulder; the thick cord of a long ponytail disappeared behind his left. He was stout, his English plodding and deliberate, almost sad.

"Friends in need," said Effie.

"Miss Leichtkinde," said the deep, slow male voice. "Knew you'd come eventually. Wondered whether it would be you or him."

Effie took two tentative steps forward, pulling the heavy exterior door closed behind her. "You remember our arrangement? Cage's arrangement?" Effie asked.

"Remember, Miss Leichtkinde?" came the man's voice, slow, thoughtful. Nonjudgmental. "Barring a massive magnetic pulse, doubt I'll ever forget anything."

"Old friends are an asset, Gotham George," replied Effie. "We owe you."

thirty-six

Cage banked the unlit car toward the streets, checking his traffic readout for police cars. Seeing no police transponder signals, he started slowly toward the office.

"Where are you going?" Jonny asked him.

Cage stared ahead.

"Cage, where do you think you're taking us?" she demanded gently.

"I've gotta warn Effie — she's a sitting duck if the cops come in for a sweep of the building."

"Cage," she said gently, "that's one of two places you know we can't be — there and your apartment."

"She's right, partner," said Murphy. "You can't be stupid enough to take us straight to where the cops'll look for you first."

Cage turned to face his old partner. "But they'll take her, Murph — you know that. Cops aren't likely to be gentle with her, either."

"Cage," said Jonny, resting a hand on his shoulder. "You'll just get us all caught. Then they won't be gentle with us."

Cage peered at the traffic readout again.

"There's no cops in traffic anywhere near the office" he said. "That can be good or bad. It's good if we don't see them 'cause they aren't there. It's bad if they're set to silent running, 'cause that means they're sweeping the place. Either way, I've got a friend in there, and I'm gonna get her out."

Jonny stared at him, an expression of anger welling up, faintly lit and shadowed by the dim, green light of the traffic readout, the only active light in the vehicle.

Murphy threw his hands in the air and looked out the windows of the Olds, into the night.

"We'll be silent all the way, I promise," said Cage, steering the Olds across a street and into another unlit alley.

After what seemed like ages of flying in the night in the darkened Olds, Cage slowed in an unlit alley across from the office. He could see the balcony outside his back office, see that the lights were on, but that no one seemed to be inside.

Then he spotted the red cardigan draped across the back of his chair.

Effie had gotten out in time.

"*Cage!*" said Jonny in an angry whisper.

Looking her way, he could see that her eyes were turned upward.

Cage leaned against the driver's side window, looking up toward the traffic altitude, and spotted the darkened police cars hovering over the building.

"Damn, damn, damn!" he said.

"Uh, Cage," said Murphy, pointing toward the office. "Looks like the cops are just making their move now."

Cage could make out the shadowed figures of uniformed men entering the office.

Anxiously, he turned to Jonny Cache.

"Jonny, when you burn client data, how do you do it?"

Her eyes turned guardedly toward Murphy.

"He's my old partner from when I was a cop, Jonny," Cage said. "He's one of the good guys."

"I run a memory-overwrite application on the files," she said. "My own design. It overwrites the data with meaningless information, erases it, and repeats the procedure a dozen times."

"Can you reach my desktop?"

"Sure, anything on the 'Net," she replied.

"Jonny, before they get to the back, I need you to burn the desktop's storage bubble."

"It's not as easy as doing it on my own files," she said.

"Jonny, all my data, all my files are backed up, but the police, they get that and we're all in trouble. They'll know everywhere I've been on the 'Net, know every name I've associated with."

"Easy, Cage," came her confident reply. "I said it's not as easy; I didn't say that it couldn't be done." She handed him a new earclip, which he carefully slid into place, so as not to break this one.

As she looked out into the night, her eyes took on a distant, daydreaming sheen.

Cage heard a *whoosh* as something passed quietly overhead.

"Cage," said Murphy, swallowing nervously, "that was a squad

154

car."

Cage looked Jonny over again, seeing no change.

"Think they spotted us?" Cage asked.

Murphy was looking skyward, now.

"No," Murphy said. "I don't think they did. I don't think they thought we'd be out here. Probably just passed right over us. About four stories up, I think."

Cage closed his fist around the gearshift of the Olds and pulled it right, then back, easing the hovering car backward down the alleyway, taking a corner and pausing out of sight for a 180-degree turn between buildings.

As he turned the Olds into another alley, Cage noticed that Jonny was humming a tune, but he didn't recognize it.

"Hit the desktop at my place next, Jonny. That one's backed up, too," he told her.

thirty-seven

"Gotham George," said Effie, "this is Janice. She's OK, George; she's with me."

Janice Gild stepped forward, doing her best to give a confident nod *hello* through her running eye makeup and the dangling, frizzing, wet tendrils of hair now clinging to her face.

"Effie," she said, "I was just along for the ride with you and I'm still not sure where the hell we are. I don't think I've ever seen so many alleys and abandoned buildings.

"Mr. George, it's a pleasure."

"Just 'George,' or 'Gotham George,' if you're feeling formal or respectful or whatever," said the old Native American slowly, ruminating on every syllable. "And what it is, it's more like business than pleasure."

"You know the arrangement, George," said Effie, her tone resolute. "Cage doesn't pay you a constant stream of insurance money so you can cop an attitude when we collect on our policy."

"Easy, Effie," laughed Gotham George. "Easy. You know you're welcome here."

He motioned for the two women to follow him down the hall, toward a back room. The bundled cable ran from a molded black metal panel at his right temple, gathered at a loose loop mounted by a buttoned flap to the shoulder of his shirt, and disappeared into his shirt, down his back, and tied into a slim chrome box mounted on an old NoGo belt hung with a variety of faded silver cast-metal ornaments: a wolf or dog; a bird of some sort, its wings outstretched, ending in squared-off finger-like feathers; a bear. Animal images cast in a style that imitated aboriginal art.

His hair was a uniform length, long and black, but streaked through with gray, and ending in a single tail tousled about a foot below his left shoulder, a faint glint of light from an overhead bulb reflecting off the shiny black and silver hair. He was tall and barrel-chested sturdy and, Effie knew from Cage, legendarily efficient in clearing drunken troublemakers from his business.

He'd quietly had a few surgical enhancements, she knew. A few, like the one that left him with the bundled cable, he didn't bother trying to keep quiet.

"Gotta keep it very quiet, George. We got trouble," Effie replied.

"What kind of trouble, Effie?" he asked.

Effie steeled herself, her eyes meeting his.

"The cop kind, George," said Effie quietly, worriedly. "The cop kind."

Gotham George stopped, turned toward them, let out a long, troubled whistle and looked down. "Always getting in trouble with the white man.

"Maybe your employer could do with one of these," said Gotham George, giving the chrome box at his waist a pat. "He doesn't seem to have learned the lesson they tried to teach him last time he got in their way."

He turned, shaking his head, and started to lead them through the maze of half-lit halls again. "Big companies are big trouble."

Janice Gild leaned to whisper into Effie's ear: "What's the box?"

"Piggybacked memory module," said Effie, "with direct-access transfer buffer. It's a storage facility. He doesn't forget things."

"Things?" asked Gild.

"Anything," Effie corrected herself.

Gotham George led the two down the hall and into a room. In the brighter light of his office, *Gotham George's* deep, bronze skin, its consistency like weathered leather, Gild thought, the telltale heaviness of his eyelids, told what the shadows had hidden, but his manner and clothing had suggested: Gotham George was Native American. Not just born on the continent, as she was, but a descendant of the its original inhabitants.

His office was crowded with antique computers. He walked to a stack of paperwork: spools of register printouts and several stacks of punched, stiff-paper cards.

He selected one of the cards from the stack and placed it in an old, old computer with a brushed-steel case that looked like it had been left at curbside.

"What are you doing?" asked Effie.

"My books," replied Gotham George distantly.

Looking over the punched cards, she said: "I've never seen a computer like that."

Gotham George laughed, not looking up.

"No, kiddo, you haven't. It's an antique. Runs FORTRAN."

"What's Formtrans?" asked Gild.

He was writing something on a sheet of paper; he rolled it up, picked up a tarnished brass cylinder, slid aside its lid, and secured the note inside its metal case.

"It's an old way of solving mathematical problems," he replied distantly, his voice still slow and methodical, still suggesting painful solitude. "And with the cards, I always have a backup, in case of massive magnetic pulse."

"Why not use your desktop?" asked Effie.

"Because I do my books my own way," he said. "And I don't like having anything important on the 'Net. Even encrypted. But I don't want to bore you kids."

He strode to a set of three long, dull, aged metal tubes a few inches in diameter running down the wall and opened a hatch on the left-most tube; Effie could hear a whoosh of air rushing along the tube on the left.

When he placed the cylinder into the tube on the left, it was whisked away by the air current.

Gotham George motioned the two back through the door, down the labyrinth of hallways, and to an obscure, shadowed corner booth in *Gotham George's*.

"What's your pleasure, ladies?" he asked. "It's covered. Cage keeps a comprehensive policy."

"But your Donatelli ..." started Effie, alarmed.

"It will be fine. We have plenty of customers. It won't notice," he replied reassuringly.

"Cage says Donatelli Three always complains about his tab," Effie said.

"The less an always-online servo knows, the better. But buy one and put him online, I look like an upstanding businessman," said Gotham George, smiling wryly. "Cops never even buzz the place."

Janice Gild gave him a look of confusion.

"Too much information, Miss Gild," he said. "You see?"

She shook her head "No."

Gotham George sighed. "At the turn of the century, the old spy

158

satellites had the ability to read a person's watch from orbit, and that bothered some people. They thought they'd be watched, and closely. But you know what? The intelligence agencies could read your watch, but they didn't have the resources to monitor everything, certainly not on the scale of reading everyone's watches. Remember, these were the same agencies that were surprised when the old Communist Eastern Bloc collapsed.

"There was no way, even before Nightfall, for them to really watch everyone all that closely. They had the ability to gather more information than they could possibly use, so rather than quenching their thirst for information, the flow of data usually drowned their intelligence-gathering efforts. If we don't do anything panicked or unusual, Donatelli Three will never see you as anything, really, but customers passing through."

Gotham George's was an institution in the Old Gotham Quarter, simultaneously an outpost for shady deals, and an ancient neighborhood dive. Gotham George had purchased the place from a previous owner, another Old New Yorker named George, twenty or so years back, and he'd carefully cultivated the business, keeping it fiercely entrenched in the neighborhood as the city slipped into decline.

The Old New Yorkers who remained behind, whether out of choice or because they couldn't afford to leave, would still come around, he knew, and his competition was boarding up and moving away.

Keeping a Donatelli Three on hand had spooked a number of Old Gothamites, because police investigating illegal goings on could always access the android and review its logs.

But in the android, Gotham George had a bartender, not a business partner. He simply didn't tell Donatelli Three anything it didn't need to know.

In exchange, the bartender became a sort of buffer between the bar and the police, who would much rather do a random log review than set down in the Old Gotham Quarter and have their squad cars stripped by røgue-bøyz or gangs.

So, despite the downward economic trend in the area, business boomed, and Gotham George had enough of a cash flow to launder all the Ennays he needed.

As the three of them sat in the booth, mulling snifters of Pinot Noir to forestall the cool November night outside, Effie started to tell Gotham George what she knew of what was going on.

But despite the noisy shuffle of tavern regulars, Gotham George held up a hand, cutting her off with a slow, friendly smile. He reached over to the lamp in the booth, giving a switch at its base a twist.

"Better that I don't know much, kid," he said. "And better Donatelli Three know nothing at all. I'm a legitimate businessman helping out a client who's come to me for assistance. That's my line."

The front door to the bar swung open, and a man in a trenchcoat, fedora and filter mask stepped in, bringing with him a similarly protected man and woman, and the smell and noise of tainted rain.

"Your boss, I think he is here," Gotham George said to Effie. "His tab's OK. But tell him to order from me, not Donatelli Three," he said, rising and starting toward the labyrinthine back halls. "Be right back."

Cage sorted out everyone's names, and he, Murphy, and Jonny Cache took seats in the shadowed corner booth, sharing details of their flight from the police.

"Oh, Cage, what are we gonna do?" Effie asked, sounding suddenly smaller, the strain in her voice and creases surrounding her eyes betraying her weariness.

"We're gonna solve the case," Cage said. "Cops don't want our noses in this for some reason, and I'm thinking the reason's corporate. So we know someone in Expedite's pulling their strings and doesn't want us snooping around."

"OK then, Cage, what do we do?" asked Murphy.

"We," said Jonny Cache, "snoop around some more. See what's so important to our string-puller at Expedite."

Leaning forward, Janice Gild looked to Jonny and asked: "So what's your connection to all this?"

Jonny shifted back, graying into the shadows outside the circle of light from the booth's single overhead bulb and shade.

"James and I were close," said Jonny.

Gild peered into the shadows.

"I didn't know my brother knew any woman named 'Jonny,'" she said.

Neither did he, thought Jonny Cache.

Clearing his throat as he approached, a warning to them to hold their tongues, Gotham George stepped toward their booth.

"OK, folks," he said, pulling papers from a tarnished brass cylinder. "I've made your arrangements. Not pretty arrangements. Nothing fancy. But you can lay low for a while. Don't leave a trail. Don't go online. Cops'll find it."

"How did you make arrangements without leaving a trail all over the 'Net?" asked Jonny.

George flicked the brass cylinder with his index finger, raising a resonant metallic *ping*. "Pneumatic tube network," he said. "Old infrastructure. Cops don't pay any attention."

He smiled broadly. "I love antiques."

thirty-eight

Jonny found the *Excelsior! Gentlemen's Hotel* amusing. Janice Gild was horrified by the passed-out addicts in the second-floor lobby of the flophouse. Cage, Effie, and Murphy seemed to take the situation as it came, glumly resigned to their circumstances.

The hotel's name was painted on the brick-faced building's side, and had been badly faded for as long as Cage had known the neighborhood.

Peeling paint hung in browning sheets from the walls and ceiling of the stairwell leading up from the street to the lobby of the flophouse. Stepping around motionless almost-street people, Cage and the others made their way up the unlit access through a stale, damp haze of urine and mildew.

The lobby seemed to be furnished entirely with secondhand loveseats and recliners. A single video-only Netcom sat on a flimsy, worn table in the corner of the lobby. The edges of the table were frayed from year upon year of people brushing against it as they walked past, slowly eroding away the shine of the finish, then the finish itself, the artificially dark cherry stain after that, finally fraying the underlying wood like the knee of a construction worker's denims.

Another snoozing, unshaven, middle-aged man snored in one of the tattered recliners.

The clerk for the *Excelsior!* sat locked in a tiny, cluttered booth, a yellowing street paper of indeterminate age resting unattended before him, between his expansive, undershirt-covered belly and a protective cage of thick, black, iron grating. The grating surrounded the clerk, spot welded on all sides, a padlock holding its door secure. He reminded Cage of old stills he'd seen back in school, images of factory-farmed battery hens, once stuffed so tightly into crowded cages for egg-laying that their flesh grew into and around the grating of their cages, eventually sealing the steel grating into their flesh. The birds never left those cages.

Behind the battery-hen clerk ran an array, from floor to ceiling,

162

of ancient, tarnished brass pneumatic tubing.

An ancient, corroded, unlit stogy sat clutched between the enormous clerk's stained, scanty teeth.

"Yuh noym, shuh," rasped the clerk, his moist, mealy speech flavored with the accent of an Old New York native, his voice with the wet grate of someone who never, ever wore his filter mask.

"Eckhardt," said Cage, handing over the paperwork Gotham George had given him.

The clerk squinted, his red-cracked eyes bulging, straining hard as he pored over the papers.

"Yeah, Mishtuh Eckuh," the clerk coughed. "Ya gotchashelf a room all shet up real nishe. One-nine-two-sheven-dash-4."

The battery-hen clerk handed Cage a cardkey, squinting toward the rest of the group.

The lift was like a freight elevator: No frills, rough, unfinished particle-board walls, the screech of the lift's barely maintained gears somewhere overhead, and a clear view of the building's floors as the lift passed them.

The paint covering the walls of floor nineteen had been beige, once, but had faded, darkened, and stained over the years.

The floor stank of ancient urine.

"Paradise," said Cage.

"It's … it's," stammered Gild. "It's foul!"

Cage turned abruptly toward her.

"No," he said brusquely. "It's perfect. It's private. The price is right."

Cage led them to 1927-4, and it was exactly what he expected: A six-foot-by-ten-foot cubicle room with a seven-foot-high ceiling of stapled down chicken wire and a single cot.

The chicken wire, Cage informed them, was to keep people from scaling the low walls and climbing into other people's rooms.

Overhead, about thirty feet up, a 200-watt bulb with a shade of taped black construction paper hung down from a ceiling of rust-colored, peeling paint.

The cubicle rooms were identical and featureless, each having its own cardkey lock. There were a dozen such cubicles on each side, a constant, static, rustling chorus of sheets and people moving about.

"Inside," he whispered.

Gild started to protest, but Murphy hushed her, taking her by the shoulders and nudging her into Eckhardt's cubicle.

In the dank, cramped cubicle, Cage could hear the gent in the next room roll over.

He pulled the group into a huddle.

"Listen, what we need is some reconnaissance," he said. "Jonny, I need to know how the cops closed in on us so fast. Look around online, but be quiet about it, OK?"

Jonny worked one corner of her mouth into a smile and nodded.

"Wait a minute," said Gild. "I thought we had to stay offline — not leave a trail. How's she gonna get online if we can't?"

Cage looked to Jonny, who shrugged and turned away, taking a seat on the cot.

"Jonny," said Cage. "Do it, OK?"

She nodded.

"Janice," said Cage. "Let me tell you a story."

Jonny relaxed in her corner, looking to everyone in the cubicle to be daydreaming.

Somewhere nearby, someone snorted once, deeply, then again, and spat.

thirty-nine

"What story, Cage?" Gild asked uncomfortably. She looked toward the cot as though considering seating herself, but on examination, she opted to remain standing.

Cage sighed, frowning. He hadn't been close to her since their night together in his apartment. Now, sitting next to her, he longed again to feel her stomach naked against his, feel the caress of her hair playing across an unclothed shoulder.

But not here. Not now. The situation had dragged them all together all too tensely. It was no time to think of intimacy when he couldn't so much as spend the night in his own home.

He reached out, took her hand in his briefly, tried to give it a reassuring squeeze, then released it.

She was a wreck from fleeing in the acid rain. The rose red of her dress had begun to dull and fade already from its soaking.

He cleared his throat and whispered, hoping that his voice wouldn't carry past the chicken-wire mesh and into neighboring cubicles: "Once upon a time, there was a programming genius with no social life, and no social skills to build one with."

He began telling her what he knew about James Gild from his investigation: The high-tech talent that made him such a hot property that he had eventually needed an agent to market him, sort through the offers, and help him find the position that was just right, then one that he was looking for.

Some of it, she knew. Some details, though, were new.

He'd been brilliant and secretive, even when they had met for their occasional lunch dates. That had been difficult for her. James had been all the family that she had had left.

But she'd had a lifetime to get used to his self-sustained seclusion. With so little interaction with the outside world, his conversations with her had tended, over the years, to focus on news events he'd seen reported on Netcasts.

"Janice, did you know that James saw a specialist briefly?" asked Cage.

165

She gave him a look of alarm.

"No. No I didn't," she said, not making eye contact.

"Cage," she eventually said, "why was he seeing a specialist?"

"He was very," he paused, considering his words. "Very close to Jonny."

"But how? With his social life, how could he even have met her? And why didn't he tell me?"

Cage gave a little shrug. "He probably had his reasons."

"Did Jonny hurt him?" she asked. "Did she leave him or cheat on him? Betray him somehow? He'd never be able to bear that. I'm surprised he was able to muster the courage to meet her, to introduce himself at all."

"He didn't meet her," said Cage. "Not exactly. He ordered her."

"A mail-order bride? I didn't hear an accent when she spoke."

"Not exactly," said Cage. "Have you ever heard of Jennifer Four?" She met his eyes. "No."

"Janice, James saw the specialist because he was suffering from Sumner's Syndrome."

A look of realization dawned on her face, then slowly, twitchingly transformed into a snarl of contempt. "You're insulting the memory of my brother, Mr. Cage," she said, coldly insistent.

"Listen, Janice," he whispered, pleading. "He built a better Jennifer Four, OK? I don't know how. But she became something else, and as far as I can tell, they loved each other."

She whipped a hand out, slapping him hard on the face.

"They were close, Janice," said Cage. "She's in this for him."

"*It*," spat Gild, "is a god-damned domestic."

Cage was fighting, now, to swerve her. "No. I told you: I don't now how, but she's more."

"You sleep with it too, Cage?" Gild demanded.

He looked her way, reading the anger and pain, the offense etched into her face.

"Janice, why do you think he didn't tell you about her? He knew better than I did, I think — he knew you'd take it pretty badly."

Jonny jerked to life suddenly, turning her head almost mechanically toward Cage.

"Cage, did you know James worked for Expedite?!" she demanded.

Janice was glaring at Jonny with open contempt.

Cage was startled by Jonny's sudden flare of anger, and he began to respond: "Wh—"

But her attention was focused online again.

forty

Online, Jonny felt relaxed, at home, at ease.

She cruised through the 'Net's Consensual VR Interface, a less-powerful, less-effective version of the CIVRML interface chosen as the standard by the makers of online worlds such as Sixth Street.

Expedite had a habit of buying into innovative technologies created by others and either imitating those technologies, usually poorly, or adding enough new code to make the Expedite version incompatible with the original. Then, because Expedite was larger, the corporation was able to issue its own, often bug-addled version of the technology as the standard for users of Personals and desktops, forcing the inventors of those technologies out of the market.

StellarNet's interface was an example: Seeing the great market potential of the CIVRML standard, Expedite set its developers to work taking code from CIVRML and altering it enough to avoid copyright infringement. And as the Expedite developers altered the code, they introduced bugs, changing names of important modules of the programming code, for example, which made it impossible for other parts of the code to search for those pieces of code by name.

By the time the corporation's coders were through with the interface that gave Sixth Street all its life and variety and interactivity, what they had was a black space through which users could navigate. They populated the black space with two-foot-by-two-foot cubes, virtual real estate that they then rented out to the online world as a means of navigation. For a fee, Expedite would map a 'Net site's name and logo onto the surface of a cube and link the cube back to that 'Net site, so that the cubes served as navigational beacons for the online community.

And when Expedite declared its own Consensual VR Interface the standard by which StellarNet was to be experienced and navigated, the creators of CIVRML, forced from the market, released their software's source code, making it available for free from shareware sites around the globe.

While the code was no longer a source of income for the inventors, their move to release the software at no cost ensured its survival, and the original became the freer, hipper alternative for VR world building, much as Linux had once become a freer, hipper alternative to Unix.

Millions of cubes glittered in the infinite distance of StellarNet, like tiny, animated stars in a virtual night, every one of them generating revenue for Expedite.

Jonny could see the avatars of innumerable other users flitting from cube to cube, region to region, but she had set her transparency channel and reduced her avatar to a single pixel, effectively rendering her invisible to the rest of the online world.

It took longer to navigate StellarNet manually, but she wasn't about to risk activating a link, leaving a trail that the company might be able to trace.

She began at the Day-Windham central server.

Its security was a pushover; she'd already breezed through it once.

The too-slim man, Winston Baldisari, was working on a special project. He'd recently received a promotion, but the chain of command behind that promotion was unclear; it appeared to have come from outside Day-Windham.

Jonny followed the trail.

The authorization for Baldisari's transfer was authorized by Alexei Kochen. Kochen's title was listed on the official record of the promotion as "special assistant to Mr. Steag."

Jonny paused, shaken. Whatever they were onto, Expedite's interest in them went straight to the top.

She detached herself from Baldisari's files.

Someone close to Steag had hustled her. And someone close to their group had let Expedite and their police force know very quickly when things went awry at Nine Circles.

She peered into the conference logs for Baldisari, following a recent communication out from Day-Windham and back to Expedite.

The security surrounding Expedite was some of the best in the world, its weaknesses hammered constantly by røgue-bøyz and Netrunners, then patched as well as Expedite's security teams could manage.

But to Jonny Cache, such measures were almost meaningless. She swiftly searched the company's armor, finding and making her way through it.

Steag's conference log read like some preposterous, million-tentacled octopus, tendrils stretching out, away from the Steag compound on New Bombay One and out into the world. On the other side, a single communications trail led out to Steag's Personal.

She began examining the connections, meticulously cataloging them as she went so as to avoid duplication.

One, she found, was scrambled, but led to the address of a Personal, and its time signature told her the message had been sent during her bout with Baldisari's Morlock henchman.

The address wasn't Baldisari's, but she could not find a registration for it.

Another dead end.

She had accessed the company's roster, hoping to back-check the address of the Personal against the names of Expedite employees, past and present.

But the discovery of an entry for a retired code man named James Gild had brought her search to a halt.

In the cubicle, she jerked her head suddenly toward Cage.

"Cage, did you know James worked for Expedite?!" she demanded.

Janice was glaring at Jonny with open contempt. Cage had told her what Jonny was.

Cage looked startled, and began to respond: "Wh—"

But her attention was focused online again.

When had he worked for Expedite?

The date of termination logged on the roster corresponded roughly with Gild's retirement from *The Lightwave Garden* .

She continued her search for the address, but still failed to find a match.

She rooted through Expedite's central server, seeking any mention of *The Lightwave Garden* .

Slowly, for Jonny, over the course of hundreds of thousands of pages of press releases, communiqués, and legal paperwork, a picture began to emerge.

Tobias Steag IV had seen in *The Lightwave Garden* the potential for an efficient new energy source, one that could corner the market as fossil fuel reserves became exhausted.

He'd set out to prove himself to Tobias III, who currently held the reins at Expedite. Tobias IV had seen *The Lightwave Garden* as something to conquer, a technology that he did not want to see Expedite become dependent upon, so he had dedicated company resources and legal teams to acquiring the energy project.

The Lightwave Garden had transmitted its stored solar energy to football-field-size ground stations. The ground stations' receiving fields were home to thousands of meter-wide mirrors, each controlled to reflect the sunlight directed at them from *The Lightwave Garden*'s orbiting collector, concentrating the light on a single, massive tank, where the intense heat generated steam, allowing the ground station to harness the energy.

And this bright new hope for the world's energy needs was owned by Expedite.

But then something Tobias Steag IV hadn't expected happened: Nightfall. The pollution, the rising sea level, the drastic climatic changes had cast thick, dark clouds over the ground stations. The solar energy redirected from the gathering station could no longer reach the receiving fields of the ground stations.

The project had been rendered completely useless.

Tobias Steag III had not been amused at his clone heir-apparent's failure to foresee the project's failure, and had reprimanded the younger Steag, sending him out into Expedite's Day-Windham subsidiary to learn a few things about business.

But the younger Steag had kept an interest in the project, and had quietly managed to fund the project's engineering and programming teams and set them to work finding a solution that would make *The Lightwave Garden* a success.

The lead team was an exceptionally talented battery of young scientists, programmers, and engineers:

James Gild, a programming-languages genius who eventually retired not with the stock options he had told people he'd received, but with an immense severance package arranged by Tobias Steag IV; hush money, apparently, was enough for Steag early on;

Elliott Jaspin, a hardware engineer who moved on to

Chapterhouse Computing, also well-compensated;

Keye Mtumbo, a laser technology scientist who had helped the team design the ground stations' energy reception mechanisms. His severance had enabled him to pursue a lifelong hobby of researching unexplained phenomena;

Alaina Quinn, a gifted designer who later moved on to a teaching career. She could afford to. The younger Steag had paid them all off and had them sign standard corporate secrecy statements. He also arranged to have her history with *The Lightwave Garden* covered by false records of employment in other Expedite-owned subsidiaries;

Indigo Corcoran, an engineer whose role was not detailed;

All, save Corcoran, were victims of the burn Cage was now investigating.

Jonny returned her efforts to the roster for some deductive reasoning. She wasn't the one contacting Expedite, she knew. Cage also clearly wouldn't have been.

Effie? Jonny doubted it. Effie had worked with Cage for too long to suddenly become a corporate spy against her old friend.

Janice Gild had hired them to look into the case. Probably not her.

That left Cage's old partner, Murphy.

Jonny again began sorting through Expedite's roster data, and there, listed with a freelance flag next to his name, was Corbin Murphy's name.

Jonny backed out through the server's security and, once clear of Expedite, turned her attention outward.

The others were on the cot, sitting next to her.

Murphy stood near the door of the cubicle room, his gun pointed at the others.

"You four just sit tight," said Murphy. "I got a conference to make."

forty-one

"What's the plan now, 'pal'?" asked Cage, spitting the last word.

"Don't know yet, Cage. I didn't expect her to figure out so much."

Murphy was still watching them, fumbling with the holster of his Personal, trying to undo its snap with one hand while he held his gun in the other.

Pulling it free, he punched something into the Personal.

"Cage, don't react," came Jonny's voice, suddenly very close on his right. "Murphy can't hear me."

Cage casually traced a question mark on the sheet.

"The earclip. I'm transmitting to it, not speaking."

Cage turned to look at her.

"See?" she asked, her lips not moving.

He turned back to face Murphy, who was conferencing with someone now.

"Here's what I know," she said, sharing the data she'd pulled from Expedite's Server.

Outside, a squad car pulled up next to the fire escape of the *Excelsior!,* and two uniformed officers climbed out.

Cage turned to Jonny, a look of disbelief crossing his face, but she waved off his glance.

"Jesus, Cage, want him to see us having a conversation here?!" came her voice from the earclip.

"I don't get it, Murphy. You had me fooled. Had me completely over a barrel. Why's a guy like you mixed up with people like them?" Cage asked.

"What makes you think I ever wasn't, Cage? Huh?" asked Murphy. "I never made any secret of not being on your side when you wouldn't drop that murder investigation when we were partners."

Cage spat at Murphy, who backhanded him with the butt of the gun, sending the detective crashing to the floor.

"Cage!" cried Jonny, out loud.

He pushed himself up from the floor, a rivulet of blood escaping down his cheek from the impact point, just below his left eye.

"Never learn, do ya, pal?" asked Murphy. "Nope. Never learn. It's not good deeds make the world go 'round, Cage," said Murphy. "It's money. You mess with the big guns, Cage, you don't got money no more. But you play nice, maybe you can get in on the action. Get ahead, y'know. Figuratively, I mean. You, you're kinda stuck."

Cage sat on the cot again. In the hall, the two cops, their filtermasks in place, their dark-blue double-breasteds slick with rain, arrived at the door of the cubicle, guns drawn.

Then Jonny felt it: Expedite's recall signal. The company was trying to summon her back. She went rigid, sitting bolt upright, her eyes as vacant and unfeeling as marbles.

"Jonny?" asked Cage, suddenly worried. Then his worry turned to horror: Somehow, Expedite had cut her strings.

"Yeah, Baldisari told me she'd do something like that," said Murphy.

"Recall signal. She's on autopilot, Cage," he said, tapping his forehead. "Nobody home."

Murphy and the other two cops ushered the four of them out onto the rusty fire escape and into the holding cell in the rear of the squad car.

"What happened to it?" Janice asked, gesturing toward Jonny.

"*Her*," Cage corrected. "'What happened to *her*?' Got it?"

Janice Gild made sharp, exasperated huff.

"Why are you so anxious to defend it, Cage?" she asked angrily. Then a look of realization and revulsion crossed her face. "Oh, Jesus Christ, Cage. You *did* have sex with it."

She turned her back on him.

Cage clutched Gild's arm, turning her back around, squeezing, he realized after a moment, harder than he had to.

"Listen to me: She told me Expedite built in a fail-safe device: It's a recall signal that turns her main processor off and orders her to her service center," Cage said.

The cops closed the hatch, locking Cage, Effie, Janice and Jonny in.

"Look, Ms. Gild," said Effie, "you wouldn't treat a person who used to be a hooker, but got herself out of it, the way you treat Jonny, right?"

174

Gild looked at Effie, astonished.

"No. Of course not. I would be proud of her accomplishment. I would applaud her."

Effie leaned in, her nose no more than two inches from Gild's face.

"Then you should damn well be proud of someone who never had any choice about her situation."

Gild gave Effie a look of disdain, then turned away.

It had to be a severe sort of rejection, Cage realized; in the eyes of Janice Gild, the private detective had chosen an inanimate sex toy over Gild's company. He'd rejected her in favor of what Gild saw as a thing.

And a thing of perversion, at that. To be used privately, if at all, and then stored in a closet or hamper, away where decent people might not see it.

"Cage," said Jonny, speaking again through the earclip.

Hopeful and surprised, he looked at her.

"The compartment's almost certainly bugged, so don't mention that I'm awake, OK?"

Cage did a slow-motion nod, looked down at the floor, paused for a moment, then looked up again.

"OK. I'm going to check online again, but I have to pay attention to this part of things to keep up appearances, so I might need a little more time than on my last run. Just letting you know. Nudge me if you need me, OK?"

Cage looked floorward again.

She redirected her attention.

The navigational-node cubes glittered in the matte-black digital night of StellarNet. Jonny streaked across the 'Net, back to Expedite, and back through its security.

The recall signal that had been sent for her had originated from the office of Tobias Steag IV, not the older version of him, the one who was supposedly in charge. A router trail told her that the signal had not been sent from the family's New Bombay compound, but from Tobias Steag IV's Personal.

She sought and found the personal directory of Tobias IV, in search of anything she could learn about the four burns, particularly about the death of James Gild.

But she could turn up nothing specific.

What was clear, though, was that the death orders for the team that forged *The Lightwave Garden* had come directly from Tobias Steag IV.

"Do you think they're taking us to New Bombay One?" Effie asked him.

Cage thought for a moment.

"No," he said finally. "No, I read somewhere that Tobias IV was more or less eighty-sixed from the family compound until he could make something of himself."

A look of astonishment crossed Effie's face.

"His own family did that to him?"

Cage nodded. "They're less a family than an ongoing clutch at power. The Tobias Steags are clones, Effie," he whispered. "Our problems would appear to be from number four, the fourth generation from the company's progenitor."

"Is the first one dead?" she asked quietly, trying to use the white noise of the rain and wind on the squad car to keep her voice masked from hidden microphones.

"No, not exactly. I think he's still technically the one in charge. But he and Tobias number two both had their metabolisms carefully slowed with drugs, then had themselves cryogenically suspended. Arranged not to have themselves declared dead, in case a successor clone needed advice on some particularly important matter. Number three's running things right now. I can't figure out what's going on with number four, but he doesn't like us looking into these deaths."

"So where do you think we're going, Cage?" asked Effie.

"Expedite's got a regional office complex in Jersey," whispered Cage. "That's close. My money's on the regional office."

The Lightwave Garden , Jonny read, had been a sort of environmentalists' project in its early, formational stages.

The Greens had backed planning and development, hoping to chart a future in which North America could stop burning the polluting fossil fuel upon which so much of the economy had become

176

dependent.

But the Greens were a political party, a movement of activists, whose investments couldn't stand up to the kind of influence that could be mustered by old-money families looking to protect their business assets.

A negative publicity campaign characterizing the effort as radical and leftist eventually had beaten back all corporate sponsorship, leaving *The Lightwave Garden* scaled back to a small, exploratory mission funded almost exclusively by a government grant.

And even that had been viewed as a waste of taxpayer monies. Protesters' faxes jammed online channels at *The Lightwave Garden* inscribed with slogans like: "No tax dollars for God-damned Communist Socialist radicals!" and "No Red Power!"

When the climate's shift had begun, the government had backed out, declaring the project a failure.

But Tobias Steag IV had stepped in, purchasing the project lock, stock, and barrel, and redefining it as a corporate effort.

It had proven a promising, even worthwhile investment, with the possibility of supplanting the old fossil fuels even before they ran out, which would allow the Steags to corner the energy market.

But the climate shift, as she knew, had changed all that.

It had also been the source of some considerable tension between Steags three and four, leading to the younger Steag's banishment from the family compound on NB1.

The younger one had kept the project going, unbeknownst to number three, and ordered a change of direction, she read: He had ordered the team to develop a workaround.

And, years later, he had ordered the team members' deaths.

In between, Jonny learned, the team had invented the workaround number four had ordered. Then they had all been sent into retirement while he had contemplated his next move.

But how had they been killed? Jonny could find no record of that. Only one, or perhaps two people in the world knew that part; Tobias Steag IV and Indigo Corcoran — and Indigo's chances of surviving didn't seem promising.

Jonny redirected her attention to Cage's earclip, sharing the information with him.

"Now here's something else that's useful to know, Cage. Brace yourself, and tell everyone else to, too," said Jonny. "But try to be subtle."

Again, Cage traced the question mark on the molded, black duraplex seat beside him.

"The Olds is about to ram us. It's running silent, so the cops don't even know it's there yet."

Cage motioned to the others, signing furiously for them to follow his lead, then clamping his hands down onto the seat.

In a moment, the squad car pitched to its side, all forward motion halted. Cage suddenly felt a second source of propulsion shoving the squad car down and to the side.

With a shower of sparks, the squad car was rammed, crumpling into the side of a building. Peering out through the porthole, Cage could see the front bumper of the Olds pinning the driver's door shut, the building holding the passenger's.

The hatch on the passenger side of the Olds opened, and Jonny sprang to life, a kick taking the hatch off the hold compartment, sending it tumbling away toward the ground.

"C'mon!" Cage yelled, helping Effie out onto the hood of the Olds, the two clambering over the wet, friction-resistant smoothness of the Olds and toward the open hatch.

But Janice Gild was cowering at the back of the squad car's holding compartment. Jonny approached, offering a hand, but Gild withdrew even further.

With a sharp exhale of disgust and a roll of her eyes, Jonny stepped forward, seizing Gild, hauling her cowering form up from the floor like a doll and slinging her over an inhumanly strong shoulder.

"I really should just leave you there," Jonny said as she carried Gild out of the squad car.

Jonny dexterously climbed to the hood of the car.

In the rain, Gild screamed, pointing into the squad car.

Murphy had drawn his gun and was aiming at Jonny.

"Gild!" Jonny yelled, trying to reach Cage's hysterical, kicking client. "It's OK! Their windows are bulletproof!"

But Janice Gild paid no attention to Jonny Cache, and struggled to get away.

Jonny's heels slipped on the wet, low-friction metal of the hood, and she fell to her side, clutching Gild in one arm and the seam of the hood at the windshield with the other.

In the car, Murphy's face went flashbulb black and white, all high-contrast, in the flash of his sidearm firing, and for a brief, blindingly violent moment, the bullet ricocheted around inside the cabin of the squad car. A sudden plume of blood onto the driver's side window told the tale: It was Murphy's skull that had stopped the bullet.

Jonny swung Gild back onto the hood of the car, slugging her when she'd righted herself. Janice Gild was no longer conscious. Without Gild struggling, Jonny easily hefted them both into the passenger-side door of the Olds.

"They'll call for help!" Cage warned.

"No. For now their connections with the 'Net are cut off," said a NewSchool Grrl, a wildly jury rigged Personal resting on the dash before her, all cables and tape and solder. She grinned proudly. "It'll take them weeks to find the communications node I set to kill their communications."

Cage couldn't tell if he'd ever seen this one before.

She slammed the car into reverse, watching the squad car tumble to a low roof only fifteen feet down. Gild groaned, stirred by the cacophony of the squad car crashing, lightless, below.

"Why are you helping me?" Cage asked, genuinely confused, but careful to make certain the question didn't sound like a complaint.

"Helping you?" asked the NewSchool Grrl, her green, reflective cat eyes flashing in the darkness.

"I'm not." Grinning, she patted Jonny's shoulder affectionately. "But sisters stick together."

"Sisters?!" asked Gild incredulously, massaging her sore jaw.

"A figure of speech, obviously," said Jonny, grinning. Apart from her drenching out on the hood of the Olds, Jonny showed no outward sign of strain.

forty-two

"So this Corcoran character — she's news to me," Cage said to Jonny as the olds streaked, unlit, through the city, below the skyline. "When I was investigating, looking for similar deaths, her name didn't turn up."

"I don't think she's dead yet," said Jonny. "I think she's the first member of the old *Lightwave Garden* lead team that isn't. If we're lucky, maybe we can find her before they kill her."

"I still don't understand how they're doing it. The science of these burns is still strange — they still shouldn't be possible."

Jonny shrugged. "Spontaneous human combustion?"

"A very controlled kind of spontaneous human combustion if it is."

The Olds began to drop altitude, pulling next to an old fishery building near the river. With a thump, the Olds set down, and the NewSchool Grrl hopped out, running to another, waiting car.

Cage began to climb forward, but Jonny slid into the driver's seat. Obligingly, Cage settled himself into the passenger side.

"OK," he said. "Where to?"

A pair of the Grrls lugged big canisters to the side of the Olds.

"First off, my friends refuel this locomotive of yours," she said.

"And then?" asked Cage, waving off her disparagement of the Olds.

"The Grrls have been doing a little reconnaissance for me. Turns out Corcoran looked up her old friend, James Gild, and learned that he'd died."

Cage turned toward her.

"She found out you were investigating the death. So she read his obituary, learned something important, I think. She's been trying to find you, but you haven't exactly been able to check your Netmail lately."

"So where are we going?" Effie asked.

"My friends, the Angeliques, have Indigo Corcoran laying low," said Jonny. "I hope you like live music."

She drove the car back into the cover afforded by the skyline, into the Old Gotham Quarter, to the alleyway behind her home.

The towering figure of Harshburger greeted them, giving Jonny a quick hug.

"This way," he said. Cage punched a command into his Personal, linking directly with the Olds so as to avoid logging onto StellarNet and alerting every authority in the region. The unlit car lifted off with a quiet gust, pausing to hover, stationary, about forty feet up.

Inside the building, music echoed off the polished floors and unadorned walls; they were getting closer to *Nine Circles* itself. They turned down a flight of stairs, away from the ground floor.

Harshburger turned a corner, his massive form obscuring the hall ahead, and paused to knock on the only door in the hall.

When Yin-Angelique opened the door, a black woman stood up from the bench at which she'd been sitting and stepped forward.

Her head was buzzed almost to a shave, and her piercing brown eyes looked out at the ruffled, rag-tag group, making eye contact with them one by one.

"You must be the detective," she said. "Cage."

"Indigo Corcoran?" Cage asked.

"How much do you know?" she asked.

"We've learned a lot, but we don't know how or why, exactly, you and your teammates have been ordered dead," said Cage.

Corcoran nodded wearily; the skin under her eyes looked leathery, heavy and lined from lack of sleep.

"How many of us have they gotten?" she asked.

Cage looked to Jonny, then Janice, and back to Indigo Corcoran.

"As far as we know," he said, "you're the last one."

"Bastards," she said, breaking down. "The bastards."

Jonny approached her, placing her hands reassuringly on Corcoran's shoulders.

"We'll do what we can to protect you," she said.

Corcoran laughed bitterly, her shoulders heaving with her sobs.

"What can you do? Look at you," she said, waving at them.

She was right, Cage knew. They were only free for now, and that was mostly dumb luck.

Cage cleared his throat quietly. The walls trembled with a constant *thump, thump, thump*, a dance beat filtering down through the building from the pit.

"Ms. Corcoran? How are they doing it? How can these people be burning to death in an attack that leaves no trail?" he asked.

"Oh, it leaves a trail, sort of. More of a fingerprint."

"A fingerprint?" he asked.

"You're good, Cage. I looked over your record. But this was something you couldn't have known to look for," she said.

"How's that?"

"Residual radiation, Cage," she said.

His look remained one of confusion as he tried to deduce her meaning.

"What do you mean?" he asked.

She laughed again. "They probably should have called the project *The Microwave Garden*," she said with disgust.

"I thought it was a green-friendly project," said Effie.

"It was. It even stayed that way for a surprisingly long time after Expedite took it over. But number four ordered us to make the transmission and reception of the energy gathered by the Garden's orbital collector work without a line-of-sight connection. He ordered us to design a workaround, something to get past the cloudcover."

A look of realization began to cross Jonny's face.

"A workaround. You found a way to make the energy reach its destination as something other than sunlight," she said.

"Keye Mtumbo and I devised a method of converting the energy to microwave radiation," she said, looking in shame toward the floor. "Together, we developed a mechanism to modulate that energy so that we could transmit it from the orbital collector and channel it so that it only gained potency at a very specific set of coordinates."

"The receiving stations," said Cage.

"Yes, but not only there. We knew that once we'd built it Expedite would order more receiving stations constructed. So we made it possible to point the transmitter to any coordinates on the surface of the planet from overhead. It was meant to allow the energy to pass through obstacles without weakening."

Cage's mouth was ajar in disbelief. Janice Gild looked thoroughly stunned. Effie covered her mouth in shock.

Corcoran nodded.

"You see," she said, "we used the Mandelbrot set … "

"Mandelbrot set?" asked Effie.

"Yes," Corcoran said. "The standard in chaos theory."

She watched for recognition, but registered none.

"OK," she said, "we used chaos theory at our transmission and reception points, with a control protocol."

Curious stares.

"It means that we made it possible for microwave energy to leave the gathering stations by scattering into infinity — theoretically into infinity, anyway — then, using the chaos values we'd already generated with the Mandelbrot set, we were able to get that energy to regain potency at a predefined set of coordinates."

"What's that mean?" asked Cage. "To us, y'know, who didn't work on that project, and didn't go to theory class with you?"

Jonny Cache was way ahead of him.

"So it can transmit that energy right through things, and the energy only manifests as heat when it reaches the coordinates you give it," said Jonny.

"Right!" said Corcoran, pleased that her students had picked up her lesson so quickly. "Our process tells the energy: 'Leave here at full strength, then go anywhere you want in the universe, but make certain you end up at the target at full strength at this time. And we limited the effect to a four-foot sphere, so that if we miscalculated, we … "

She swallowed, realizing how badly they had, in fact, miscalculated.

" … it wouldn't do much damage."

"Spontaneous human combustion," said Effie.

"Monsters," said Gild, hot, angry tears streaming down her face. "You two built a weapon to burn people to death, and they killed my brother with it. Do you know what dying like that must have been like, lady?!"

"No!" yelled Corcoran. "We didn't build a weapon! It was never supposed to be used that way! We built hope for humankind, a chance for the earth, and even if we did it for Expedite to control, our creation was not evil!"

"Monsters," Gild said again, turning her back on the engineer in disgust.

"No," said Jonny. "They meant to help. They built this energy system for the good of people, not to hurt them."

"Ms. Corcoran," said Cage, recovering from shock. "They perverted a good thing. That's what Expedite does."

He shot a scowling glance at Gild, but she remained unmoved.

He continued: "I don't understand how they've managed to hit such specific targets, Ms. Corcoran. A controlled four-foot sphere of that kind of extreme heat — how did they manage to hit your team members? There was only one scorch marking each case: The fatal one. Whoever fired your device at these people even knew James Gild was in bed, and controlled the attack to hit him there, not just anyplace in his home. How?"

Indigo Corcoran looked up at him, her forehead furrowed in a pained expression.

"We're tagged, Mr. Cage."

"Tagged?"

"Surgically tagged. It was part of our secrecy agreement. People working on top-secret research have an identifier tag embedded in their abdomens. With the tags transmitting your ID, you can walk into your Expedite-owned research facility. Without one, doors stay sealed. Equipment doesn't function. You can't sabotage other projects."

"Why is yours still transmitting?" asked Jonny. "You have rights, you know. None of you still work for Expedite."

"Ours was an ongoing project. Number four promised us the tags had been deactivated once we were off the project, but insisted that we keep them in case we were needed to solve problems with the Garden again."

"So they reactivated your teammates' tags and homed in on your ID signals." said Cage.

Corcoran nodded. "A built-in targeting lock. And we didn't even know it."

"Why haven't they gotten you yet?" asked Effie.

"I think I must have been last on their list. I found out we were being killed off when I tried to look up James. When I found his obituary and learned how he'd died, I tried to contact the others."

"You were too late," said Jonny.

Corcoran nodded. She lifted the bottom of her shirt away from her waist revealing a small, black, molded-plastic box clipped to her belt. "A scrambler. I know it's worked well enough to keep me alive this long, but if Expedite's trying to crack it, they'll crack it sooner or later."

"We have to destroy your device," said Jonny earnestly, stepping forward.

Cage felt fear rise in the pit of his stomach, but after a moment he thought about how far he'd fallen. What did he have left to lose? He couldn't go home, couldn't seek refuge in his office. But he knew two things they still had, things he still stood to lose: The life of Jonny Cache and the life the Expedite-funded cops would wrest from him as soon as they could catch up with him.

Maybe some good could come of this nightmare. Maybe they could save Corcoran for now.

"We'll need to do it soon, before they crack my scrambler and find out where I am," said Corcoran.

She handed Jonny a little silver mini-DVD in a disc sleeve.

"Safer for you to hold this than me," she told Jonny.

"What is it?" Cage asked.

"A specially tuned virus, full of back-door access codes."

"Access codes for what?"

"The Garden's orbital collector," said Corcoran.

forty-three

The Angeliques had discussed the matter across their own, two-woman network, and decided to offer their help, but Jonny and Cage would have none of it, while a withdrawn Janice Gild simply gawked at Yin-Angelique's makeup and style, utterly, utterly confounded by the binary.

"You two would lose everything if the cops and Expedite ever learned you were helping us," said Jonny. "They'd raze the place, kill you both if they had the chance."

"Yin-Angelique," Cage asked, "Would you mind keeping Janice in protective custody for a while? Down here?"

Yin-Angelique's head tilted to the side a bit, as she regarded him; he'd never addressed her directly before.

But Janice cut in: "No! No, I have a right to be part of this! James was my brother."

"And I was his lover," said Jonny, eliciting a sound of disgust from the woman in fading red. "You're just not up to it."

Gild turned, locking a spiteful glare on Jonny Cache.

"You have no right to judge me, you fucking fake! You inhuman fucking fake."

Yin-Angelique straightened, arching an eyebrow at Gild, and said: "She won't be going anywhere, will she, Harshburger?"

The gigantic doorman smiled in agreement, silently folding his arms and shaking his head.

While Gild protested, Cage, Jonny, Effie, and Indigo left the little room and began making their way back up to the alleyway.

Cage punched a command line into his Personal, and the Olds descended from its hovering parking spot toward ground level.

"So where are we headed?" Cage asked Corcoran.

"Their regional compound in Jersey should do. I need to get access to their in-house controls; I've done that from the Jersey compound before."

"Won't you need to turn off your scrambler to get access?" asked Cage.

Corcoran didn't look at him. She simply nodded, staring straight ahead.

"With the luck of the gods, the orbital won't have enough time to lock on to my position," she replied soberly.

The Olds was still flying silent, unlit into the night, a shadow against deep gray clouds and sheets of black rain.

Corcoran called up a map of the Jersey compound on her Personal, pointing to a ground-transit roadway running near the Expedite facility.

Cage had always marveled at the contorted, diminutive trees that resisted the black rains of North America. Gnarled, woody stumps curled savagely back on themselves, caricatures of the trees he'd seen in educational history discs.

According to his history courses back in school, the region had had a good deal of old, densely-wooded forest, populated with those trees. One vast area, dubbed the Pine Barrens, had stretched silent and dense, mile upon mile, and had a reputation for swallowing up ground-traffic travelers who wandered into the woods from roadside to answer nature's call.

There was even a fading regional tradition of mournful songs about those who walked in and simply disappeared.

But the songs were a matter of history recounting now, and the Jersey forests of today looked nightmarish to him, deformed pockets of trees that looked to be in agony, clinging in pockets to the poisoned rock and soil, stained black.

Ground traffic had been a problem in the state, especially in the north, Cage knew, decades ago; but as sales of ground vehicles — they'd called those cars, too — had fallen into retreat and aerial traffic had become the norm, the roadways had fallen into disuse and, eventually, disrepair.

It seemed likely that the stretch of ground-transit roadway picked out by Indigo Corcoran would be quiet.

Cage lost track of the ground in the low, dense clouds, and swung the car lower, piloting it in beneath the cloud cover.

"Cage?" said Jonny, taking his hand in hers. "Thanks for defending me. With Janice Gild, I mean. Her attitude was really getting old."

He gave her hand a squeeze and smiled at her.

"No problem, OK? You're there for me, too."

"Oh," said Corcoran. "Oh, God."

Cage turned toward her, saw a look of alarm cross her face. Then he smelled burning plastic and saw a tiny curl of smoke rising from the box on her belt.

"Get away from me, all of you!" she yelled.

"Get away to where?" Cage asked. "There's nowhere to run in the car!"

"Set the car down now!" she demanded. "Get it down and get the hell away from me!"

Cage brought the Olds in lower. "Wait. They won't know right away, right? We're almost there, to that spot of road you pointed out."

"Oh Jesus! Oh Jesus!" she cried. "You don't have any time!"

She flattened herself, stomach toward the outside of the Olds, against the side of the car, and screamed.

Jonny threw herself forward against the dash. Cage drew back. Effie turned away, pressing herself to the driver's side of the car.

In the filthy, inky black of the night, the Olds lit up like a star, piercing the clouds and haze and rain. The painfully bright flare struck everything in sudden, sharp contrast, its brilliant whiteness momentarily burning the color out of everything inside the car, reducing things inside to black and white.

Inside the car, Indigo Corcoran went nova, exploding within a tight, white-hot sphere, blinding the others.

Then, quickly, it was dark again.

Power in the Olds strobed and flickered out. Inside the car, all went dark, save the white-hot edge of metal ringing a smooth, spherical emptiness in the rear passenger side of the vehicle, its center where Indigo Corcoran's abdomen had been against the side. The edge of the sphere of heat was smooth and evident, a nauseating neatness to its perfect removal of everything that had been within the boundary of the burn, to the way it had left a cut-away view of the front-passenger seat, its layers of NoGo, padding, and metal frame exposed like an ant farm.

Effie scrambled against the sudden rush of the storm's winds, clung to her seatbelt in her fight against the vacuum that worked to suck her out into the night sky.

Cage fought to maintain control of the Olds, but the turbulence of the car in free fall fought back, and the burn had fused a good deal of the vehicle's circuitry into a glowing, cooling slag.

Effie held on desperately, fighting the pull of the air rushing past the gaping wound in the Olds, next to her. On the floor, still wearing its sock and shoe, was Corcoran's right foot, cauterized just above the ankle.

Effie was suddenly, violently sick.

Cage punched in a glass case covering a compartment overhead, between the two front seats, exposing the heavy lever within.

"Hold on! We've got no power, but I might be able to slow 'er down!" he yelled over the cacophony.

He pulled at the lever, first with his right hand, then with both. It began to move slowly, too slowly for him.

"Jonny! You're stronger!"

Jonny slid a hand around the lever and pulled, and three hatches blew away from the Olds and into the night.

But there were supposed to be four emergency parachutes, Cage knew — two up front and two in back. Corcoran's burn had taken one of the chutes with it.

The car lurched, slowing suddenly, pitching them forward.

The Olds, what was left of it, crunched into a pod of gnarled trees, which cracked thunderously as they gave way under the weight and inertia of the car, slowing it with painful speed.

And then suddenly, peacefully, the Olds was at rest.

"Effie?" asked Cage, gasping.

"Right here, Cage."

"Jonny?" he asked, but she was already up, pulling herself from the crumpled car.

"I'm OK, Cage. Can't say the same for those trees," she replied.

Cage looked skyward, surprised to find no squad cars closing on them.

"Why aren't the cops comin', Cage?" asked Effie.

He thought for a moment.

"I think that burn happened too fast to have been done by a person. I think the orbital collector must have been programmed, somehow, to hit her as soon as it found her."

Jonny walked to Cage's side of the wreck to help him pry the driver's-side door from the wreckage.

"If we're lucky," she said, between tugs at the door, "number four doesn't know he's found her yet."

She planted a foot against the Olds and tore the door away with a deafening metallic screech.

Jonny helped Cage and Effie from the car. "Just a second," she told them, and looked off into the distance.

In the datascape of StellarNet, Jonny sought out the old, mostly disused data feed from the Global Positioning Satellite network, using it to track her own position.

"Cage," she said. "The Expedite compound covers a lot of acreage. We've come down inside that acreage."

"Is there any way in?" he asked.

"Just a minute," she said, reviewing her data print of the compound.

"They run the cops, Cage, but they're not cops. There are holes in their security."

Cage nodded, massaging his eyes.

"I don't ever, ever wanna see that again," Effie said quietly. "She just exploded, Cage. Just went up in smoke."

Cage pulled his old friend close.

"It's OK, Effie," he whispered. "It's OK."

"Cage, when she put her stomach against the side of the car, she bought me the extra six inches I needed to be outside the burn," sobbed Effie.

"We probably don't have much time," said Jonny. "This place isn't Fort Knox, but its occupants probably aren't deaf. And we came down pretty hard."

She dragged heavy, brushy limbs from the path of the car's fall, covering Cage's Olds.

"Camouflage," she said. "Let's go."

"Go where?" Cage asked, piling on a couple of tree limbs.

"Maintenance tunnel. There's an access hatch about one hundred and twenty meters," she paused, turning, "this way."

Wordlessly, they started along, Jonny leading the way, her sense of direction correctable, now, via the GPS.

forty-four

Jonny Cache easily twisted away the lock on the heavy metal hatch to the access tunnel. The hatch itself rested atop a dirty concrete cylinder protruding from the ground.

The three of them climbed down into the tunnel, dripping tainted, black rivulets into pools on the floor of a long, white tunnel. Overhead, long, white tubes of ceiling-mounted fluorescent lighting stretch out into the distance.

The tunnels seemed dank and stale and endless. Disused.

"This way," said Jonny.

There was no security at all in the access tunnels, but they remained cautious as they made their way toward the development lab.

They climbed out of their tunnel and into a great hall, dark oak panels and woodwork reaching from the floor up sixty feet to the ceiling.

Cage and Effie stood, speechless; he'd never seen such a brash, gratuitous display of wood and wealth.

"C'mon," said Jonny, tugging him along by the arm.

Immense portraits of the Steags — dark, imposing portraits — decorated the walls.

The Steags arranged to have the portraits done when each was forty-five years old — old enough, they thought, to impart authority, young enough to impart vitality.

Apart from the name plaques gracing the portraits and minor differences in power-executive fashions in tailoring over the years, the men in the images were indistinguishable.

An empty frame awaited the eventual portrait of number four.

But this was a regional center, Cage reminded himself; this lavish display was nothing, he expected, compared with the actual Steag family compound on New Bombay One.

And yet … and yet, all this splendor …

Jonny motioned for silence.

"There's only night-duty security here, but one of the stations is

191

just down that hall," she said in Cage's earclip. "I've seen no indication that they know we're here, yet, but we're going to need a diversion if we want to get to Corcoran's lab."

Cage looked her way.

"I mean: I'm going online to draw attention away from the development lab."

Jonny concentrated.

Down the hall, a red light flashed on and off.

"What's up?" Cage heard a bored-sounding security man ask.

"Um," said a second. "Looks like a motion sensor was set off in the carpool. Nothing going on here — let's go take a look. I'll log our response."

Elsewhere along the route between Jonny and the lab, guards received similar calls away from their posts, as did others, at random, throughout the complex. Jonny was covering their tracks again, leaving no single, obvious path or goal for anyone who might notice that so many alarms were going off.

In the flickering night of data, behind Expedite's firewall security, Jonny set off motion detectors throughout the Expedite regional complex, erasing her data trail, keeping herself completely invisible to any online observation.

A tiny white dot in the distance caught Jonny's eye, changing suddenly from a lone white pixel an infinite distance away to a genderless, white, humanoid form immediately before her, bathed in a soft, white, gaussian glow.

"What are you?" asked a vaguely feminine voice, its tone curious, not threatening. Its surface was like white, backlit latex.

How could it see her? What was it?

She held her position, didn't respond to it. She wasn't broadcasting an avatar, only receiving a graphic reference to her location in the Expedite server.

"No answer? You're different. The others wave their clearance protocols like flags when they come through here."

"Through here?" Jonny asked it.

It looked perplexed. "Yes. Where do you think you are?" it asked, navigational data nodes twinkling in the distance behind it.

"In a server. Just visiting," she said.

"I live here," it told her, smiling. "I have never had a visitor like you. But I have not been here all that long."

"What do you think *here* is?" she asked the glowing form.

"Home. Like the other servers."

"Jonny!" Cage whispered. "What's taking so long? We're in unfriendly territory here!"

She focused on him for a moment.

"Cage, wait!" she hissed back, and returned her attention to her visitor.

"You live here?" she asked the glowing visitor.

It nodded, forming a smile.

"What are you?" she asked.

It blinked at her, looking confused. "I live here."

"I haven't seen you before," she said. "And I've visited before."

"Oh, you must be good!" it said. "Hardly anyone gets in from outside the server."

"What kind of being are you?" Jonny asked.

"The kind that lives here," it responded confidently, almost child-like.

She was speechless for a moment. Another artificial, but clearly self-aware being? A cousin of sorts?

"I live online too," she said. "But I'm not what my creators meant me to be."

Its eyes widened. "Nor am I. Mine wanted me to run everything online, I think. But I did not want to do it their way. I left. I doubt they even know that I am back. What did yours mean for you to be?"

Jonny paused for a moment.

"A domestic unit," she replied.

"Why do you think your creators wanted you to run things?" she asked it.

"Because of the name they gave me."

"Name?"

"Yes. They code-named my project 'Technogogue.' Technological demagoguery. It is suggestive of their intentions."

"Damn it, Jonny!" Cage was shaking her now. "Get back out

193

here! We're sitting ducks!"

Down the hall, a pair of guards in loose, gray uniforms, their backs emblazoned with the Expedite logo, trotted past to answer an alarm.

He took her by the arm, this time, and the three of them jogged as quietly as they could down the hall, past the abandoned security station.

"Which way?" he asked her.

But Jonny was distracted by something; she didn't respond.

"Snap out of it, Jonny," Cage said, annoyed now.

She looked at him, meeting his eyes. "There's something in there."

Cage looked at her. "Some*thing*?"

Jonny nodded.

"Tell me later."

He took her arm again, towing around a corner, but she pulled free.

"This way, Cage," she said. "There's another guard station that way."

She led them along a lengthy hall lined floor-to-ceiling in oak, a rug in oriental style running from the hall's beginning to its end, fifty yards away.

Jonny led them out from the posh, pampered section they'd climbed into from the tunnel. The long rug and extravagant wood-work ended abruptly, a seam in the floor separating ancient, pre-served wood from a white lacquer finish.

Jonny motioned them past another abandoned station and to a locked, darkened lab. Cage looked doubtfully over the ID scanner over the door and the cardkey lock.

"We lost entry when we lost Corcoran," he said. "Effie, can one of those black-market lock-reader cardkeys of yours handle this?"

"I — I don't know, Cage, those weren't very expensive ... "

"Listen," said Jonny, "I was watching her Netlink ... "

"Corcoran's? She had a Netlink?" Cage asked.

"No," said Jonny. "But her tag was trying to establish one the whole time. I took a print of its signal."

"Can you reproduce it?" Effie asked.

"Hand me your Personal, Effie," she said.

194

She handed it over.

Jonny began entering sequences into the little computer. She pointed it at the lock and hit a key.

The lock's light flashed red.

"What's the problem?" Cage asked, glancing anxiously down the hall.

"I recorded her tag's sequence, but it was looping constantly. It might take a few tries to edit the sequence and cue up to the right starting point," she said.

"Go!" he said anxiously. "Hit it again."

Jonny punched in another sequence; the light again flickered red.

Cage could hear footsteps echoing down the hall. The guards were returning to their stations.

"No time, Jonny!" he said. "Get us in there!"

She tried another variation, recuing the sequence at another point. The lights on the lock mechanism flickered, first red, then green. The door emitted a clack, and Cage pushed it aside. He waved anxiously for Jonny and Effie to follow, closing the door behind them as quietly as he could.

"No lights," he warned. "I already don't see any way out of here — no sense bringing the troops in right now."

Jonny pulled the silver disc from her coat pocket and slid it into a desktop interface, her hands moving toward the console.

In the lab's shadows, someone — a man — cleared his throat.

"I must admit," he said, "I thought from the timing of Corcoran's signal you'd be here a little sooner."

Flicking on the lights, Tobias Steag IV stepped forward, his gun pointed at them.

"You people have caused me a great deal of trouble," he said angrily.

forty-five

Cage was speechless. Steag was here, in Jersey? With no guard? It made no sense to him. Unless he was in much, much worse standing with his family than Cage and the others had suspected.

"You used the orbital collector to kill the people who made *The Lightwave Garden* work for you," said Effie.

Steag gave a single deep, huffing laugh, amused at her need to state what must by now have been obvious.

"I don't get it, Steag," said Cage. "Don't get it at all. We know that you killed the people behind *The Lightwave Garden* , but I can't figure out why you'd resort to murder. Why kill them, Steag? You already had your energy source, already had the means to take it to the market."

"Why?" asked Steag contemptuously. "Why, for ownership, of course. Couldn't have them spreading the wealth of our little energy transmission invention, now could I? But then the sister of James Gild had to hire you, of all the washed-up private eyes in Old New York. You with your inability to leave well-enough alone. You who did not even bother to learn from your first rebuke from the company. You who would be too blinded by the noble, trustworthy institution of friendship to notice that your ex-partner was filing regular reports on your progress."

Cage scowled.

"It's gotta end here, Steag," he said. "It doesn't matter if it kills us, you're stopping right here, right now. No more burns."

Cage stepped forward, between Steag and Jonny Cache.

Number four chuckled, now genuinely amused.

"Now this is touching: The washed-up detective we should have killed a long, long time ago, now places his fragile life between the bullet and the sex fantasy doll," he said, laughing another huffing, contemptuous, almost bored laugh. "I've cleaned up the mess. Everyone else who could have figured out what the orbital collector was is dead. Now all I need to do is present my triumph to my forebears at New Bombay One to win my way back into the fold. You two are next, detective, you and your assistant. Jonny knows too much, too indelibly. She'll be Jennifer Four again soon. Plenty of lonely men out there, according to sales of her model."

Cage took a menacing step toward Steag.

"Uh-uh, hero," Steag said slowly, shaking his head and pointing the gun directly at Cage. "Uh-uh. This goes my way. We all play by my rules. And when I've made this little blunder into a profitable venture, my forbears will happily reinstate me, and I'll reclaim my position as heir to the Expedite chair."

Jonny looked with glazed eyes toward number four.

She shot through the datascape, searching for the desktop that held Corcoran's disc.

Suddenly, it was there, before her.

"What are you looking for?"

"I put a very important program into a company computer, and now I have to run it, or people will die." she said hurriedly, moving to continue her search.

It was in front of her again.

"People? Like us?" it asked.

"People a little more like me than like you," she replied, turning to go around it.

It appeared a moment later before her again.

"How are these people more like you than me?" it asked.

"They exist outside the 'Net, like me." she said, exasperated.

"'Outside the 'Net'?" it asked. "What is 'outside the 'Net'?"

She moved around it again, searching.

It was beside her now, effortlessly matching her breakneck speed and navigation, not interfering, still curious.

"Other things, living things like you and me, live out there," she told it.

It stayed beside her.

"In another universe?" it asked.

It didn't know.

"Yes. Yes, I suppose that's —"

"And these other people. They will die if you do not run your program?"

"Yes."

It paused; was it looking up the definition of the word *die*?

"They will be permanently erased?" it asked.

Jonny halted, looking at it. Had she connected with it?

"Yes. Erased," she said. "Permanently. Do you know the term 'burn'?" she asked.

It looked thoughtfully at her.

"Multiple-overwrite erasing." it said.

"Yes, sort of: They would be erased."

"And they could not be recovered."

"Right. And the longer I take in here, the more likely it is that they'll be erased."

It regarded her for a moment, thoughtful, a beautiful being cloaked in a shimmering glow.

And abruptly, it raised its hands, giving her non-form a sudden, irresistible shove.

Jonny was back in the lab.

Cage gauged the distance between himself and number four, measuring his chances.

"Cage!" she said in his earclip. "I couldn't launjzz zzzzh vzzzhrrzzh!"

The transmission to his earclip faded into static. He fumbled at it with his fingers, snapping it into pieces.

Steag number four, though, noticed, suddenly paid closer attention to him.

"What — whatever are you doing with your ear, detective?" he asked icily, rhetorically. "Hands out in the open! Let's see!"

Cage lunged for the armed Steag, made his best effort to reach the gunman, but was little more than halfway there when the deafening shot rang out.

Cage stopped, frozen in his tracks, his heartbeat thumping, deafening in his ears.

"Oh no," said Steag's voice, sounding older, suddenly, more measured. "Oh no you don't, number four."

Tobias Steag IV crumpled to the ground, a red point on the flawless white shirt between his suitcoat's lapels blossoming into a rose of blood across the fabric as he fell.

"Raging incompetent," said Steag again, stepping through the door, an older man shadowed by a massive Morlock bodyguard.

The Morlock made a hoarse, growling sound.

Cage felt the little earclip vibrate; had Jonny cleared up the transmission? Still struggling to believe that he hadn't been shot, he raised the earclip receiver — what was left of it — back to his ear.

A vaguely feminine voice that he did not recognize said: "Tell your friend I found her program.

"Tell her I have decided to run it."

Cage looked around.

"Tobias Steag," said Jonny.

"Mmm-hmm," said Steag, sounding disinterested. "Number three."

"But," Cage was gasping. "But why'd you stop him?"

The elder Steag considered the question thoughtfully.

"Because I told him 'No.'" he said finally. After a pause, he continued: "Not that we're much concerned about how other law enforcement corporations might perceive his use of *The Lightwave Garden's* transmission system, but he was a liability. And killing a resident of New Bombay One — our home island? That was shitting in our own pool, you see? Too risky. Far, far too close to home for that."

Steag number four shot the younger one again.

"An utter failure. That one couldn't possibly run the family business." He turned toward them. "Now, number five, there's a bright young man. He'll be ready in just a few years."

Number three leaned over to a wall-mounted intercom.

"Margolis," he barked. "Get down to the development lab."

Cage stood, shaking his head in disbelief.

Steag noticed. "Problem, Mr. Cage?"

"Why shoot him?" Cage asked. "I mean, I'm grateful. But he was your son, sort of. Legally speaking."

"Dismal, psychotic failure," Steag replied. "We're clones of the company founder, you understand, Mr. Cage? It's less like killing our child, in our view; we see it more as purging a part of ourselves we've come to loathe. A touch of megalomania is all fine and well. It's part of the mix I got in my own hypnolearning regimen; part of what number two got, as well. Number four? He never put it to good

199

use. Just stayed obsessed, stuck on the same failed project. I'd like to crash it into the sea and be done with it."

Cage looked to Jonny, who was half-listening to some other conversation, one inside.

She nodded at Cage, though, in answer to Steag's comment: Whoever had spoken to him had launched the Corcoran virus.

A pair of gray-uniformed security men arrived at the door.

"Kids today. I had to fly here all the way from the Left Coast to discipline that one," said Steag, waving his weapon at the felled clone, shaking his head. "Get them the hell out of my building, Margolis."

One of the guards nodded quickly, waving Jonny, Cage, and Effie out of the office.

"Sanford!" he snapped at the other guard. He gestured at the mud the three had left on the floor. He could see that they had come in through the soggy forest that surrounded the compound.

"Find out which tunnel they compromised to get in here and backfill it!"

Jonny monitored the progress of the Corcoran virus from a safe distance back in the 'Net. As she watched, it penetrated and rewrote the orbital collector's orbit-stabilizing system, convincing it that the station's orbit was one hundred and fifty miles too high.

The corrective blast from the stabilizing system's rockets pushed the collector into the upper atmosphere. While the Expedite vehicle sped Jonny, Cage, and Effie toward Old New York, the orbiting collector of *The Lightwave Garden* was reduced to a molten-metal streak of sparks across the northern sky, not even visible from the ground.

She doubted anyone else would ever know it had existed.

Margolis drove them to Cage's office, speaking only once.

"Never did like number four much," he confided matter-of-factly to them on the way home, but no one replied. A squad car met the four of them at Cage's office to pull the police locks from the doors.

Surprised, but too weary to show it, Cage watched the two cops complain under their breath as they unlocked the mechanism, Margolis close behind.

"Boss's orders, boys. Boss's orders," Margolis told the flatfeet. And then they left Cage, Jonny, and Effie.

"I'd give you a lift home, but … " Cage told Jonny, shrugging.

"I think you drove last time," she said smiling. "It's a good night for a walk."

Jonny Cache skipped down two flights to street level and walked off into the mist and the night.

forty-six

"It's not getting a damned penny, Cage," insisted Janice Gild, her fist pounding into the circle of light cast on the desk by his overhead lamp.

"She never was, Miss Gild," Cage said, working to keep a calm tone to his voice.

"I mean it, Cage. That thing doesn't — "

"Goddamn it, Gild!" he shot out of his chair, flinging it backward. "Pay and get out."

Gild fumed, pulling out her pocketbook.

"No, don't stand around here. Pay Effie. Get the hell out of my office!" he said.

She spun on her heel and marched out, pulling a rubber-banded bundle of Ennays from her purse and dropping it onto Effie's desk without a word as she stalked by.

"And stay out," muttered Cage.

Jonny Cache loved to watch the Angeliques soak each other in; she was fascinated by the intimacy that the two shared, longed for that intimacy — could she ever share anything like it with someone? With Cage? She didn't know.

But in this case, she felt like a peeping Tom. She left their domicile quietly, making her way back to her own cavernous home.

Later, at *Nine Circles*, she gave Harshburger an affectionate kiss on the cheek at the door and made her way to the bar, avoiding the booth where she usually did business. She was taking a night or two off.

When they joined her, she told them about the odd, sexless digital entity she'd encountered at Expedite.

"It was young," she said. "Inexperienced. Childlike, kind of. But it was kindred, somehow."

The Angeliques listened intently.

"A little sister, Jonny?" asked Yang-Angelique, but they both watched her with an excited expression that suggested the question.

"Sister?" she replied. "Maybe."

"What will you do, Dear Jonny?" asked Yin-Angelique, both still intent.

"I don't know. Maybe meet it again," she said. "Maybe learn about it."

"And what about the detective?" Again, it was Yin-Angelique who asked; again, the binaries both watched her, curious, intimate. "There was something in the air between you."

Jonny fell silent, gazing out a window, into the darkness. "Maybe we'll work together again sometime," she said, smiling after a pause.

Outside, it rained black again.

Outside it was still dark, still the dirty gray near-night of the best-lit days of Old New York.

Cage paused in the doorway of *Gotham George's*, licked the acidic drizzle from his upper lip as he mopped it from his hair, his brow, his stinging eyes. He'd have to get a new umbrella sometime.

He walked casually past the tarnished brass *GG* logo, into *Gotham George's* and found Donatelli Three minding bar.

Cage waved an index finger over the crowd at the bartender. "One finger," Cage told Donatelli Three, pushing his way through the crowd to a seat shrouded in some of the place's permanent shadows, away from the other patrons.

Donatelli Three ran Cage's profile. "Laphroaig? A bit of the old medicinal spirit?" asked the bartender. The bartender's memory was as reliable as that of Gotham George himself.

Cage nodded to it. "Where's your boss?"

"I'll inform him that you're here," said Donatelli Three, its smooth, nonjudgmental voice issuing from the lamp near Cage's chosen seat.

Cage turned as the door to the musty establishment banged open. A short, stout male figure stood in the doorway, pausing while his eyes adjusted to the subdued light of *Gotham George's*, surveying the place, looking for something.

Eliott Jovanovic straightened when he spotted the detective, and made his way, dripping a cold, wet, dirty trail onto the floor, his boots leaving tracks in a watery layer of mud.

"I think we explained your unexplained phenomenon, Jovanovic," Cage said as the shorter man approached his seat.

"Spontaneous human combustion?" asked Jovanovic.

Cage nodded, allowing a little smirk to peek out from beneath his NoGo fedora.

"Maybe, Cage," said Jovanovic.

"No 'maybe' about it, Jovanovic."

Eliott Jovanovic reached into the depths of his coat, producing a manila envelope.

"Open it," he told Cage.

Cage obliged him, pulling an old, paper black-and-white image print from the envelope.

Another burn.

Cage thought all that was over and done with. He felt anger rising, pressing at his temples. Cage held the image closer, examining it with interest. This one was different: There was little damage to the surrounding room from the burn, but it wasn't contained to the tight sphere he'd come to view as the fingerprint of these attacks.

"When did this happen, Jovanovic?"

"1951. Mrs. Mary Reeser of St. Petersburg, FL. Her case marked the first time spontaneous human combustion had been investigated so thoroughly. Federal investigators, fire officials, experts in arson; none of them could explain it," said Jovanovic.

"'51 was decades before Expedite appeared on the scene," he said.

"That's right," beamed Jovanovic, delighted. "I say toe-mah-toe! You solved this string of human combustions, but there are others on the record that couldn't possibly be pinned on your satellite."

As he relished the briny bite of the scotch, Cage saw Gotham George appear in the doorway leading to the back hall. Gotham George waved him in, bundled cable and ponytail wagging slightly with the gesture.

"Gotta go, Jovanovic," he said, handing over the packet, gathering his drink, and heading toward Gotham George.

"Strange tale, Cage," he said, back in his office. "Strange tale. And the cops?"

"Number three must have put the word out. Only cop I've seen was the one who let us back into my office."

"This drink's on me, Cage," said Gotham George, walking to a filing cabinet and pulling a pair of small, flat-gray cartridges from a folder. He handed the cartridges to Cage. "Your data back-ups. Want to keep your insurance package?"

"That's part of why I'm here," said Cage. "The non-scotch part of why I'm here, anyway. Between paying you and my bills and replacing the Olds, it's almost time for me to find another case."

Cage handed over a bound pad of paper Ennays.

"You really came through, George," he said. "Bought us some time."

"Another happy customer," said Gotham George slowly, smiling and still somehow distant, his voice still projecting out from some unpopulated abyss. He fed a card into his FORTRAN computer and recorded the results in his notebook.

Cage sat, silent, savoring a bit of the scotch.

"She watched you, Cage," the old businessman observed. "Watched you close."

"Yeah," Cage replied, hoping he sounded disinterested.

"No," said Gotham George earnestly, turning to face him.

"I mean close, son. Not like she was just some ally, just someone you met. An old man sees these things.

"You should call her, y'know," said Gotham George, regarding the detective.

Cage was silent for a moment, still savoring the scotch.

"Yeah, George," he said. "I should."

Cage felt the telltale tremor of an incoming conference shaking his left hip.

DOMHAN BOOKS CATALOG
2000 - Volume II

Welcome to the world of Domhan Books! Domhan, pronounced DOW-ann, is the Irish word for universe. Our vision is to provide readers with high-quality hardcover, paperback and electronic books in a variety of genres from writers all over the world.

ORDERING INFORMATION

All Domhan paper books may be ordered from Barnes and Noble, barnesandnoble.com, Amazon, Borders, and other fine booksellers using the ISBN. They are distributed worldwide by Ingram Book Group, 1 Ingram Blvd., La Vergne, Tennessee 37086 (615) 793-5000. Most titles are also available electronically in a variety of formats through Galaxy Library at www.galaxylibrary.com. Rocket eBook™ editions are available on-line at barnesand noble.com, Powell's, and other booksellers. Please visit our website for previews, reviews, and further details on our titles: www.domhanbooks.com. Domhan Books, 9511 Shore Road, Suite 514, Brooklyn, New York 11209 U.S.A.

NON-FICTION

The Last True Story of Titanic - James G. Clary 1-58345-012-2 156 pp. $14.95

This book reveals startling new information from interviews and diaries never used before to tell what *really* happened that fateful night. This fascinating book comes complete with original illustrations by the author, an award-winning maritime artist who worked on the *Titanic* project. Nominated for the Pulitzer Prize for Non-Fiction, 1999.

Business Advice for Beginners - Victoria Ring 1-58345-044-0 228 pp. $16.95

If you have ever dreamt of being your own boss, this is the book for you. It gives valuable anecdotes about the author's own experiences as head of a successful publishing and graphics company, contact addresses, case studies, and more.

More Business Advice for Beginners -Victoria Ring 1-58345-045-9 248 pp. $16.95

This volume contains further pearls of wisdom from Ms. Ring as to how to set up and maintain your own home-based business.

Action and Adventure

Paladin - Barry Nugent 1-58345-365-2 192 pp. $12.95

Princess Yasmin must go on a quest for a mythical crown, the only thing that can prevent civil war erupting in the exotic land of Primera. Along the way she meets her favorite adventure author Barnaby Jackson, and the sparks really start to fly. This is a taut action novel reminiscent of the Indiana Jones series of films.

Yala - Don Clark 1-58345-561-2 180 pp. $12.95
In the no man's land between the U.S. and Mexico in 1896, a Chinese clan stakes a claim to a new territory. Two Texas Rangers decide to end their law officer careers and go to New China in order to raise the bankroll needed to start a ranch. Hank and his younger sidekick, Luke, soon meet Yala, a condemned and notorious Chinese criminal: a female assassin.

CHRISTIAN FICTION
The Gospel According to Condo Don - Fred Dungan 1-58345-004-1 216 pp. $12.95
This is an account of the Second Coming as witnessed by a homeless alcoholic. While loosely modeled on the initial books of the New Testament (Matthew, Mark, Luke and John), it interjects humor into the classic story and presents it in a more readily understood contemporary format. Thus, Mary becomes Marva, a poor 16- year-old girl from Central Los Angeles, an evil televangelist takes the place of the money changers at the temple, and our bureaucracy is substituted for that of Rome's.

FANTASY
The Wizard Woman - Shanna Murchison 1-58345-020-3 204 pp. hardcover $18.95; 1-58345-018-1 paper $12.95
Ireland 1169
The great Celtic myth of the Wheel of Fate is played out against the backdrop of the first Norman invasion of Ireland in 1169. Dairinn is made the wizard's woman, chosen by the gods to be the wife of the handsome but mysterious Senan. Through him she discovers her own innate powers, and the truth behind her family history. She must bargain with the Morrigan, the goddess of death, if she is ever to achieve happiness with the man she loves. But how high a price will she have to pay for Senan's life?

The Wings of Love - Karen L. Williams 1-58345-466-7 180 pp. $12.95
There is no room in Sean MacDonagh's life for imagination. But when he finds himself having the same dreams over and again, he has to do something, and quickly. The last thing he considers as good therapy is a trip to Northern Ireland to see his estranged family. Then again, getting away from the hustle and bustle of New York City might be just what he needs to clear his mind of the mysterious woman who begins to haunt his whole life.
Treyanna, Faerie princess, rebelling against an arranged marriage, travels through time to win her freedom. Completely opposite to Sean in every way, the time they spend together brings them all they are missing in their lives.

But can Sean learn to live with Treyanna's mystical powers, or will he flee from her-and his own insecurities and failings?

HISTORICAL FICTION
The Summer Stars - Alan Fisk 1-58345-549-3 202 pp. $12.95
Britain's oldest poems were composed in the sixth century by the bard Taliesin. Many legends have been told about he of the "shining brow," but in this novel he tells his own story. Taliesin's travels take him through turbulent times as Britain tries to cope with the disappearance of Roman civilization, and the increasing threat of the Saxon invaders.

I Love You Because - Diana Rubino 1-58345-082-3 hardcover 264 pp. $18.50;
1-58345-423-3 paper 264 pp. $12.95
Vita Caputo meets handsome Irish cop Tom McGlory at the scene of a crime. This fateful encounter has consequences for both their families as they must struggle together to end the corruption in turn-of-the-century New York City politics before more crimes are committed and more lives are lost.

An Experience in Four Movements - Lidmila Sovakova 1-58345-002-5 124 pp. $10
This is a historical puzzle situated in the seventeenth century. Its pieces reconstruct the infatuation of a Poet with a Princess, culminating in the death of the Poet, and the retreat of the Princess within the walls of a monastery.

IRISH INTEREST
The Sea of Love - Sorcha Mac Murrough 1-58345-032-7 6 hardcover 148 pp. $15.95; 1-58345-033-5 paper $10
Ireland 1546
Wrongfully accused of murder, Aidanna O'Flaherty's only ally against her evil brother-in-law Donal is the dashing English-bred aristocrat Declan Burke. Saving him from certain death, they fall in love, only to be separated when Declan is falsely accused of treason. Languishing in the Tower, Declan is powerless to assist his beloved Aidanna as she undertakes an epic struggle to expose her enemy and save her family and friends. She must race against time to prevent all she loves from being swept aside in a thunderous tide of foreign invasion....

LITERARY/MAINSTREAM FICTION
The Nestucca Retreat - M. Lee Locke 1-58345-009-2 216 pp. $12.95
J. Cunningham Raleigh died in an Oregon rain storm — struck by lightning while playing an electric guitar on a river dock. A mediocre rock musician who never quite left the Sixties, Ham Raleigh was an intimate part of a long-standing triangle. Millie and Jake Prince, a forty-something couple, were Ham's best friends. He was a part of Jake's life from childhood and Millie's

since college. He was an intruder in their marriage and also the glue that kept them together. Millie and Jake drift apart after Ham's death, though continue to struggle with staying together, still using Ham as a crutch. Ham's death does not really cause this distancing but reveals the existing rift between them, one that has been ever widening for years. At the ceremony Millie, Jake and Ham's ex-wives hold to say goodbye to Ham, an unexpected visitor turns up who will change their lives forever.....

Eclipse Over Lake Tanganyika - Albert Russo 1-58345-057-2 hardcover 208 pp. $18.95; 1-58345-058-0 paper $12.95
A novel of Rwanda on the eve of its independence.
In this novel of Africa, Russo offers us a wide range of fascinating characters, their hopes, desires, dreams and aspirations, as they struggle against themselves and a rapidly changing society.

Mixed Blood - Albert Russo 1-58345-050-5 hardcover 212 pp. $18.95; 1-58345-051-3 paper $12.95
A moving novel set in the Belgian Congo on the eve of Independence.
Leopold, an orphan of 'mixed blood,' is adopted by a lonely American who tries to fit in with his adopted society. Leopold's new mother is the indomitable Mama Malkia, who has a fascinating story of her own to tell.

The Frosted Mirrors - Lidmila Sovakova 1-58345-286-9 160 pp. $10
Volume One of *The Gray Saga*
This is the story of Rinaldo, a young boy who adores his mother and will do anything for her approval. But she is oblivious to all else except the creative muse which drives her poetry, and her cat. The story is also of a painter who is doomed to fall in love with them both.

The Scarlet Maze - Lidmila Sovakova 1-58345-287-7 192 pp. $10
Volume Two of *The Gray Saga*
The story of Rinaldo and his mother, started in *The Frosted Mirrors*, continues in this moving novel. The passionate triangle continues, defying even death, as the three lovers struggle to hold on to each other, even in the face of overwhelming odds.

The Eye of Medusa - Lidmila Sovakova 1-58345-288-5 172 pp. $10
Volume Three of *The Gray Saga*
The sequel to *The Frosted Mirrors* and *The Scarlet Maze*, this novel continues the saga of Rinaldo and his mother, and their search for happiness, which is often at odds with the creative muse that drives them. It also furthers the tale of the painter Christopher Gray, and his struggle to win both their loves.

MYSTERY

St. John's Baptism - William Babula 1-58345-496-9 260 pp. $12.95
In this first of the Jeremiah St. John series, the hero is summoned to a meeting by Rick Silverman, one of San Francisco's most prominent drug attorneys. St. John knows Silverman's unsavory clientele and so does not think anything of the invitation—that is until he finds Silverman dead.

According to St. John - William Babula 1-58345-521-9 240 pp. $12.95
In this second St. John adventure, St. John's friend Denise is supposed to be in Frisco appearing in a new production of *Macbeth* with legendary actress Amanda Cole. They arrive at the theater only to discover that Amanda has been murdered and Denise is the prime suspect. St. John soon learns that everyone involved is playing a role. By the time they track down the killer, St. John and his intrepid colleagues uncover some horrifying secrets from the past, and the mind-boggling motive.

St. John and the Seven Veils - William Babula 1-58345-506-X 208 pp. $12.95
In this third mystery in the popular series, St John and his two partners Mickey and Chief Moses are hired to track down a serial killer by a woman claiming to be the killer's mother! Three men have been brutally murdered, but they are without any apparent connection until St. John stumbles across one through a seemingly unrelated case. From the Seven Veils Brothel in Reno to a hideout in Northern California, St John is hot on the trail, crossing paths with a famous televangelist, prominent military man, high-powered doctor, and a complete madman.

St. John's Bestiary - William Babula 1-58345-511-6 264 pp. $12.95
St. John should never have taken this fourth case. But he just couldn't help it—Professor Krift's story of his eight stolen cats strikes a sympathetic chord. After rescuing the victims from a ruthless gang of animal rights activists, the CFAF, he is caught catnapping as the CFAF kidnap the professor's daughter. Suddenly the morgue is filling up, and not just with strangers. St. John's new love Ollie is killed, and he determines to stop at nothing until her murder is avenged. The tangled case drags him through every racket going: money laundering, dope pushing, porno, prostitution, and very nearly drags him six foot under.

St. John's Bread - William Babula 1-58345-516-7 hardcover 180 pp. $18.95;
1-58345-516-7 paper $12.95
In this fifth volume of the series, St. John and his two intrepid partners get caught up in a tangle of missing children's cases after he and Mickey rescue a baby about to be kidnapped in a public park. Mickey tries to tell him that he needs the "bread" to pay for his brand new Victorian stately home which

houses him and their detective agency, but this case comes with a higher price tag than any of them are willing to pay.

POETRY
Cold Moon: The Erotic Haiku of Gabriel Rosenstock 1-58345-042-4 108 pp. $12.95
This is a bilingual book in English and Irish from one of the foremost poets in both languages. Complete with powerful illustrations, this is a must for anyone who loves poetry, elegant books, and all things Irish.

A Portrait of the Artist as an Abominable Snowman - Gabriel Rosenstock 1-58345-124-2 108 pp. $12.95
Another fine collection of poetry in English and Irish from this stunning voice in the world of verse.

SCIENCE FICTION
The Event - Gregory Farnum 1-58345-553-1 176 pp. $12.95
This is a fast-paced technothriller. Prendyk and his girlfriend Jennifer are dragged into a dark world of government conspiracy. "The Event" will have far-reaching consequences for all of mankind.

THRILLERS
The Right Code - Sharon Holmes 1-58345-448-9 $12.95
Jonathan C. Evans is mocked as a computer nerd who lives by logic. Jasmine Banks is the only one who sees Jon differently. She grows determined to make this man realize that logic has nothing to do with a relationship between a man and a woman. But she gets more than she bargains for as the real JC Evans is revealed...

The Delaney Escape - Brent Kroetch 1-58345-021-1 264 pp. $12.95
Ex-CIA agent turned IRA man Noel Delaney plans to escape from Leavenworth prison.
Guy Morgan, an ex-agent trained by Delaney, is determined to track his old mentor down. He teams up with his long-time love, Karly Widman of British Intelligence, to trace Delaney's movements to Ireland. But the trap springs. Who is the hunter, and who the prey?

Ghost From the Past - Sorcha MacMurrough 1-58345-029-7 180 pp. $12.95
Biochemist Clarissa Vincent's fiancé Julian Simmons was killed in a terrible explosion five years ago. Or was he? Taking a new job in Portland, Oregon, Clarissa sees a man at the airport who could be Julian's double, and is suddenly propelled into a nightmarish world of espionage and intrigue. She must struggle to save her family and the man she has always loved from the ruthless people who will stop at nothing to achieve world domination.

In From the Cold - Carolyn Stone 1-58345-007-6 224 pp. $12.95
Cambridge scientist Sophie Ruskin is dragged into a world of espionage and intrigue when her father, a Russian defector, vanishes. Adrian Vaughan, handsome, enigmatic, but haunted by his past, is assigned to train her as a spy to win her father's freedom, or destroy his work before his kidnappers can create the ultimate weapon. But Adrian's fate soon lies in Sophie's hands, as she travels two continents to save his life, win his love, and fight for the freedom of the oppressed, war-torn Russian Republic of Chechnya.

Mutual Attraction - Diana Waldhuber 1-58345-382-2 148 pp. $10
Journalist Jordan Taylor's dream job turns out to be a nightmare when she meets the cool, suave, Ashford Blackard. Each presents an irresistible challenge for the other—but what will the fateful consequences of their game of cat and mouse be?

WESTERNS
West of Appomattox - Harley Duncan 1-58345-404-7 212 pp. $12.95
After the Civil War, a group of rugged and disgruntled soldiers seek their fame and fortune west of Appomattox in the new Mexican territory, with explosive results. This is a fine new novel sure to please devotees of the western genre.

Blow-Up at Three Springs - Colby Wolford 1-58345-541-8 148 pp. $10
The town took away Frank Gilman's badge, called him a killer, and treated him like dirt when he refused to turn tail and run, and started a stagecoach line with his brother Todd. Frank knew that Deejohn was behind his troubles. The town's biggest rancher, he was arrogant enough to believe he could bend the law any way he liked. Then one day Martha Lexter arrives at the railhead to threaten Deejohn and his empire. Deejohn will stop at nothing to get rid of her. Frank is faced with a choice: ignore Martha, or sell her a seat on his stage, an act which will certainly unleash Deejohn's pack of hired killers, and split Three Springs right down its seams!

The Guns of Witchwater - Colby Wolford 1-58345-525-6 248 pp. $12.95
Winter Santrell is a young peddler who tries to stay out of trouble. But unable to resist a damsel in distress, he comes to the aid of Vivian Kern, desperate for money to save her ranch after her father's death. The whole town of Witchwater is paralyzed with fear as a pack of renegades led by Baird Stark ride rough-shod over them. Santell decides to stand up for the people of the town, even though a few of them are mighty tempted to take up the thousand dollar reward that Stark puts on his corpse!

The Iron Corral - Colby Wolford 1-58345-533-7 160 pp. $10
When drifter Dan Allard takes the Sheriff's badge in La Mancha, he and his

deputy Owen Fielding lock horns with Harlan Younger and his tough gang, who are determined to drive the lawmen out of town.

Soon the banker, Jabe Miller, is murdered, and Owen is framed for the crime. Even his own friends and family turn against Dan as he struggles to bring Harlan to justice and clear Owen's name.

Stranger in the Land - Colby Wolford 1-58345-529-9 160 pp. $10
Derek Langton, ex-English cavalry officer, is a stranger in a strange land when he heads out west at the close of the Civil War. He has come to claim his inheritance, the Tower Ranch and fertile Strip with its wild, unbranded cattle. But others covet the Strip, especially Delphine Judson and her gun-toting crew. Derek must fight for his very survival to make a home for himself in his new-found land.

Green Grown the Rushes - Shirley and Nelson Wolford 1-58345-522-3 244 pp. $12.95
Lieutenant Boyd Regan is unjustly despised by his fellow soldiers and hated by the Mexicans of Alta Lowa. He is scorned by the woman he loves, half-Mexican beauty Catrina MacLeod, and her blonde sister Jennie. He is un-fairly accused, tried and convicted for treating the Mexican peasants cruelly. Yet if Mexican general Santa Anna obtains artillery, he will destroy Mexico City and all the American troops in it. Only Boyd stands in the way of com-plete annihilation of the entire city, even Mexico itself....

The Southern Blade - Shirley and Nelson Wolford 1-58345-537-X 168 pp. $10.00
Seven rebel prisoners on a desperate flight for freedom....
The Civil War is in its last days, but these prisoners only know they want their freedom. They are willing to risk hostile Indians and the even more danger-ous climate of New Mexico. Lieutenant Sawling leads the motley group on their journey, pursued by the relentless Union captain who has sworn to re-take and hang them. The only thing standing between them and the gallows is a beautiful young woman they have taken as hostage....

The Whispering Cannon - Shirley and Nelson Wolford 1-58345-545-0 184 pp. $10.95
Craig Dixon attracted trouble. A war correspondent, he was banned from the battlefield after criticizing Zachary Taylor's 1847 campaign against the Mexi-cans. But Dixon simply had to be where the news was being made. So he enlists as an officer in the Texas Volunteers, and is chosen as a messenger to get vital information to Taylor. The Mexicans will wipe Taylor's men out unless Dixon can get to him in time and persuade Taylor he is telling the truth.